The two great discoveries th— life were the Sat Nav and — of direction, Carol spent way too long poring over maps, missing turns, getting utterly and completely lost and hoping that she'd get there in the end—which she invariably did, but usually flustered and late. The arrival of Irish Sean into her life changed many things. She soon learnt that if she just carried right on sooner or later he'd re-navigate and she'd reach her destination.

Carol also spent way too long poring over application forms—she's been a typist, a nurse, a fruit-picker, a backpacker, and has also applied to be a policewoman and to study midwifery, psychology…the list goes on. They all appealed—just not *enough*. Since the age of eighteen she's dabbled with writing, but it was a rather sporadic effort at first—then finally she decided to take it more seriously. The biggest thrill in Carol's writing life (and it still is to this day) was typing, for the first time, the words "The End". For so many years there had been chapters and outlines and endless stop-starts, but having a full story, from start to middle to end, gave her a rush she had never expected. Of course it was rejected, but she'd got the bug and kept going till she was accepted.

These days she takes an awful lot of fish oil, and keeps a pen and paper by her bed, in her bag, in the kitchen, in the car. She loves that she can talk to friends at length about the people who pop into her head and not get looked at too strangely for it. Being published, sitting down to write every day—finally she found direction and a whole lot of new friends. A whole new way of life, really. Now, no matter what life throws, when she pushes the button for home the answer is always the same: at the end of the day, sit down and write.

Find out more about Carol at www.carolmarinelli.com

putting *Alice* back together

Carol Marinelli

MIRA

First published in Great Britain 2012
MIRA Books, an imprint of Harlequin (UK) Limited,
Eton House, 18-24 Paradise Road,
Richmond, Surrey, TW9 1SR

© Carol Marinelli 2012

Cosmic Love by Yasmin Boland used with permission

ISBN 978 1 848 45059 2

60-0312

MIRA's policy is to use papers that are natural, renewable and recyclable products and made from wood grown in sustainable forests. The logging and manufacturing processes conform to the legal environmental regulations of the country of origin.

Printed and bound by
CPI Group (UK) Ltd, Croydon, CR0 4YY

For Sam, Alex and Lucinda
with love always xxxx

putting *Alice* back together

Prologue

Little Alice

'That's the Munchkins sorted.' Mrs Evans smiled. 'Now we can move on to casting the main parts.' Everyone was nudging, all sitting cross-legged on the gym floor—a mix of eager and dejected faces, because anyone left after this would be in the chorus. 'The Wicked Witch of the West...' Mrs Evans announced, and I held my breath. If I wasn't going to be Dorothy I didn't actually mind being her, but I could feel the sweat beading on my forehead as Debbie Carter got the part.

'The Lion...' I knew this next lot of roles would go to the boys.

It was between Louise and me—she was so pretty and blonde she'd be lovely as the good fairy.

I knew I was good at drama. I knew I had a role and that there were only two girl ones left—and with my curly hair I wouldn't make a nice neat calm fairy. And given that my hair was red too...

I was going to be Dorothy!

Jonathon Phillips actually walked like the Tin Man as he stood up.

'Choose me, choose me...' I had my fingers crossed under my little fat shaking knees. I was trying to pretend I didn't care, that the lovely gingham dress and ruby shoes didn't matter so, except they did. I made my wish at the wrong second, though. Everyone was cheering. Louise was patting me on the back and Mrs Evans was grinning widely as, red in the face, I stood up and crashed my way through all the crossed knees.

I was Alice Lydia Jameson—the Scarecrow.

One

'How could she not know?' Roz snorted.

Hugh was at the table, filling in tax forms.

Roz and I were watching the news when a story came on about some woman who hadn't known she was pregnant and had flushed it down the loo...

'For God's sake.' Roz, lovely Roz, who was usually non-judgmental, was so opinionated and scathing as she said it again. 'How could she not know? How can she say that she didn't even know?'

And I gave a half-laugh, topped up my wine and carried on watching the news. But my face was burning, just as it did during a love scene at the movies when I felt as if the whole cinema was watching me and gauging my reaction; just as it did when Dr Kelsey asked all those questions.

I couldn't hear the scratch of Hugh's pen any more and I was sure he was watching me.

I just felt as if he knew.

'Of course she knew!' Roz insisted, even though I wasn't arguing, and I wanted to turn around and correct her. I wanted to tell her to shut the fuck up, but instead I took a swig of wine and almost missed my mouth, my hand was shaking so much. She turned her attention to him. 'What do you think, Hugh?'

Only I didn't want to hear what Hugh thought.

I didn't want his educated opinion.

Do you know, every time some poor cow flushes a baby down the loo, or it turns up in a rubbish dump, or she arrives in Emergency with abdo pain and produces a babe, or pops a foetus into her hand luggage and tries to head for home, the comments are the same—*she must have known*.

No.

No.

No.

She didn't know.

She *couldn't* know.

Because once she did, *then* it was real.

I didn't need Hugh's opinion and I didn't need Roz's either.

I could see how it happened.

I knew how it happened.

Because, Once Upon a Time, it had happened to me.

Two

Alice

It's not something you can just blurt out, though.

I mean, when do you slip that little gem into the conversation?

You can't.

Ever.

Not to anyone.

You just learn to live with it.

To run from it.

To live your life around it.

There's so much that hinges on silence.

I don't really know where to start.

If I go back even just a few weeks, it wasn't something at the forefront of my mind. Really, I didn't think about it at all, or I did everything I could not to—I was too busy being normal. I had a job, a fantastic wardrobe, brilliant friends, massive credit-card debt, all the usual stuff. Okay, I had a few problems, but don't we all? I spent a lot of my lunch breaks in the self-help section at the bookshop, looking for the book, the answer, the reason. I'd tried Reiki, hypnosis, Indian scalp massage…

Forgive me if it's jumbled at first, I suppose I was too.

Nic was leaving for the UK; her cousin Hugh was coming to stay at the flat. There was a small leaving do for her, which I was a bit late getting to—see, I was just busy being normal.

'You've met Christopher,' Nicole said, as she made the introductions, and though I'd heard her moan about her boss often enough, we'd never actually met, which Christopher quickly pointed out.

'Actually, no.' His voice had that bitchy upper-class ring to it and I wasn't sure if he was English, as Nicole and I are, or if he'd been privately schooled here in Australia. As he shook my hand he held on for just a fraction too long. 'I'd certainly remember.' He smiled that capped smile and I returned it, but only briefly. I mean, he was way past forty, for God's sake—I was so not flirting with him.

'Where's Dan?' Nicole asked.

'He's working.' Christopher's eyes were still on me as I made Dan's apologies, but there was no real need—I could see the relief on Nic's face when I told her that Dan couldn't make it.

'And Roz?'

'She'll be here soon,' I said, and I knew Nicole wished that Roz wasn't coming—Nicole hates her friends and colleagues being together. She jumps out of her skin if we meet someone we know out shopping or at a bar. It is as if she's terrified they might find out she actually has a life outside law—that she isn't always this poised and groomed.

That she can actually talk about something other than work.

Oh, God, you should have heard them. It was Nic's leaving do. Well, she's not leaving—Nicole's been in Melbourne for five years and she's taking six weeks' annual leave to catch up with her family and new boy-friend, who she met while he was on holiday here. But, instead of enjoying the party, they're talking about some sub-clause in some clause or something. And for all their money, they were mean. No one offered to buy a drink. They just sipped on their tasteful choices and I knew it was going to be a long, mind-numbingly boring night or worse, as I saw a couple of them glancing at their watches, it was going to be a short, complete fizzler of a night, which would kill Nicole.

Why did I feel that it was my problem?

That I had to make conversation, do something to en-tertain—that it was up to me to salvage the night from being a disaster?

Because Nicole's my best friend, I guess.

I went to the bar and looked at the wine list. My pay should have gone in and though I *knew* I couldn't afford it, I ordered two of the second cheapest bottles of spar-kling wine and ten glasses.

'I'll take care of that.' Christopher made his way over and I felt a mixture of annoyance and relief as he changed my order and took out his credit card. 'You're Nicole's flatmate?'

'That's right.' I felt a bit awkward, obliged to stay and talk to him now that he was paying for the drinks.

'You're English too?' he checked as he waited to sign the bill and, instead of noticing his blond hair or blue eyes, I saw the fan of lines around his eyes and the acne scars on his jaw.

'I am.'

'Nicole never said.'

I gave him a very brief smile, thanked him for the wine and made my way back to the group. Normally, there would have been a quick reminisce, or a moment taken to find out where the other was from, how long they've been over, that sort of thing, but he'd got that sharky look, like a real estate agent sensing a deal, so I headed back to the table and took a seat on the sofa furthest away from him.

Nicole seemed to have developed a tic—her head kept twitching in the direction of the toilets and once the champagne had arrived and we'd all wished her well for her trip back home, I excused myself and headed over there. Maybe fifteen seconds later Nic flew in.

'Where the hell were you?'

'I had to go back to the flat and get changed.'

'Any messages?' she asked, and I shook my head as I touched up my lipstick. Peering into the mirror, I could see a good quarter of an inch of ginger roots, so I fiddled with my parting to mess it up a little and made a mental note to see Karan. 'Thank God, you're here,' Nic carried on, and even if she didn't want Roz and Dan along, clearly she was relying on me. 'It's been awful. They're all just sitting there. Any minute now they'll go.'

'Nobody's going,' I soothed. 'Let's just get out there and have a good time.'

'Alice, you have to do something...'

See—it was my problem. As much as Nic didn't want her worlds colliding, I was supposed to be the entertainment. I was the one who had to ensure that everyone had a brilliant time. I just didn't get why it always fell to me.

'Come on,' I said. 'We can't have a party in here.'

'Don't let me drink too much,' Nicole begged, and that made me smile. Nicole practically gave up drinking the day she met Paul. She used to love a night out, or a night in with a couple of bottles. Now she was constantly putting her hand over her drink, terrified you might fill it.

'And please, Alice, be nice to Christopher.'

'He's awful.'

'I know.' Nicole cringed. 'But please, just be nice.'

'I am being nice.'

'You just gave him the brush-off.'

'I didn't.'

I hadn't!

Okay, I hadn't engaged in conversation. I hadn't asked when he was next going back to the Mother Ship and if he could get me some clothes from Next and some of that amazing moisturiser from Boots, but I hadn't given him the brush-off.

Or had I?

'He's a sleaze,' I pointed out, because he absolutely was. 'Did someone take an ice pick to his face thirty years ago?'

'Alice, please,' Nicole begged, even though she laughed. 'He's been a right bastard since he found out I was going back to see Paul. He knows I might…'

And I felt my throat tighten as her voice trailed off. Nicole had never admitted it, but I knew, I *knew* that she was thinking of moving back to England—she had just confirmed it. I couldn't believe she'd give everything up for Paul but, then, that's what she does with men, over and over.

God, Nic knew how to pick them.

Nic always thought she was in love.

Always insisted that this was the one.

Until he dumped her, hit her, or his wife found out.

Nicole's love life was like a really bad soap opera. Every weeknight at six-thirty she flew through the flat door with the latest instalment and, even though you knew how it was going to end, knew it was heading for disaster, still you found yourself watching from behind your fingers, scarcely able to believe someone could really be so stupid where men were concerned.

And she was *surely* heading for disaster.

Big time.

Which meant, yet again, yours truly would be left to pick up the pieces.

'Christopher was a manager at the London office,' Nic said, but I just added another layer of lip-gloss. 'He knows everyone there. I don't want to leave on a bad note.'

'You're not leaving, though—you're going for a holiday.' I gave her a smile. 'It's going to be a great night— just relax and enjoy it.'

'The thing is, Alice…'

I just didn't want to hear it here—I mean, it was supposed to be her party. 'Come on,' I said instead. 'We'd better get back out there.'

The champagne hadn't buoyed the mood and I knew it was going to be hard work. We were all sitting on low sofas and I told a couple of funny, indiscreet stories about the newspaper where I work—and I don't know how I do it, Nicole doesn't either, but the mood was suddenly lifting. People started to open up, to loosen up and then Jason—or was it James?—shocked everyone by admitting that his wife had left him at the weekend and Christopher, well, he had the gift too, because he laughed and said, 'That's a reason for more champagne,' and called the waiter over. I could see Nicole beaming, relief starting to flood in, because her leaving night was going to be a success.

'There's Roz…' I waved out of the window to where Roz was sucking down the last of her cigarette and Roz waved back and carried on puffing away.

She just didn't get it.

I smoked sometimes, but it's so unfashionable these days, you didn't do it at places like this. If you did, you went right away from the window and doused yourself in perfume and sucked mints before you came inside. But not Roz. She came to the door blowing out the last of her smoke, and she was so out of place there that for an appalling moment I thought the doorman was about to refuse her. I called out her name loud enough for him to hear and, realising she was with the posh, champagne-drinking lawyers, he let her in.

'Christ!' Christopher soon showed his bastard colours. 'Who the hell is that?'

'Roz,' I answered tartly. 'She's a friend of ours, she works with me at the paper, she's studying accounting…' My voice trailed off, because he wasn't actually interested in Roz.

His reaction was a familiar one—he'd dismissed her instantly.

Before she'd even walked through the door.

She was in cargo pants and a sloppy T-shirt and sandals that were about to snap from lugging her bulk around and she'd put on *more* weight. Her divorce had just come through, all her old friends and even her daughter had turned against her, and though she insisted that she was happy that her marriage was over, every day she seemed to go under a little bit more. She was really letting herself go.

Dan didn't like her. He said she brought me down and he couldn't stand the way that she looked. Yes, elegant and chic weren't two words that sprang to mind when Roz was around, but I wished people would take a bit of time to get to know her. Roz was the kindest person I knew, she'd do anything for me, for anyone.

She's just lovely.

'I can't imagine her as an accountant.' Christopher made some caustic comment about her not fitting in and I bristled as Nic's face coloured up, not in anger at Christopher but in embarrassment at her friend.

'No,' I agreed with him, 'because she's not boring enough.' Out of the corner of my eye I could see Nic tense, and I remembered then that Christopher was a financial lawyer, but instead of offending him I'd made him laugh. I didn't see the acne scars any more, or the lines around his eyes. His eyes were blue and he was smiling at me and I found myself smiling back.

'There's drinks here.' I dragged my eyes away and I called to Roz because I knew she hated going to the bar. I moved along on the sofa to make room for her.

'I'm Christopher.' He introduced himself and poured her a drink and he was being really nice to her, but somehow I knew it was for me. I knew, because he apologised that he couldn't hear what Roz was saying and came over to our side of the table and squeezed in between us.

There was a frisson of excitement that flooded my veins, an awareness, and even though he was talking to Roz, and I was entertaining the table, I knew he felt it too.

I knew because I could feel the press of his thigh on mine.

An hour ago I'd have stabbed him in the leg with my keys.

I didn't press back. I pretended not to notice.

But I didn't move my leg away either.

I was half listening as they spoke about their children. He had a sixteen-year-old too, it turned out, *and* a twenty-year-old.

He must be ancient.

I mean, Roz had Lizzie really young and she's thirty-four.

The table was becoming rowdy and everyone was chatting away, me included, but my head was like an abacus, trying to work out his age. As he dropped his phone, I *expected* the brief brush of his hand on my calf and he delivered.

It was my turn to have the nervous tic—I tried to catch Nicole's eyes to get her to come to the toilets and tell me how best to handle this. I mean, there's being nice and being *nice*—what the hell was I supposed to do?

'I won't be long.'

I excused myself—I had to side shuffle along the sofa to get out and I was acutely aware of my bottom passing his face. They must all have thought I had a bladder the size of a thimble, but I just wanted to escape. I walked calmly to the toilets even though my heart was hammering. I wanted to be away from him.

He must have been mid-forties.

Nicole had missed my frantic signals because she didn't follow me in. I waited a few minutes then I started to walk back out to the party, deciding that I would wedge myself in beside Nicole.

'Alice.'

I heard his voice from the disabled toilet.

I turned. And, to my shame, I went in.

I'll spare you the details.

I'm trying to spare myself from the details too.

It didn't take long.

He went back and I stayed there for a moment or two.

I tried not to look at myself in the mirror as I put on my lip-gloss and sorted out my hair.

I could not have hated myself more. I wasn't even pissed—I'd had two glasses.

How did I get here?

How had my life got to this point?

Why was I like this?

I wanted to hit rewind. I wanted to go back and start the night all over again.

How did he know? I mean, of all the women out there…

I wanted to go home. I wanted to go out through the rear of the restaurant. I wanted to hide, to curl up on the disgusting floor—anything rather than go back out—but instead I closed my eyes and took a deep breath. Or tried to.

I couldn't get the air in.

I scrabbled in my bag but I couldn't find them. There

was an appointment card for 4.30 tomorrow, which I tossed back, and searched some more, then felt the relief as my fingers closed on a thin white box. It was a short-lived relief because there was only one left and after that there would be none.

Alice Lydia Jameson

Diazepam 5 mg.

One tablet twice daily as needed.

Avoid alcohol.

I didn't know if they worked, I really didn't, or if it was just knowing I had them that helped—because even before the little yellow pill had dissolved on my tongue, I felt calmer.

I headed back out there, scorching with shame but trying to act as if nothing just happened.

'Where did you get to?' Roz asked, but she didn't wait for my answer. 'Are you coming out for a cigarette?'

Nicole was enjoying herself. Christopher, having ordered more champagne for the group, was saying goodbye, though he didn't extend a farewell to me.

'Have a great night, Nicole.' He kissed her on the cheek and she smiled back at him.

'Thanks for coming.'

Only then did he smirk in my direction. 'It was no trouble at all.'

I stood outside with Roz and I didn't have a cigarette, I just breathed in the cool night air and tried not to think about what I'd just done.

'I can't believe she's going into work tomorrow...' Roz was chatting away. 'She's flying tomorrow night...'

'That's Nic.' I went into my bag for my cigarettes and I pulled out the appointment card too.

'I'll come back to the flat with you after work and we can all—'

'Actually…' I hesitated. I didn't really know how to tell Roz. 'I'm leaving work a bit early tomorrow, I've got an appointment.' I knew she was curious, that she was waiting for me to explain, but I didn't and Roz would never push. 'I'll be back in time to pick up Nic. You can meet me back at the flat.'

'That's fine,' Roz said. 'I'll just meet you at the airport.'

I'd been intending to cancel.

Or just not show up.

I had no intention of examining my past, but I needed a prescription and, I reluctantly admitted, perhaps I should speak to someone—not about *it*, of course, but about other things.

Maybe this Lisa could help.

Three

Another Alice

I liked the piano. It was my first instrument, the violin my second, but it was the piano I loved.

I hated the lessons, but I sort of understood I had to have them.

Young Mozart I was not—but I *could* read music.

I just could.

To me, it was easier than learning to read English— a quaver was an eighth of a whole, that dot meant you lengthened the note.

I supposed I had not talent as such but, as my mother would tell everyone she met, her youngest daughter had an 'ear for music'.

I lived and breathed music—the classics, hymns, anything I heard I wanted to play.

And as a teenager it had been considered nerdy.

Seriously nerdy.

Especially as I'd also sung in the church choir.

Of course I'd got teased at school and hated it when

people found out about my other life, but I loved hymns and singing and a couple of times I even played the organ.

Yep—a serious nerd.

There's nobody musical in my family. Mum's a nurse, dad's in sales and marketing, Eleanor is my oldest sister and basically does nothing apart from look good—well, she has to, she's married to a cosmetic dentist. Then there's Bonny the middle one, who takes after Mum and is a nurse too. It really took a lot of convincing from my teachers for Mum to realise that she wasn't being ripped off when the school suggested that if I wanted to pursue a career in music, then I needed some extra private tuition. (I was fifteen then. Dad and Mum had just broken up so it caused a few rows, Dad said he was paying Mum plenty—Mum said…well, plenty.)

So, with things a bit tight, instead of more lessons with my regular music teacher, Mum found various students from a school of music to coach me. I was doing fairly well and looking at a career in teaching. As well as lessons and choir and choir practice, I had to practise my instruments for hours every day—though I didn't mind practising the piano. In fact, I lived for it. It was the lessons I hated.

Still, as I said, I understood that I had to have them and just put up with them, I suppose…

Till Bonny's wedding loomed, when *everything* changed.

As far as I can remember, Eleanor's wedding just seemed to happen without fuss. I was ten and, along with Bonny, I was a bridesmaid, but I don't remember the whole world stopping in preparation for Eleanor's big day—I just remember the church and the party afterwards.

Oh, and the gleaming teeth in the photos.

One minute Eleanor was dating Noel and the next we were in the church, or so it had seemed.

Whereas Bonny's wedding was the full circus.

Bonny's *life* was a full circus, but the wedding and the preparation were the worst.

It was to be a New Year's Eve wedding—it was the only way Lex's relatives could all get over for it, and Mum, devastated that her middle child would be moving to Australia as soon as she took her final nursing exams, would do anything to please and appease. And, as much as I love Bonny, boy, did she take full advantage of the situation.

I was seventeen and full of teenage angst and wondering if I'd ever lose my virginity, especially since I'd never even been kissed. I was heavily in love with Gus, my latest music tutor, and I was also very aware that I was behind on piano practice and my exams were just a few months away. Which sounds ages, but it really wasn't.

Not that any of this mattered to Bonny.

Lex, Bonny's fiancé, was a sexy six-foot-three Australian who worked for some international pharmaceutical company and was helping to compile statistics both here and in America. They had met at the hospital Bonny worked at, had fallen in love and within three months had got engaged.

Everyone said Bonny was too young to marry, but Lex refused anything less. He didn't want to live with her—

if she was going to take the leap and move to Australia, then it would be as his wife.

He's a nice guy, Lex.

A really nice guy, and even if Bonny was a bit young, I could understand why she didn't want to let him go.

I had a crush on him—of course I did—I had a crush on everyone!

Bonny went a touch crazy in the weeks before the wedding: it was colour schemes and flowers and cakes and invitations. The whole house was wedding central. I couldn't practise my violin or piano for two weeks before the big day. Really, I didn't mind missing the violin, I could make up the time later, but I don't think I'd ever been even two days without playing the piano. I didn't just practise…I played. If I was tired, if I was depressed, if I'd been teased, if I'd had a shit day, I'd play. It didn't lift me, instead it met me. I could just pour it out and hear how I was feeling.

Sometimes I glimpsed it—this zone, a place, like a gap that I stepped into and filled with a sound that was waiting to be made.

There's no one else I can talk about it with, except for Gus—he gets it. Gus says that playing is a relief.

He's right, that's what it feels like sometimes—relief.

An energy that builds and it has to be let out somewhere.

It's more than relief—it's release.

Or it would be if it didn't upset Bonny.

Everything upset Bonny.

Everything was done to appease her.

Which was why I had been forced to wear pink.

A sort of dusky pink, which was fashionable, my mum

insisted—as if she would know. As if a size twenty, middle-aged woman with bad teeth and the beginnings of a moustache would know.

I hated it—I hated it so much, there was no way I was going to wear it. But my threats fell on deaf ears. It was Bonny's Special Day—and what was a bit of public humiliation to a seventeen-year-old as long as the bride was smiling?

So I wrote reams of pages of 'I hate Bonny', 'I want to kill Bonny' and 'I want to gouge out her eyes' as I lay on my bed the afternoon before the wedding with the beastly pink dress hanging up in plastic on my wardrobe. I had my period and was having visions of flooding in the aisle, and to add to the joy, the hairdresser was here and, as anyone with frizzy red hair would understand, I wasn't looking forward to that either.

I lay down and imagined that it was me getting married and not Bonny.

That sexy Lex only had eyes for me.

Then I felt bad—I mean, I might hate her but she is my sister—so I moved my fantasy over to Gus instead.

Except he was already married…

Apparently you couldn't wash your hair on the day of the wedding, because the spectacular style Bonny had finally chosen after several screaming trips wouldn't stay up on newly washed hair. So she was being blow-dried while I washed my hair and then the hairdresser would dry it with a diffuser and put in loads of product and then pin it up tomorrow. We'd had a practice a couple of weeks before and it had looked suitably disgusting but, again, I'd been told to shut up and not complain because it was Bonny's Special Day.

So I washed my hair and I sat sulking in the kitchen as Bonny's hair was being blow-dried, and then Eleanor's was blow-dried too. Mum wasn't having hers put up, so she was getting 'done' tomorrow, and as I moved to the stool, perhaps seeing my expression when the hairdresser took out her scissors, Mum tried to appease me. She couldn't give a shag that I hated hairdressers and hated, hated, hated getting it trimmed—no, she just didn't want me making a scene and upsetting Bonny.

'It's just a little trim,' Mum warned, clucking around and trying to pour cold water on the cauldron of hate we were all sitting in before it exploded. 'Oh, I didn't tell you, I rang Gus and you can have an extra piano lesson,' Mum said to my scowling face. 'He's working over the holiday break and he can fit you in on Monday.'

Now, *that* did appease me.

You see, Gus wasn't like the usual, scurf-ridden, vegan tutors that Mum had found for me in the past. He was as sexy as hell, with brown dead-straight hair, no hint of dandruff and dark brown eyes that roamed over me for a little bit too long sometimes. He smelt fantastic too. Sometimes when he was leaning over me, or sitting beside while I played, I was scared to breathe because the scent of him made me want to turn around and just lick him! Like Lex, he was from Australia (they must make sexy men there—I was thinking of a gap year there to sample the delights). Gus spoke to me, instead of down to me. He spoke about real things, about his life, about me. Once when his moody bitch of a wife walked in on our lesson and reminded him that he'd gone over the hour, it came as a surprise to realise that we had. Instead of playing, for those last fifteen minutes we'd been talking and laughing and I felt a slight flurry in my stomach, because I knew that when I left there would be a row.

He started to tell me more and more about his problems with Celeste and I lapped every word up and then wrote it in my diary each night—analysing it, going over and over it, looking for clues, wishing I'd answered differently, wondering if I was mad to think that a man as sexy as Gus might somehow fancy me…but I felt that he did. He told me that he had intended that the sexy Celeste, who—and Gus and I giggled when he told me— played the cello, would be a fling. Well, she was now almost six months pregnant, his visa was about to expire, and he and Celeste would be going back to Melbourne once the baby was born—but for now he was broke and miserable and completely trapped. The sexy cello player he had dated was massive with child and the only thing, Gus had told me bitterly, that was between her legs these days was her head as she puked her way through pregnancy—not her cello, and certainly not him.

I loved Gus—he wasn't like a teacher. And even though I knew Mum was paying him to be one, for that hour, once a week, I was more than his pupil. I was the sole focus of his attention—and I craved it.

He was so funny and sexy, and I couldn't stand the thought of him going back to Melbourne, or even understand why the hell he put up with Celeste and her moods.

She was a bitch. She didn't say hi to me, didn't look up and say goodbye when the lesson was over. Occasionally she'd pop her head in and say something to Gus and look over me as if I were some pimply teenager, which of course I was. She thought she was so fucking gorgeous, wearing tight dresses and showing off her belly and massive boobs, but I knew how Gus bitched about her.

Actually, at our lesson yesterday he'd told me a joke. He knew I was as fed up with Bonny's wedding as he had been with his and as I packed up my music sheets and loaded my bag and headed for the door, he called me back.

'Hey, Alice.' He smiled up at me from the piano stool. 'Why does a bride smile on her wedding day?'

I could feel his dark eyes on my burning cheeks and I shrugged—I hate jokes, I never get them, oh, I pretend to laugh, but I never really get them.

'I don't know.'

'Because she's given her last blow job!'

I didn't really get it. I laughed and said goodnight. I knew what a blow job was, sort of—I hadn't even kissed a guy. I even told Bonny the joke when I got home but she wasn't too impressed.

It was only that night as I lay in bed that I sort of got it, that I realised he was talking about Celeste.

I lay there feeling grown up—thought about Mandy Edwards and her snog with Scott, thought about Jacinta Reynolds and her fumble with Craig, a boy in lower sixth.

Gus was twenty-two.

It made me feel very grown up indeed.

Four

I was expecting offices. Nice, bland offices, but as I turned into the street I saw that it was a house, and better still there was a large sign that displayed to all and sundry that I was entering a psychologist's practice.

Really. You'd think they'd be more discreet and write 'Life Coaching' or something.

A very bubbly receptionist greeted me and handed me a form to fill in. She told me to take a seat with the other psychopaths and social misfits and that Lisa would call me in soon.

God, I so did not belong here. There was a couple, sitting in stony silence, who were presumably here for marriage counselling (and from the way he rolled his eyes when she had the audacity to get up and get a drink from the water cooler, I didn't fancy their chances much). Then there was a huge guy with a face like a bulldog who had probably been sent by the courts for anger management. There was, though, one fairly normal-looking guy, who was reading a magazine. He was rather good looking and he gave me a smile as he caught my eye, but

I quickly looked away—I mean, normally I'd have been making conversation by now, but I had some standards, and refused to be chatted up in a psychologist's waiting room. I mean, God alone knows what he was there for.

And what would you say when people asked where you met?

Mind you, I did feel guilty for snubbing him and when I saw him look at me again, I gave him a sort of sympathetic, understanding smile, just in case he was normal and was here for grief counselling. I started on the form and the disclaimers, telling them who my GP was, my job (er…why?) and filling in all the little boxes. I ticked my way merrily through the form—though it was completely unnecessary. What business of theirs was it where I worked? Or if I was at any risk of blood-borne diseases or had heart problems or had been involved in a workplace accident. I was here for a chat, not cardiac surgery. Mind you, I almost ticked 'No' to allergies, but quickly moved my pen to the 'Yes' box and in the bit below, where I had to elaborate, I wrote: 'Hazelnuts— cause shortness of breath and lips to swell.'

And on the bit about current medication I made sure to remind this Lisa why I was here and boldly wrote my order.

Valium.

I put Roz down as my emergency contact, even though she had no idea I was here.

A woman, presumably Lisa, opened the door and gave me a patronising smile as she took my forms, then invited me to follow her.

On sight I didn't like her.

I certainly couldn't imagine myself *relating* to her,

or her to me. She was a big woman, about sixty, with massive, pendulous breasts. Worse, she wore a really low-cut olive top, so you could see her crêpe chest and cleavage. Add to that a flowing A-line, snot-green skirt, green sandals. And she had accessorised with—in case we hadn't noticed her colour choice for today—a huge jade necklace.

There were four seats for me to choose from. No doubt the one I chose would *mean* something, and I hesitated for a moment, before settling for the one in the middle.

'Excuse all the furniture...' She gave a pussycat smile. 'I had a family in before you.'

Lucky them, then.

I put down my bag, checked my keys were there, zipped it up and sat back. There was a bowl of sweets on her desk, cola bottles, snakes, wine gums, all my favourites really, and I stared at them instead of her.

'So...' Lisa finally broke the silence. 'What brought you here today?'

I *so* did not need this. Last night had been a one-off drunken mistake, I'd by now decided, and I'd learnt my lesson—I was never mixing alcohol with Valium again.

'Okay,' she said to the ensuing silence. 'Why don't you tell me about Alice?' I could feel a really inappropriate smile start to wobble on my lips. I couldn't believe I was sitting in a psychologist's office being asked to discuss *me* in the third person. 'Alice is English?'

'She is,' my twitching lips answered.

Well, we skirted around for a bit, I told her I had to leave promptly, that my flatmate was going to the UK and I had to take her to the airport.

'Nicole's English as well?' Lisa checked.

'She's been here five years,' I said. 'She'd never leave.'

Lisa wrote a little note but I couldn't make out what it was.

'You'll miss her?'

'I guess,' I admitted. Though lately we hadn't been getting on too well. Not that I'd tell Lisa that, so instead I mentioned that Nicole's cousin Hugh, a doctor, was arriving in a couple of days and staying till he found somewhere near the hospital to live.

'You don't look too pleased.'

'I like my own company.' I shrugged. 'I was looking forward to a few weeks to myself.'

Actually, that had nothing to do with it.

Normally I'd be thrilled to have the good doctor to myself, but I'd found out from Nic that he was a red-head—need I say more?

I know that sounds anti-redhead, but I'm allowed to be, because I am one.

Think Ronald McDonald meets Shirley Temple.

I had the kind of hair that stopped old ladies in the street, made them pat it as they chattered away to my mother.

'Beautiful hair. Of course, she'll hate it later.'

I hated it already. By the time I was six it regularly reduced me to tears. Hour after hour was spent in front of my mother's dressing-table mirror trying to brush out the curls. Night after uncomfortable night was spent sleeping with pins speared into my scalp in the hope of producing a straight fringe by morning. And as for the colour! I'd barely hit puberty before I bought my first hair dye and even now a very significant portion of my monthly pay cheque is spent on foils, serum, ceramic straighteners, regular blow-dries and, if I ever save up enough, I'm getting that Brazilian keratin treatment.

Though I digress, there is a point—my hair is now strawberry blonde and straight. For the first time in my life I'm actually pleased with my hair and I do not need a reminder of the *au naturel* version of myself walking around the flat.

Not that Lisa needed to hear that.

Honestly, it was the most boring, pointless hour of my life.

Yes, I suppose sometimes I did get a bit homesick.

Yes, I'd been here for nearly ten years now since my sister Bonny had got married and emigrated.

'But you only initially came to Melbourne for a year?'

'That's right.' I nodded. 'I just loved it, though. I got a good job…'

'Doing what?'

'Working on the classifieds section at the newspaper. Well, it was a good job at the time.'

'And you're still there?' She peered at the form I had filled in.

I felt myself pink up just a little bit. 'I'm a team manager now and I do web updates.' I gave a little shrug. 'It's not my ideal job, of course…'

'What is your ideal job?'

'I don't know…' another shrug '…something in music, I suppose. My exam results weren't great. That was one of the reasons I came in the first place—to have a break and work out what I was going to do.'

We chatted some more, or rather she dragged information out of me. 'And are the rest of your family here?'

'Just Bonny. My mum and Eleanor, she's the oldest, live back in the UK.'

'And your father?'

I felt my face redden. I mean, I hadn't meant to leave him out. 'He's in the UK too.' I waited for her to scribble something down, but she didn't. 'They're divorced. I speak to him and everything…it's no big deal.'

'When did they divorce?'

'When I was fifteen.'

Well, it would seem that I had my Valium. She pounced on the fact my parents were divorced. Really, she worried away at it for the rest of the hour. How did I feel when they broke up, had there been rows? I couldn't convince her that it hadn't been *that* bad. I mean, you hear all these terrible tales, but the truth is, Mum let herself go after I came along, Dad met Lucy and left. We still saw him. Every Friday night we stayed over while Mum did a night shift, and then on Saturday lunchtime he took us to the pub for lunch, just as he had done when they were still married. Mum had been upset, of course—depressed, in hindsight—but it really wasn't that much of a big deal at the time. I told Lisa that as she started jotting down a little family tree and making copious notes.

'Look, I'm not here about that.' And I supposed, if I wanted the prescription, I was going to have to tell her. 'I had an anxiety attack.' My cheeks were flaming as I cringed at the memory of Olivia's leaving do last week. Everyone gathering around, offering me water, paramedics, being strapped to a stretcher and taken down in the lifts and out onto the street. 'Really, I'm not even sure that it was an anxiety attack—the doctors at the hospital thought it might be an allergic reaction.' She frowned. 'I had a similar thing when I was seven and I ate hazelnuts.' But still she just sat there. 'The medicine they gave me at the hospital really helped, though.'

'The Valium?'

'Yes.' I gave a little swallow. 'I'm worried it might happen again, but if I had some Valium, just till I get the allergy tests done…'

'You could just avoid hazelnuts!' I swear her eyes crinkled. Honestly, I felt as if she was laughing at me, which she couldn't be, of course.

But then she did.

She laughed.

I couldn't believe it. She didn't sit there and roar, but she gave a little laugh that made her shoulders go up. The type you do when you say something amusing, only this wasn't funny.

I'd get her struck off.

If she didn't give me my script.

'Okay.' She glanced at her watch and managed to contain herself enough for another little scribble on her pad. 'If you can make an appointment again for about two weeks' time. Now, don't be surprised if you feel a bit unsettled over the next couple of days—we've touched on some sensitive areas.'

Which was news to me.

'But what about…?' I gave a nervous swallow as she stood. 'The doctor said I should see a psychologist if I needed more Valium. He was only comfortable giving me ten.'

'That's very sensible.'

God, she wasn't making this easy—I wasn't asking her to buy them, just to write the bloody script.

I decided to go for direct. 'Do you think you could write me up for some?'

'I don't prescribe medication.'

What the hell? My ears were ringing from her words as she droned on. I'd been through all of this, *all* of this, and she still refused to write me up for drugs—what did she suggest then? Was she some sort of alternative psychologist, was she going to suggest meditation? 'I'm happy to write a note for your GP explaining that you are seeing me.'

'But the doctor at the hospital said I should come and see you.' I could hear my voice rising. I'd taken my last Valium yesterday and I had none left.

None.

'The doctor was recommending counselling, Alice. Your GP, if she does feel you need medication, is likely to suggest the same.' She read my stunned expression and twisted the knife. 'Even if I thought you needed it, I'm not qualified to prescribe medication.'

Well, what was the bloody point of that? I huffed, as I paid and left.

I was late for Nic. I'd wasted an hour talking about a stupid divorce that had happened more than a decade ago, and she'd charged me one hundred and twenty dollars for the pleasure. I hadn't even got a script—let alone a single bloody insight.

I was not best pleased, I can tell you.

Five

I hate airports.

You know at the beginning of *Love Actually* where Hugh (Grant, not the ginger one that's coming to stay) says you just have to go to the Arrivals at Heathrow to witness love, or something along those lines?

Well, there's a flip side to that.

Departures.

If there is a hell, then for me it will be Departures at an international airport.

I won't be shovelling coal for eternity into a furnace. Instead, one by one I'll have to say goodbye to everyone I love and watch them disappear. It will be constant, it will be perpetual, and once I've said goodbye to everyone, just when I think I've got through it—it will start over again.

That's my hell.

And contrary to Arrivals, after which you drive home with your loved ones and you can't stop talking because there's so much to catch up on, so much to say, the drive *to* Departures is a nightmare.

Every time.

Nicole was furious with me because I didn't get back till ten to six and she wouldn't let it drop.

'I wasn't late!' I could see the picture of an aeroplane on the road signs for those who can't read or can't speak English. I needed to change lanes or we'd miss the turn-off, and I actually thought about it—honestly, that would have given her something to moan about. 'You said we had to leave by six and we did!'

'You're so bloody selfish sometimes, Alice. You didn't even answer my texts. Could you not just have come home? What was so important?'

'I got stuck at work.'

I heard her snort and I turned and glared at her, which wasn't a good idea, given I was going at a hundred down the freeway. 'What? Just because I'm not some hotshot lawyer, I can't be busy at work?'

'Alice!' Nicole was shrinking back in her seat and I turned my attention back to the road, but I was so angry I could spit. Just because I didn't work in some top-notch job she assumed I couldn't possibly know busy.

'Why didn't you tell me Paul rang last night?'

'What?'

'You know what, Alice?' I didn't want to know, but she told me anyway. 'I think you're jealous. I think you're jealous of me and Paul.'

It was me snorting then.

I couldn't stand Paul.

I mean, I could not bear him.

He was the most arrogant man I'd ever met.

And he's stupid.

I've nothing against stupid people—but stupid people

who think that they're clever just set my teeth on edge. Never mind Nicole's a lawyer, *he's* opening a coffee shop. It's all he talks about. From the day I met him till the day he—thankfully—went back to the UK, it's *all* he spoke about.

He's going to have a loyalty card for his customers. For every ten coffees they get a free one and—wait for it—on their birthdays, if they have their driver's licence with them and can prove that it is their birthday, well, they'll get a free one on that day too. Oh, and he's got this really good idea about providing the daily papers and *current* magazines for his customers. I kept waiting for the punch line. I kept waiting for him to walk into any other coffee shop in any other street and have a complete breakdown because someone had stolen his idea. Honestly, I have sat there cross-eyed listening to him droning on and on so many times.

And Nic thought I was *jealous*.

'You've done everything you can to dissuade me from going.'

'I'm driving you to the airport,' I pointed out.

We were at the turn-off and I felt like pulling over and dumping her stuff on the side of the road and letting her walk.

'You knew I was worried that he hadn't called, you knew I was panicking he was having second thoughts whether he wanted me to come, and you didn't even tell me he'd called. You didn't even write it down.'

'I forgot, okay?' We were at the short-term car parking and I wound down my window to press the button.

'Use your credit card,' Nic said. This, from a woman who pays her monthly balance in full and sometimes a little extra too on the day her statement comes. 'It'll be easier for you getting out.'

Not with *my* credit card. I pushed the button and took a ticket and I heard her irritated sigh because I hadn't taken her advice.

I couldn't stand this.

She was going.

In an hour or so she'd be gone and I didn't want it to end on a row.

'I just…' We were through the barrier and going up the levels. 'He rang just as I was dashing out. I knew you were waiting and I couldn't find a pen—I just forgot, okay? I'm sorry.' The place was packed and we drove around but ended up going up another level and I knew I hadn't mollified her.

I didn't want her to leave on a row.

I didn't want her to leave on a row because it would make it easier for her to never come back.

'I'm not jealous, Nicole.' I found a parking spot, it was narrow and it would be hell getting out, but I squeezed in. 'I'm just…'

'Just what, Alice? Go on, just say it.'

How, though?

'Just what, Alice?' She insisted to my rigid face. 'Come on, if you've got something to say then I want to hear it.'

'I'm worried about you.' I turned and looked her square in the eye and she stared right back. 'Remember how badly you took it when Dean broke up with you?'

'Paul's nothing like Dean.'

'Off course he's not,' I said quickly, and then paused

for a moment. 'But he does live on the other side of the world. I'm just worried how you're going to be if it all ends.'

'It might not end,' Nicole said firmly, 'and if it does then I'll deal with it. You don't have to worry about me, Alice. I'm not like I was when Dean broke up with me. I know I was a mess, I know I must have been a pain to live with and how great you were and everything, but that was years ago.'

'There have been others since then, though,' I pointed out gently. 'And you always seem so...' I struggled to find a softer word than the one that was on the tip of my tongue, but none was forthcoming. 'So devastated when you break up with someone. You've got so much pinned on this trip; I'm just scared you're...'

'Heading for a fall?' Nicole asked, and I nodded, not sure how she'd take it, so I was infinitely relieved when she leant over and wrapped me in a hug.

'Oh, Alice, that's so like you.' She hugged me tighter. 'Always worrying about other people, and I suppose with my track record...' She gave a little laugh and pulled away. 'I know I've been an idiot over guys in the past, but I've grown up since then. I'm a lawyer, I see women every day moving on with their lives after their relationships break up—I'm not going to crumple in a heap if Paul and I finish.'

'I know. I'm just concerned for you, that's all.'

'Well, you don't have to be,' Nicole said, but her words were gentler now.

'I'm sorry I forgot to tell you he rang.'

'I'm sorry for bringing it up, I was being stupid.'

And I left it at that.

We were friends again.

That was all that mattered.

We made an odd little group. We were rarely all to-gether but Nic seemed genuinely delighted that we'd made the effort.

Dan was there waiting, the most beautiful man on God's earth, and his face lit up when he saw me. I just fell into his arms and stayed there for a moment.

He knows me better than anyone.

He knew, more than anyone, how hard tonight was for me.

He just didn't know it all.

'She'll be back,' Dan said, and kissed the top of my head and held me for a moment. 'How was last night?'

'Great.' My face burnt in shame against his chest for a full minute before I could bring myself to look up. 'You missed a good night.'

Roz was there too. In contrast to Dan and his suit, Roz was in last night's cargo pants and T-shirt.

'Come on,' said Dan as he let me go. 'Let's go and have a drink.'

'I can't, I'm driving.'

'You can have one,' Dan said, but I shook my head and the three of us found a seat as he went to the bar.

I never got that—I mean, what is the point of having *one*?

Why would you sit there nursing one gin and tonic when you know you can't have another?

I'd rather just go without.

'What time do you have to go through?' Roz asked, and Nicole glanced at her watch.

'Not for another hour.'

My lips pursed a touch—all that carry-on and we had to sit here for an hour.

Dan was up at the bar, ordering the drinks, and I was thinking that maybe I should have one after all, because sitting here trying to make small talk, trying to pretend that in fifty-six minutes we wouldn't be saying goodbye with that awful music hitting every nerve, was more than I could bear.

You know those two-way mirrors at airports?

I assume you think, like I used to, that customs officers are standing behind them, checking you out. Watching how you walk in case you've got half a kilo of crack cocaine concealed in your privates.

Well, they're not.

Instead they're standing there pissing themselves laughing as they choose the next song and watch the public's reaction.

I swear that's what they're doing.

It's bad enough your loved ones are leaving, but to have to sit and listen to that...

I love music, I love songs, I love lyrics, I love notes, and every last one at the departure lounge is, I'm sure, designed to encourage suicide.

And that won't end it though, oh, no, because suicide's a sin, so you'll end up in hell. A hell I've just upgraded, because not only will you perpetually be saying goodbye to your loved ones, they'll have the music that most gets to you, playing over and over, as you do.

'Here you go.' Dan hadn't listened to me and had got me my one gin and tonic and I was glad that he had.

I glanced at the clock.

Fifty-three minutes now.

Oh, and they were having fun in customs, they were really cranking it up.

We'd had Mike and the Mechanics, 'The Living Years'.

And then the customs officers were all nudging and grinning behind those two-way mirrors because they'd unearthed an ancient New Seekers song, and, lucky me, it's the one Mum played over and over when Dad left— 'I Wanna Go Back'.

And I was really trying to smile and chat to Nicole, but I wanted to go back too.

'I Wanna Go Back'. I couldn't help it, I was starting to cry.

'It'll be sodding "Leaving on a Jet Plane" next!' Dan grinned and put his arm around me.

'I'm going to go through,' Nic said, because she could see I was upset and, as she doesn't smoke, she was quite happy to be on the other side trying out perfume in the duty free. I could tell Roz was relieved because she wanted to get outside for a fag.

And suddenly we were there at the silver doors and it's the place I hate most on this earth.

One of my self-help books said that the universe repeats our life lessons till we've learnt them, or something like that. Well, I'd learnt it, thanks. I hated goodbyes. I hated this very spot, but over and over I found myself there. I hated saying goodbye to Mum, kissing her and knowing when I saw her again she'd be two years older.

If I ever saw her again.

'It's six weeks, Alice.' Nicole hugged me and tried to

reassure me, and I hugged her back and didn't want to let her go.

It wasn't six weeks.

She was going through those doors and again everything was changing.

She was changing.

She wasn't coming back, or if she did come back it would just be to leave, and in my heart of hearts I knew that.

'Be nice to Hugh,' she warned. 'You will remember to pick him up? I'm sorry Mum didn't send a photo. You can just hold up a sign.'

I wouldn't need a sign.

Ginger with glasses and a cousin of Nicole's.

Oh, I wouldn't need a sign.

She cuddled Roz.

Roz, all practical and stoic, reminded me of my mum the day Bonny had left for Australia. Overweight and trying to smile.

Lisa was right, it *had* unsettled me.

I didn't want to remember that day.

But I was standing there doing just that: Bonny and Lex leaving for Australia. Mum spilling out of her shoes and skirt, trying to smile and failing, because Bonny was her baby, Bonny was her favourite and she had to let her go.

Nic had one of those hand luggage bags on wheels and she headed to the door, jaunty and shiny and *ready*. We waved her off and thank God Dan's arms were around me as I did the right thing and forced a smile and made myself wave.

But I kept remembering.

Dad there with Lucy, his new girlfriend, dainty and pregnant.

Bonny bawled her eyes out and Lex hugged me, just briefly, even though I knew he didn't want to, but it would have looked odd if he'd missed me out. I could feel the contempt and disgust as he reluctantly embraced me.

'Take care, Alice.' That was all he said. Lex still wasn't able to look me in the eye and I couldn't look at him either.

I didn't want to think about it.

I *couldn't* think about it.

So I blew my nose and I wished Dan would come back to the flat, but he had a new car and was taking it to visit his family. I couldn't stand his father, so I was more than happy that he hadn't asked me along.

'I'll come back with you,' Roz said, because she's nice like that.

She sort of mothered me a bit, I guess.

'You should have used your credit card,' Roz said, as I rummaged in my bag for money for the car-park machine. 'It's so much easier.'

I could see my hands shaking as I put in the coins and dropped one. I felt the impatience in the line behind me.

I *couldn't* think about it.

Except I couldn't *stop* thinking about.

And worse, I knew that lately, sometimes, Lex was thinking about it too.

One mistake, one stupid mistake. I wanted to live my life without having made it. I wanted to have my life back.

I didn't want to remember, but details, details, details

kept flinging themselves at me, chasing me, cornering me, and I knew they were about to catch me.

Why couldn't Big Tits just have written up a script?

'She'll be back,' Dan said, and it was a funny thing, because it was his new car that was blocking in mine. It was a sign, I was sure, that we were meant to be together perhaps, or, given how he'd parked, that he takes up all of the bed.

He gave me a cuddle as Roz waited.

I could hear the steady thud-thud-thud of his heart as mine leapt up to my throat and I wanted him to come home and lie down beside me.

'Love you lots,' he said to me.

'Love you lots too.'

It's our little thing.

'It's good she's gone to see him,' Dan added. 'She might finally work out he's a complete wanker.'

And I laughed, got into my car and I chatted to Roz.

Put my ticket in the machine and the boom gate went up and Roz and I headed for home, and Nicole wouldn't be there.

Only it's wasn't Nicole that was upsetting me.

Somehow I knew that.

I didn't want to think about it.

We stopped at the drive-through bottle shop on the way.

'Are you okay, Alice?' Roz checked when we got back to the flat.

'I'm fine,' I said, because I was pouring a nice glass of red, and I would be in a moment.

'I know you're upset about Nic going, but is there

something else?' Roz pushed. 'Is there something on your mind?'

'Nothing,' I said, because I didn't *want* it on my mind. I didn't *want* to think about it.

Just, lately, it was all I seemed to do.

Six

As you can imagine, as I sat there in the kitchen, having my split ends trimmed and trying to block out Bonny's moaning, another hour with Gus was such a nice thing to think of. So much so that as the hairdresser gave me a 'little trim to tidy things up', I wasn't concentrating—instead I was having a lovely thought about Gus leaving miserable Celeste, and me and him setting up and playing piano and…

'What the…?' She'd given me a fringe… Okay, that doesn't sound so bad if you don't have curly hair, but if you do have *really* curly hair, you will know this was a crisis.

'I've left plenty of length,' the hairdresser was saying, but I could sort of hear the wobble of panic in her voice, because even if she had cut it to the bridge of my nose, as she tried to drag the wet curls down with her finger, they were already coiling up into knots in my hairline.

'It will be fine.' Mum was reassuring.

'With lots of product.' The hairdresser was plastering on serum to weigh the curls down. I was crying, not just at the prospect of the wedding but seeing Gus, and, worse, Bonny was screaming, completely hysterical.

'Look at it!' She was staring at my hair in horror. It was like the day the nit nurse at school found nits in my hair and I could feel everyone staring at me in disgust. I sat there humiliated as Bonny screeched out what a shit bridesmaid I'd make, what a mess I looked, how I'd ruin the photos.

For months I'd put up with her histrionics. For months I'd shut up and put up and been good...

'I don't want to be your bridesmaid.' I didn't.

'I don't want to wear that disgusting pink dress.' That was certainly true.

'And you don't have to worry about people talking about your ugly bridesmaid.' I ripped off the towel from my shoulders. I was so angry, so ashamed, so embarrassed that I couldn't even cry. 'They'll be too busy looking at the back end of the bride and sniggering at her massive arse. I thought brides were supposed to lose weight before the wedding.'

Mum slapped me.

We're not talking a little slap either, she slammed her hand across my cheek, and Bonny's screams quadrupled—not, may I add, because her sister was being beaten (well, maybe not beaten, but it bloody hurt) but because someone had dared to mention Bonny's increasingly ample figure. Her dress had been let out four times.

It was Eleanor who stepped in.

She took Bonny through to the lounge and Mum to the dining room. I was left with the bloody hairdresser. With much running from room to room by Eleanor, urgent peace talks were under way.

I, through Eleanor, reluctantly, extremely reluctantly, mumbled that I was sorry for calling her fat—which I believe was translated to 'She doesn't think you're fat at all, she's just jealous and you know how crazy she goes if anyone talks about her hair. She thinks you look fantastic.'

I don't think Bonny apologised. All I got from Eleanor was 'She's just worried about tomorrow...'

And as for Mum, well, there was no formal apology—in fact, it was I who apparently apologised, through Eleanor, for upsetting Bonny on the eve of her Fucking Special Day... And then we were all back in the kitchen.

They speared it down with pins. I was ordered not to cry any more or my face would look like a pizza. I think Mum did feel a bit bad for hitting me, because she even gave me a glass of wine to calm me down. It was not the usual thimbleful we got on a Sunday—so she can say she is sensibly introducing her girls to alcohol and it won't be a mystery—no, I got a full glass of red. And when Bonny started getting upset again Mum pulled her aside and told her to calm down, that she was making things worse. I filled up my glass and felt calmer. It would look better in the morning.

I fell into bed, and bloody hoped that it would anyway.

I also hoped I'd have a bruise.

Enough that make-up would cover.

But enough, too, that Mum would notice.

It didn't look better in the morning.

And, sadly, there was no sign of a bruise.

The pins came out and my hair was still orange, a mass of orange ringlets with a stupid crinkle fringe. I had a thumping headache, and just wanted to crawl back to bed and hide till it grew out (say around eight months or so), but the hairdresser was back earlier than planned and all bubbly and bright (and reeking of brandy), and had a much better idea.

'We'll straighten it.' She pulled out a bottle and started squirting me with water. I protested but Mum gave me a warning look as Bonny came into the kitchen. She was even allowed to smoke inside because it was her Special Day. I sat there, as my head was dragged and jerked backwards and sideways, and my scalp burnt with the heat of the hairdryer. It took about forty minutes—I have loads of hair, just loads and loads of hair, but the strange thing was, as the hairdresser worked on, Bonny's mood lifted. She had sworn to kill the hairdresser last night, and her entire family too, yet she was chatting away to her now, and Mum was beaming as they all stood and watched.

'There!' The hairdresser beamed, and so too did everyone. Even Eleanor, beautiful, stunning, gorgeous Eleanor, gaped as she walked into the kitchen.

'Oh, my God!' she screeched when she saw me. 'Straight suits you.'

I ran up to the bathroom and stood there.

Yes, it was still bright orange, but it was straight, smooth and sleek and the newly created fringe fell over one eye and...

It was me.

For the first time in my life I felt as if I was staring at my reflection and recognised the person that was staring back.

Seven

I soon cheered up.

It was nice having Roz back at the flat but it wasn't just her company I wanted. There was conversation that needed to be had.

Dan had a point.

In all honesty, I sometimes got a bit embarrassed when I went out with Roz.

It wasn't just that she didn't make an effort—it was as if she tried to look like she hadn't made an effort, if you know what I mean. I knew she was hurting, I knew her ex-husband Andrew had displayed her as some sort of trophy wife and had got really narky if she put on a bit of weight or didn't get her nails and hair done religiously, but to go so far the other way was only hurting Roz.

We chatted about Nicole. Then there was a half hour or so listening to her bang on about Andrew's new girl-friend Trudy. Then I sat through the saga of Lizzie, her daughter, and their latest row and then, when she'd worn herself out talking about the bitch that is her daughter, she waffled on about Hugh.

'He might be nice.' Roz raised her eyebrows.

'He's living with someone called Gemma. (Nicole had told me *after* I'd agreed he could stay.) Nicole reckons they're serious.'

'Well, they can't be that serious if he's coming out here. He's a consultant.' Roz nudged. 'You never know.'

Oh, I knew.

'He's Nicole's cousin,' I said, because it covered so many things—anally retentive, frigid, uptight, driven. 'I only agreed because if Nicole told me one more time about Aunty Cheryl and her mother's row, and how this would really help, I'd have strangled her.' But we weren't here to discuss Lizzie or the impending arrival of Dr Hugh Watson, so, rather skilfully I thought, I moved the conversation around to this fabulous new body moisturiser and a hot oil hair treatment I'd bought from my hairdresser Karan as Roz pretended to listen.

Yes, pretended.

I could sense her distraction and it infuriated me. I wasn't doing this for my benefit—I didn't have a halo of pubic hair on my head, I wasn't slobbing on the couch in khaki oversized cargo pants and a T-shirt you could house a Third World family in.

'Roz!' She jumped to attention as I held up the pack. 'Let's have a girls' night in—maybe we could do each other's hair or something…'

'I don't know, Alice.' She shrugged, then flicked her cigarette somewhere near the ashtray and for an appalling moment I reminded myself of Nicole as I sucked in my breath. 'I'm just past all that.'

'Past all that.' I shook my head firmly. 'You're only thirty-four, Roz. You're nowhere near past it, though with that attitude...' My voice trailed off as again Roz shook her head.

'It's nothing to do with my age.' She gave a wheezy laugh, which turned into a cough. Then just when she managed to finally get her breath back, when the blue tinge left her lips and the broken veins bulging on her cheeks faded somewhat, she stubbed out her cigarette and lit another. 'When I say past it, I mean I'm over it.'

'Over what?'

'Trying to please people—I had enough of it with Andrew. No matter how thin I was, no matter how good I looked, it was never enough. Look, I see how long you spend on your hair...'

'It makes me feel nice,' I smarted. 'Believe me, Roz, I don't want to spend all those hours, but better that than walking around like I've got my finger in a plug socket. It's important to take care of yourself.'

'I'm not going there again.'

'Looking good isn't just about pleasing people, Roz,' I answered tartly. 'This is about pleasing yourself, about self-respect.'

'Perhaps,' Roz mumbled. 'It just seems like such a lot of work and for what?'

Okay, so softly, softly wasn't going to work here. I'm not very good at being firm, but really I know I sound like a bitch, I know I sound superficial and I know I probably am all those things, but I truly wasn't being bitchy or superficial at that moment. I was actually in a real predicament—one I hadn't even told Dan about.

Roz smelt!

I would never say it to Dan because, well, with Dan it would be bitching, but it wasn't just me who thought it. Since Roz started on my team I'd had four complaints about her personal hygiene. Yes, she smokes, but it wasn't just that—I smoke, half the team smokes.

The fact was Roz smelt.

I really did think Roz was depressed, I mean properly depressed. I truly didn't know what to do about it and I had no bloody idea how to approach her questionable hygiene, but I had to, because if I didn't deal with it, I'd be complained about. One of the managers, like Claire, would then no doubt have a less than sensitive word with Roz—which would kill her.

I'd bought her smellies as presents, but that was as far as I'd got. How do you tell a good friend, and one who is very sensitive, that, on occasion, she reeks?

'Why don't I rub in this hair mask for you and then we can both put on face-packs and then you can have a shower…'

'I really can't be bothered.'

'Come on, Roz—you have to get back out there!' I paused for effect, gave her a wide-eyed, very direct stare. 'I mean, I understand you might need a break after your divorce but sooner or later you're going to want to start dating again, and when you do, well…'

'I've got a date.' Her broken capillaries darkened, and she gave a shy smile.

'When?'

'Tomorrow night?'

'Who?' My mind raced. When had this happened? The only person Roz went out with was me, and there wasn't one person at work I could think of…

Unless.

'Trevor.'

'What?'

'The computer whiz, the one who comes around...'

'Oh, please!' Roz was coughing again, clearly appalled at the suggestion, and in fairness I'd be appalled at the suggestion too. Trevor had Roz's split-ends problem only his covered the whole of his face, and deodorant clearly wasn't at the top of his shopping trolley.

'Then who?'

She shook her head. 'I don't want to talk about it, Alice; I don't want to jinx myself.'

I saw an opening.

'But you want to look nice?' I nudged the pack across the table.

'I guess,' she said slowly, and I felt her waver, took it as a positive sign and moved quickly to build on it. 'I know it's what's inside that matters, Roz, but you've only got a small window of time to make that first impression. I read that it takes less that a second for a person to form an opinion, less than a second,' I reiterated as Roz started to frown. 'You can be the nicest person in the world but if you don't look the part, no one's going to come over and find out.' She was frowning deeply now, so I put it in simpler terms: 'It's fabulous you've got a date, Roz.' A bloody miracle really, I almost added, but held back. 'It's fabulous that you're getting back into the swing of things. And whoever he is, he clearly likes you for who you are...' She opened her mouth to speak but I overrode her. 'Surely you want to show that you've made a bit of an effort for him.'

She didn't answer, just stared into her empty glass,

and for an appalling moment I thought she was going to cry. Actually, it wasn't even a moment. About ten seconds later she started to howl, not delicately (this is Roz we're talking about) but great throaty sobs that caught in her throat and made her cough at the same time.

'God, Roz, I'm sorry.' So much for softly, softly. So much for helping. Here was poor Roz blubbering on my sofa, crying her eyes out and feeling fat and ugly and worthless, and it was all my fault. 'Don't listen to me,' I said, appalled at what I'd done, wrapping my arms as far around her shoulders as I could and squeezing tight. 'What would I bloody know? You look fabulous,' I said firmly, so firmly even I thought I sounded as if I meant it. 'You're going to knock his socks off...'

'No, Alice.'

'Yes, you are!' I insisted as Roz took a deep breath and calmed herself, finally looking up as I cracked open a bottle of Baileys. 'Feel better?'

She gave a sort of sorry nod, forced a bit of a watery smile and stared at me as I handed her back a very full glass.

'Tell you what,' I said frantically, terrified she might start crying again or—even worse—leave, 'why don't I ring for a pizza?'

'You don't eat carbs.'

'I'll pick at the cheese,' I said quickly, 'and smoke.' I held my breath, held it so hard I thought my lungs were going to explode but finally after the longest time she nodded.

'Better?' I asked again, and this time she gave a firmer nod.

'Much.'

'You're not just saying that?'

'No.' She gave a loud sniff and I thought the tears were about to start again, but to my utter relief she started to laugh, really laugh. 'Oh, Alice!' She shook her head and then picked up my fifty-dollar cream and started massaging it into her hooves. 'Oh, Alice,' she said again, and something in her eyes didn't add up, because for all the world I felt as if she were placating me, as if she was going on with the charade just to please me, when it was the other way around.

'Tell you what...' Roz gave a loud sniff and picked up the hair mask and read the back. 'How long do I have to leave this stuff on for?'

'Half an hour.'

'Will you play?' Roz was always doing this—always trying to get me to play the piano. The flat has one. It was there when I first moved in. Roz starts crying sometimes when I play and goes on about how I'm wasted at the paper. But that's Roz—I could play 'Trotting Pony' and she'd tell me I was fantastic.

I didn't want to sit at the piano, with Nicole gone and everything, though if it meant that she stayed...

'Deal!' I grinned, dropping the mask in a cup and grabbing some towels from the bathroom.

In fact, it turned out to be a great night. I played for forty minutes—I went through some of my old exam recital and then we had a little sing-along. She even let me pluck her eyebrows and a fun time was had by all working our way down a bottle of Baileys. By the time we were at the sucking on ice cube stage, she was so pissed I even managed to persuade her to stay over and it was kind of nice hearing her snoring from Nicole's room.

Not that I could sleep.

Playing the piano always unsettles me.

Oh, not when it's 'Coming Round The Mountain' or 'My Old Man', but when I play the classics, when I'm stretched, when I have to reach inside myself, I feel, for a while at least, as if I'm coming apart.

Eight

'Hey!' Gus gave a smile of appreciation as I walked in. I had washed in the sink for two days, avoiding steam from the bath, and even dragging a couple of emerging curls out with the hairdryer myself in anticipation of this moment.

And it was worth it.

Oh, it was so, so worth it.

'You look great,' Gus said. 'How was the wedding?'

'Great.' I beamed, because the wedding had been awful, but at the end of the reception I had got off with this guy, Lex's best man, in fact, and finally had a decent snog and then a bit of a fumble in the loos.

Celeste didn't comment on my lovely hair, just scowled up at me from the kitchen where she was standing. I didn't smile back—I had heard them rowing from the street when I arrived, and it made Gus's smile all the more worth it, that he could manage to be nice, unlike Celeste.

We went through and I set up my music.

It was my favourite piece.

Tchaikovsky, 'January', from *The Seasons*.

I'd been focusing, amongst others, on this piece for a good few months now. It was for my exam and it was so bloody hard.

Not so much technically, but my playing strength is emotion and that is the hard part to explain. At home when I was practising, every now and then I got it. Sometimes I played it so well, even I cried. I just had to work out how to do that for my exam.

You see, my sisters think it's just a matter of playing. They can't understand that it might take a year to learn one piece of music, but Gus understood, and he was so patient—except he wasn't this evening.

'You haven't been practising.'

'I have.' I screwed up my face as I lied.

'Pianissimo!' he said. 'It's supposed to be soft but it's like a herd of fucking elephants.' I didn't mind that he swore—it made me feel older. I knew he wouldn't swear with some of the little kids. Over and over we went but we never got past the first page—and I could hear the mistakes and feel him wince. It must have given Celeste a thumper of a headache, because when we went over the hour, she came in.

'How much longer, Gus?' She didn't even look at me.

'When I'm done!' Gus didn't look at her either, just sat in silence as Celeste slammed the door.

'I'm sorry.' I felt as if the row was my fault; I mean, it wasn't exactly a row, she'd just slammed the door, but I knew he was proving a point when, instead of closing my music, he told me to go from midway.

God, I loved this bit; there's a lot of hand crossing and I ached to play it right—I yearned for the day I did it perfectly, but still I messed up. He was behind me, and he played the right hand and I played the left. He did it so much more easily, and then he mucked up too—well, he had an excuse because he was over me, and not sitting down, but he laughed at his own mistake and then I laughed too, and everything suddenly felt a bit better.

Anyway, there we were, me trying to sort out the hand-change thing and he was still leaning over and I messed up.

His hands went over mine to show me a move, just as he did in every other lesson, I guess, but it was different, I could feel his fingers. Before it was like he was showing me, but now I could feel them.

He moved his other hand so that his arms were under my armpits and he played for a moment. I could feel his arms against my breasts. They were sore; my period had finished so it wasn't because of that. It was a nice sore, sort of heavy, and achy.

I was looking down at his fingers, but all I could see were my breasts. The nipples were sticking out, and it was like I'd never seen them before. They were like thimbles under my dress and he was still playing the tune. I could feel his breath on my cheek but I had no breath. I wasn't breathing; my breasts hurt and as his arms pulled back his hands brushed them.

It was like watching in slow motion. His hands had the palms facing inwards, and as they slid from my chest they stroked the sides and I don't know if they paused; as I lay in my bed that night I wondered if they had, but I don't think so. They just slid against the sides and I wanted them to slide back, but they didn't.

'Okay.' His voice sounded normal. 'Let's leave it there

for now. Practise, Alice.' I was closing up my music and I dropped a couple of sheets and I turned around to pick them up—I was head level with his crotch and I saw his erection. I wanted to touch it, but of course I didn't. I stood up.

I pretended that I hadn't seen it.

I wasn't even sure if I had, but as I lay in bed that night all I knew was that I was having another lesson in a couple of days.

Nine

I hated my own company.

That's not what I said to Big Tits because I knew it wasn't how I was supposed to be. I knew, because I'd read all the self-help books. I was supposed to have inner reserves, to be able to spend a thoughtful evening alone, lighting candles and playing music that meant something to me, as I spoiled myself by soaking in an aromatic bath with a deep and moving book. But the simple fact was, I hated being by myself.

Hated bouncing questions I already knew the answers to.

Hated watching a film when there was no one to pass the tissues to and share the ending.

And where was the fun in candles and soft music and bubble baths when you were alone?

Anyway, the flat didn't have a bath.

Roz had taken her weary liver out on her date and Dan hadn't returned my phone calls all day. By evening I re-sorted to texting him saying I was *really* worried about work and needed his advice and he eventually texted back and said he'd come over.

You see, Dan's a careers counsellor: he goes around schools telling sixteen-year-olds they can be whatever they want to be and he takes it all very, *very* seriously, so I knew if I dangled that little carrot, he'd bite quickly. That he might manage to tear himself away from Matthew for five minutes.

Yes, Matthew.

Sorry to disappoint you—believe me I felt the same when I found out too.

Worse!

Dan, you see, was possibly the love of my life.

Lisa, I'm sure, if she knew about Dan and me, would say that I was comfortable with Dan *because* he was gay, that because there was no sexual tension I was able to be myself and to relax with him.

Bullshit.

I loved him long before I knew he was gay.

I wasted months, wondering what the hell I was doing wrong.

You just wouldn't spot it—okay, the fitted shirt, the Pilates and, I guess, the fact that he exfoliates might have been missed clues—but loads of guys look after themselves now.

His friend Michelle was my flatmate at the time— they weren't going out or anything—and Dan used to come around and I'd pull out all the stops.

Then he became more regular at the flat and I stopped pulling out all the stops and he still liked me. I could answer the door in baggy pyjamas, still orange from a new spray tan and walking with my toenails splayed with cotton wool because I was painting them, and he still liked me.

Then I got drunk and slept with some football player to make him jealous. Well, suffice to say it ended in tears—with a blotchy face and a rather fat lip (the football player *did* have anger issues). Dan was the one who held the ice pack.

Dan was appalled when I confessed that I'd done it to make him notice me.

And then he'd told me the truth.

And he also told me just how much he hated the truth.

That he'd rather slash his abdomen and dissect his own intestines than fess up and tell the world that he was gay.

At first it had been a whoosh of relief—so *that* was why he didn't fancy me.

Then I had decided that, if I tried harder, one day he might—he had assured me he wouldn't.

He wasn't bisexual; he said it as a warning.

He was gay.

So I got angry...

And we fell out, but we missed each other and made it up, though we hadn't yet come full circle. There was still this...this...bitterness there on my part.

I mean, how unlucky was I, that the perfect guy for me, the one guy who actually loves me, just wasn't technically wired that way?

I hated all the crap about 'Oh, I'm not homophobic—my best friend's gay'.

I actually HATED it that he was gay.

I cried at every episode of *Will and Grace*.

I hated it that I would love the smell of him coming

out of the shower for ever, that he could make me laugh with just a twitch of his lips, that he's just the most amazing guy in the whole wide world, that he can pull me in his arms and make me feel safe—and that, faults and all, somehow he loves me and yet somehow he can't.

He loves me.

Just not in that way.

However, Dan had been a bit off recently. Every time I rang he was always just on his way out, and call me paranoid if you must, but whenever I got the answering-machine I swear he was home, hovering over the receiver and not picking it up because it was me. It wasn't fair. We'd been through everything together. When he was in the closet, he'd been only too happy to drag me to every family function imaginable and pass me off as his girl-friend and then, when he was coming out, night after night had been spent metaphorically holding his hand as he worked up the courage to tell his family and friends. And once out! Oh, yes, he's Mr Bloody Sensible now, but he was wild for a while there, dragging me along to gay bars where I'd sit and pretend not to notice how long it took him to go to the men's room.

Now, though, when *I* needed him, he was too busy being happy with Matthew.

I was making lime margaritas—there was a mountain of limes that I was juicing and I had all the ingredients lined up to whizz in the blender but Dan filled the kettle.

'I'm not drinking,' he said, which meant that he wouldn't be staying.

'I got a couple of movies, though.' More and more it was getting like this with Dan. Since he had started going out with Matthew I was slotted in, like a dental appointment or a quick dash to the shops on a lunch break. 'Stay the night, Dan, you haven't for ages.'

'I can't.'

'Okay.' I knew not to push it. 'At least stay for a while, have a drink...'

'Actually, no.' He looked uncomfortable, six feet two and in his suit he looked bloody gorgeous but, actually, nervous. 'You and I...' he gave a tight smile '...well, it's causing a few problems with Matthew.'

'What?' I was about to turn on the blender, but instead I laughed. 'How, for God's sake? We've established you don't fancy me. Can never fancy me... Surely to God you're allowed friends.'

'Of course I am...' He was working his way up to telling me something and suddenly I didn't want to hear it, so I turned the blender on instead, but you can only blend a margarita for so long and after a moment or two I had no choice but to stop. I could feel his chocolate-brown eyes on me, but I didn't turn and look at them, instead focusing a great deal of attention on salting two glasses as he spoke to my back.

'Every time I come here I get smashed and end up staying.'

I had the salt in lovely perfect lines, the glasses were icy cold from the fridge, and I slowly poured two drinks before I answered.

'Don't get smashed, then.' Now I did turn and look at him, angry, because how the hell was it my fault? Since when did his boyfriend decide it was up to me to police him? 'I'm hardly pouring drinks down your throat and tying you to the bed, Dan.'

'I know that.'

'If you don't want to be here, don't use Matthew as an excuse.' He closed his eyes and I could hear him drag in a deep breath.

'I do want to be here.'

'Then tell Matthew that.' I was near tears, I was so angry I felt like crying—bloody Matthew was so jealous he hated Dan out of his sight for anything more than five minutes. Every time we went out he texted about a gazillion times and if Dan did have the guts to stay over, his phone would start bleeping at the crack of dawn.

'I have told him,' Dan said. 'I'm here, aren't I? It's just...' His voice trailed off and then, because he knows me, because he knew that even if I wasn't boohooing, even if there were no tears, I was actually crying. We had promised, *promised* that no relationship would ever come between our friendship, and now it seemed one was.

Dan gives the nicest cuddles.

I stood in the kitchen and I just leant on him, I smelt him and it was the nicest place in the world to be and I didn't want to let him go, I didn't want him going back to Matthew, but I knew if I stamped my foot too hard, then it would be a long time till I saw him again. That Matthew would up the bloody curfew, so I trod carefully.

'Make me a coffee, then,' I said to his chest.

'Serious?'

'Sure.' I felt him smile, felt him relax as I made it easier for him. 'Anyway, I've got to ring Mum tonight and sometimes she talks for hours.' He kissed the top of my head and then he loosened his arms and smiled down at me and I smiled back.

Dan, the only guy on this planet I can look straight in the eye.

'I love you, Alice.'

'I know.'

'I am here for you.'

'I know.' Yeah, take that, Matthew, I thought, you can bitch and moan and whine, but you'll never break up our friendship.

'One won't kill, I guess…' He picked up the margarita and rolled his eyes in bliss as he took a sip.

'You'll get me in trouble with Matthew,' I warned.

'We just won't tell him.'

I felt a rush of relief as he came back to me, a whoosh of euphoria as whatever crisis had loomed was somehow averted.

Dan was back and together we always had a ball.

We just didn't that night.

He asked about my work, but I didn't want to just talk about that. 'I'm worried about Roz,' I said, hoping that would get him going. He loved a gossip, but Dan rolled his eyes.

'I really think she's depressed.'

'I'd be depressed if I looked like that,' Dan said. 'No wonder her husband left—you'd slash yourself if you had to wake up to that face every morning.'

'But he didn't leave her.' I frowned as much as my Botoxed forehead would allow. 'It was the other way around—Roz left him. Though God knows why, he was gorgeous. *Gorgeous*,' I added for effect, and Dan shot me a look of disbelief. 'She says they married way too young and that she felt stifled, that she needed to *find* herself.'

'Find a bigger McDonald's outlet more like.' Dan pursed his lips and then he glanced at his watch and I felt a flutter of panic, so I quickly changed the subject to Dan's favourite.

Me!

That was a joke.

My career, or lack of it.

I hated my job. I knew, *I knew*, in these times it was good to *have* a job—but, frankly, I didn't know if I would for much longer. I did the website as well sometimes, thanks to Dan pushing me to do a course, but mainly I sat with headphones on, typing up birth, marriage and death notices, announcements, stuff for sale, jobs, that sort of thing. We used to do more dating ads, that was fun, but everything was moving to the internet, not just dating—and what with eBay (love it, love it), I couldn't see my job lasting much longer.

So I told him all about my worries, that I was sure management was up to something, hoping he'd be so consumed by my problems, that he'd fill up his glass. 'I'm probably just being pessimistic.'

'You're being realistic,' Dan said, which made the knot in my stomach tighten. 'Everyone's cutting back. You need to get some real qualifications.' I hadn't really wanted a doom-and-gloom careers appraisal. I wanted him to say that I'd been there nine years, that of course my job was safe, but Dan had said all he was going to. He looked at his watch again and I knew, despite the win with the margarita, I was about to lose my audience. 'I've got to go, Al,' he said. 'I'm exhausted.'

It wasn't even nine, but I followed him to the door,

determined not to push him to stay again, and I accepted his hug and kiss goodnight.

'Think about it,' Dan said.

'Think about what?'

'What we spoke about the other week—you really need to think about going back to your studies.'

'I could never afford it.' I thought of my credit cards, the rent, the car payments, but Dan disagreed.

'You can't afford not to, Alice. You've got talent. Don't waste it. Take a package if one's offered and get yourself to university.'

I knew he was right. I guess he'd said what I wanted deep down to hear, even if I didn't really want to hear it now.

I tried to ring Mum but the line was busy, so I tried Bonny, but her line was busy too.

I tried Mum again and guessed she must be talking to Bonny.

I even contemplated ringing Eleanor, but she was so much older, we just weren't that close and it was always awkward when I called.

So I tried Bonny again and I got Lex.

'Oh, hi.' I was surprised. Normally Bonny answered the landline.

'Bonny's in the bath,' Lex said. 'Do you want me to get her to call you?'

'It's nothing important. How are the kids?'

'Feral! Look, while I've got you…' And then there was a pause. 'Let me just close the door.' I felt my insides turn to liquid. 'Sorry, I don't want her to hear.'

My hand was shaking so much I could barely get my

drink to my mouth. 'You haven't forgotten about next Saturday.'

'Of course not.'

'It's just…' And then I heard Bonny's voice in the background and Lex lowered his. 'Can you make a special effort?' And then his voice was back to normal. 'It's your sister.'

I chatted to Bonny, but my heart wouldn't stop thumping and thankfully, given she was dripping wet, we didn't talk for long.

I was all unsettled. I took the blender over to the computer and filled up my glass. I searched universities and entrance criteria and it was just too confusing so I checked my horoscope, which said now was a good time to give up bad habits but there was nothing about my finances or love life improving.

So I checked another and I checked another and then something caught my eye.

Cosmic Love by Yasmin Boland.

A step-by-step guide to cosmic-ordering the perfect guy.

It was all about manifesting, apparently.

Build it and they will come sort of thing.

It was an eBook, which was just as well, because I'd have been too embarrassed to go into a shop and buy it. I typed in my details and waited for my credit card to be declined, but—well, the universe must have wanted me to have it because, despite my late payment, or rather no payment, there it was in my inbox.

I loved it.

It was so positive. All I had to do was write lists (well, there was a bit more to it than that, but I went straight to the good stuff) and tell the universe what I wanted in a partner.

And not some vague wants either, a specific order.

So I did.

I did everything Yasmin told me.

Well, except the clearing-out stuff part, but Nicole had had a big tidy before she left. And I didn't bother with the cleansing shower to get rid of past loves, and visualising and snipping the threads that bound and letting them go and all that mumbo-jumbo crap.

Be sure that you are ready, Yasmin warned, and that you've done your preparation.

Oh, I was ready.

I *loved* this book—I toddled off to the kitchen and made another jug and got some scissors so I could cut out the pyramid that came with it.

If I had ink in the printer.

I did.

It was all aligning that night.

I had to write what I wanted—I could be as specific as I liked and for a second there my mind did flick to Dan, though Yasmin had warned me not to manipulate—and really, even if I could turn Dan straight, would I want to? I mean, you'd never relax, would you? Anyway, Yasmin said it was better to trust the universe, that the right guy would always come back if he was the one.

I had to print out the pyramid again because when I was cutting it out I chopped off the end.

God, I was pissed.

And, yes, I trusted the universe and everything, but not completely.

I wanted blond or raven, not someone with my

affliction. I mean, I had to think of our children and, anyway, people might think we were brother and sister when we went out. So I knew it couldn't be Hugh. Nicole's cousin held no charm for me, but perhaps he was a means to an end. One look at me, and Hugh's eyes would widen. 'There's the type of girl to take to the neurosurgeons' Christmas party. That's the type of girl who would look marvellous at the Kids with Cancer Christmas fundraising ball.'

Well, maybe not Kids with Cancer, just underprivileged or burn victims or something and I'd be there, radiant and smiling all ready to meet the love of my life.

I added a few little extra requests, and then I wrote MR.

It stood for Mr and Massive Ring.

Clever, huh? No one, if they found my list, would work that out.

I followed the instructions as best as I could, but I didn't have a compass, so I guessed as to the south-west corner of the flat. And then, given I was sorting out my love life, I decided I might as well go the whole hog so I went back to the computer and read again the application procedures and the qualifications required to be a music teacher. I even filled in some forms to ask for them to send me some forms. It was all so daunting—the more I looked, the more overwhelming it seemed. Impossible, actually.

I had barely scraped through my exams at school. Even if by some miracle I was accepted, how could I give up my job? I was in debt to the eyeballs as it was.

I thought of the pile of unopened envelopes stuffed in my drawers and under my mattress, the credit-card statements that were too scary to open—let alone think about—so I didn't.

While my credit card was behaving I bought an online tarot reading and then poured another margarita instead.

Ten

I woke at two.

Just shot awake, wondering what had woken me, my heart racing and trying to catch my breath, sure that I must have had a nightmare—except I still couldn't breathe.

I was soaked in sweat, and I dragged myself into the bathroom, gulped icy water from the tap—it didn't help. I had to concentrate on breathing. It wasn't happening. Every breath was an effort and I couldn't seem to get enough in.

I rang Roz—I knew she was on a date, but surely she'd be home by now. I didn't even care at that point.

'Roz…' I could barely get the word out as her voice came on the phone. 'I can't…'

'It's okay…' I could hear she was groggy and asleep but just the sound of her voice calmed me. At least someone knew, I mean, if I collapsed this second Roz would send for help. 'I'm on my way.'

She didn't even dress—mind you, Roz's sleepwear is pretty much the same as her day wear: tracksuit bottoms and a vast T-shirt, except, horror of horrors, she wasn't wearing a bra.

All this I noticed as she bundled me into her little car. My breathing was a bit better. Since I had known help was on the way, it had improved a fraction. And as we drove to the hospital I managed to get my breathing into some sort of a rhythm right till we got to the doors. Security was waving her on.

'You can't park here, love.'

'She can't breathe!' Roz said.

'Then she's in the right place, but patient drop-off is down there.'

Roz was muttering and swearing and then I saw my hands do this strange thing: they were tingling but it was like my hands were spastic, my fingers all curling up, and I couldn't straighten them.

'She's going unconscious…' I could hear Roz panicking, but the security didn't panic, he rolled his eyes and got a nurse, who helped me out of the car. She didn't seem to be particularly worried either.

They took me straight into the triage room; the nurse put a little probe on my finger and told me to calm down.

'I can't breathe…'

'Your oxygen saturation is ninety-nine per cent' There was a bored note to her voice which infuriated me as she wrapped a blood-pressure cuff around my arm. Did she have any idea how hard it was to get it to that? Breathing should be natural, you shouldn't have to think about it, but I did. I had to pull in air and hold it in, and it still didn't go deep enough. My hands were doing strange things, and she was giving me a bloody paper bag and telling me to breathe in and out slowly.

'You're having a panic attack.'

'No!' I pushed the bag away.

'How much have you had to drink tonight, Alice?'

What did that have to do with anything? 'I'm allergic...'

'To what?'

'Hazelnuts.'

'Okay...' the nurse said, 'you can wait in the waiting room. Just keep breathing into your paper bag.'

'I can't.' I couldn't. I could not face going out there, but the fucking nurse wouldn't budge. 'Your girlfriend can let us know if you get worse.'

Now, a quick explanation here. In Australia, and it took me a while to get used to this, but a friend who's a girl is called your girlfriend. I've been back to London and it's used more that way there too now, but there was something about the way she said *girlfriend* that had me frown. I looked over at Roz, who was blushing bright red and then she led me out.

'She thinks we're...'

'I know,' Roz mumbled, blushing to her roots. 'Just breathe into the bag.'

It wasn't helping. My lips were tingling, there was just so much noise, so much going on, I couldn't stand it. I stood up and paced. I honestly didn't feel safer in the hospital. I actually thought I might *die* here, and then they'd be bloody sorry. Panic attack indeed!

I was up at the big plastic shield that separated the staff from the waiting room now, and the nurse was refusing to look over. I could see stars and spots and I was like a cartoon character then, pressed to the glass. I thought I was dying and Roz was calling for help. Finally they realised that I wasn't putting it on, that their stupid paper bag wasn't going to work, because a buzzer went and a nurse came with a wheelchair and I was sped through.

Okay, not sped, and I didn't end up in Resus with George Clooney saying, 'On my count...'

Instead I was given a gown and told to get undressed and put it on, and Roz helped. I couldn't have done it on my own. My lips were completely numb now. Then this twelve-year-old that was dressed up as a male nurse asked me to explain what had happened.

I wheezed away as he put an IV into the back of my hand, which hurt, I might add, as Roz did the talking for me.

'We were in with the same last week. She's got a nut allergy...' And finally I got a response, because the twelve-year-old looked worried. He checked my blood pressure then dashed off to get a doctor as Roz wrapped her arms around me and told me I was going to be fine.

'Just keep breathing into the bag, Alice.'

'It's not helping.'

Well, my ten seconds of concern lasted till the arrival of the emergency registrar, which coincided with the arrival of my old notes. He listened to my chest and confirmed the triage nurse's diagnosis.

'She's having an anxiety attack.'

'No...' I shook my head. I was crying, and not able to breathe. 'I woke up and my lips were swollen and tingling...' Well, they hadn't been then but that was what they had asked me last time. The emergency doctor sort of hummed and haaed for a minute before he wrote me up for 10 mg of diazepam and some oral steroids. 'In case a mild allergic reaction triggered the anxiety attack.'

Bastard.

Still, I didn't argue, I didn't have the breath. And in a moment the twelve-year-old had returned with a little plastic cup with six pills. The white ones, he explained, were prednisolone and I would have to take a reducing dose for the next few days. The blue one was Valium.

I took the blue one first.

It took about twenty minutes—actually, maybe a bit less. Roz was so kind and reassuring, and the bright lights and all the equipment were starting to reassure me too, and when twelve-year-old took my pulse and said it was slowing down, I forgot about my breathing for a moment. I lay back and it was such a relief to not have to remember to breathe. Of course, as soon as I re-membered, my breathing got harder and I had to remind myself to do it, but gradually it was just happening, even when I thought about it.

I lay there thinking about hypnosis tapes as Roz held my hand.

I'd bought loads, I had the lot, but I hated that they all, at some point, told you to concentrate on your breathing and the natural rise and fall of your chest, or the effort-lessness of breathing. As soon as they said that, I swear, it didn't happen naturally. If I could find a shagging self-hypnosis tape that didn't tell you to concentrate on your breathing, I would have given up fags and booze and kept all my new year's resolutions years ago.

'Better?'

The doctor roused me from my slumber. Roz had just gone to the loo, he explained, and he wanted to have a word with me. Now that I wasn't dying I noticed that he was actually nice looking, in a sort of Hugh Laurie *House*-type way. Well, actually he was ugly, really, but he was a doctor and sort of crabby, and that reminded me, I had one coming to stay in the morning. I toyed with telling him, maybe it would give me reciprocal rights or something, maybe then he'd believe me.

'Much!' I said, but then I remembered twelve-year-old saying that the steroids might take a while to kick in. 'Well, still a bit itchy,' I said, scratching at my ribcage.

'Itchy?' He sort of hauled me up and checked my back then laid me flat on my back and looked at my stomach and then my legs, and then he scratched the inside of my arms with the end of his knee-jerker thingy and I willed just a little welt to appear.

It didn't.

Had I brought my handbag I could have whipped on some lip plumper made of cayenne pepper and he'd have believed me, but my bag was sitting at home. I looked towards the curtains he had pulled and willed Roz to appear. She'd put him right, but he must have read my mind.

'I've asked your friend to wait outside so that I can talk to you. How much have you had to drink, Alice?'

'A friend came over,' I said. 'He made margaritas, I've never had them before, maybe I'm allergic...'

'You had a full-blown anxiety attack.'

'I didn't,' I insisted. 'I was asleep...though I did eat some leftover Chinese; I think I saw a cashew...'

'Alice, you might convince Brent, but you won't convince me—that was a full-blown anxiety attack. The tingling, the numbness, the hand spasticity were because your oxygen and carbon dioxide levels were out of balance—that's why we got you to breathe into a paper bag.'

'I wasn't anxious,' I insisted. 'I was asleep.'

'Is there anything on your mind?' I remember feeling sort of vaguely touched. The place was steaming, there were *really* sick people, I could see the trolley wheels and feet whizzing past beneath the curtain, hear the shouts for help, and House was being nice to me. But there wasn't anything on my mind—okay, I had more than fifty grand in credit-card debts, but he was hardly going to write a cheque. Still, I did concede a touch.

'I've got a few money problems.'

'Okay.'

'I'm getting on top of it.'

'Good,' House said. 'Anything else?'

'Isn't that enough?'

'You tell me.'

He smiled at me and he actually wasn't so ugly, he was really quite nice looking—with a bit of luck he was thinking of breaking his ethical code.

I gave what I hoped was a sort of brave smile.

'Nothing…' I racked my mind for something that would make me sound stoic and brave, but there really was nothing.

'Anxiety doesn't just go away, Alice. A lot of people have money problems, but they're not in emergency at four a.m. with an anxiety attack. You need to talk to someone.'

'And I will,' I lied.

'Good,' he clipped. 'Right, Brent will dispense your script—I've given you a reducing dose of steroids. It's important that now you've started you take the course—you have to finish them, Alice,' he reiterated, 'and I'll write you up for twenty diazepam tablets, one or two a day as required... You need to go and talk to your GP and give him this letter, I've suggested that you see a psychologist.'

Well, he could suggest what he liked. There was no way I was going back to Lisa—except I wasn't really listening to him now.

Twenty diazepam.

If you counted tonight, that was three weeks' worth.

I *would* give up drinking. Take tonight. Had I been able to relax, to switch off, I wouldn't have had so much to drink. But now I had three weeks' supply. I would go on a diet too—absolutely no carbs. No, better than that, I would do the lemon detox diet. I would start it this very morning. I would buy nicotine patches, and cleanse my body and exfoliate every night, and in three weeks' time I'd be glowing and calm and radiant.

I was delighted.

'You will see your GP?' House checked, and I gave an assured nod, signing for my goodies when Brent appeared. I was dressed and ready and actually smiling when an anxious-looking Roz was allowed back in.

'All okay?' she checked.

'Fine.'

'What did the doctor say?'

'That I have to see my GP...' As we walked out to the car park the cool night air hit me and I was a bit wobbly and shaky, and Roz took my arm. 'He thinks I have an underlying allergy, though they're not sure to what. I have to have some bloods and that done.'

'You poor thing,' Roz fretted, seeing me in first, then walking round to the driver's seat.

It was nearly five a.m. by the time Roz got me home.

Woozy from the Valium, all I wanted to do was sleep, but Roz found me trying to set my alarm.

'What are you doing?'

'I have to pick up Hugh.'

'I'll pick up Hugh. And you're not going to work to-morrow. You're staying in bed.'

'I haven't got any sick days left.' I climbed into bed, too tired to pull the duvet up.

'I'll ring them for you—I'll ring the hospital if you like, get a note.'

'I won't get paid if I don't go in.'

It was the closest I'd come to admitting how broke I was, that I couldn't ring in sick tomorrow, that I needed my crap hourly rate, and thankfully Roz didn't push it, just tucked the bedding in around me.

'Sorry I rotted up your night,' I said.

'You didn't.' Roz smiled.

'You were on a date.'

'About three hours before you rang.'

'I didn't disturb anything?'

'It was our first date—I was hardly…' She didn't carry on: we both knew our version of first dates were different.

'Thank you.'

'Go to sleep, Alice. I'll crash in Nicole's room.'

'You don't mind staying?'

'Of course not.' Roz paused before she left. 'Alice, is anything worrying you?'

'I told you, nothing.'

'Okay—but if you were worrying about something, you know you could talk to me.'

'I know,' I lied.

'If there is something on your mind, you can share it—I might even understand.'

I looked at her kind, tired face.

A woman who'd married at seventeen, who was studying to be an accountant, who had it all so together she didn't even use conditioner, and as much as she might think she'd understand, I knew that she couldn't.

'I'm fine.'

'Good.'

'I really am.'

I was tired, but I still couldn't settle, so I took one of the Valium and read one of my self-help books as I waited for it to kick in.

I was to picture myself as a child apparently, to love the little me, and I managed a wry grin at that.

If only she'd seen what I'd looked like!

I lay back on the pillow, I could hear Roz snoring and it soothed me.

With Roz in the flat, I could almost stand to think.

Eleven

I pulled out some money from my savings and on
Thursday after school I went to the hairdresser and got
it straightened again. It looked even better this time than
it had at the wedding. She smoothed it with serum, and
then, after I went home and thankfully Mum was out, I
washed myself and I shaved my legs. I pinched some of
the perfume Lex had bought Bonny.

I wanted to change into something, but I always went
in my school uniform and I didn't want him to think I
was making an effort or, worse, for Celeste to think that
I was, so I didn't bother.

Celeste was poisonous; she warned him that they had
to leave at seven for the antenatal class as we headed to
his study.

'Like I want to learn to change nappies!' Gus said as
he closed the study door.

But whatever had happened on Monday had gone. He
was very businesslike, and really pushed me. He even
told me off a bit when I messed up, and said that if I
wanted to pass then I had to practise more.

Celeste came in at ten to seven and told him they had to leave now.

'Alice has paid for an hour,' Gus said. 'You don't mind spending it, Celeste; well, I have to earn it. I'll meet you there.'

She slammed out of the study again and then out of the house.

'I can go...'

'No.' Gus shook his head. 'Play, Alice—she moans about the noise. Jesus...' He hissed out his frustration, closed his eyes and I felt so sorry for him. He was doing his best, trying to earn some money, and all she did was moan.

And I told him so.

'She's lucky to have you.'

'Well, she doesn't think so... We went to this sodding class last week. I'm doing everything right—I've married her, I'm supporting her and there's not even a sniff of appreciation, not a sniff of anything.'

'Then she's...' I didn't know what to say—I sort of knew he was talking about their sex life. I didn't understand Celeste. How could she not want him? She had him, why wouldn't she try to keep him?

'Come on,' he prompted, 'let's go through it again.'

I messed up—and he told me to do it again, then stood up, and then he put his arms in to show me how my fingers should go... His hand was over mine but not as it had been. I could hear him breathing a bit hard, feel his hands sort of capture mine, placing each finger on the key. Instead of pressing down on the keys, I pushed my fingers up, sort of entwined them with his.

'Play.' His voice was lower and he moved his hands,

and I played, or tried to, because his arms slid away. This time his hands did pause at my breasts, just at the sides, and I was still playing, and they were still there, a pause as still I played on. I felt dizzy. I wanted to stop but it seemed imperative that I keep playing, because if I did stop, maybe so would his hands. They were stroking the sides now, then moving round to my nipples.

His hands were on my breasts. I looked down and his fingers were opening the buttons of my blouse. I was going to bite him, but I didn't.

I breathed in tightly.

I was somewhere between relief and fear as his fingers slid into my bra, then the fear slid away and my breath blew softly out.

It felt nice.

Twelve

'I hope I didn't wake you!'

I jumped out of my skin when I shuffled into the kitchen at midday and saw Prince Harry filling a kettle, dressed in jeans and T-shirt. He was all sort of untucked and rumpled and I instantly wanted to smooth him and tuck him in.

Well, not Prince Harry exactly—his hair was a little less red, and his cheeks a little less ruddy—but I *do* like Harry: for a redhead he's sexy and he's fun and he's naughty... Where was I...? Oh, yes.

I will give you rapid details so that you will understand what I suddenly found myself dealing with.

I was expecting, I don't know, someone with bright orange hair to greet me—instead I found myself gazing upon dead straight hair, a touch redder than strawberry blond, and he had a long fringe that was flopping in his face (given he was already in transit when I wrote my requirements, I think the universe had amended my order as best it could).

Glasses—but oblong black ones that I have to say looked fantastic.

A big body—not fat, just sort of big and male, and taking up the kitchen—and he wasn't white. This is a very important point. I glow in the dark I am so white— that is why I have a fair-skinned spray tan once a week and apply holiday moisturiser for fair skin each night.

I sent a silent thanks to the universe for the spectacular, rapid delivery of my order. In eBay terms the feedback was five-star, fab, better than expected.

'Coffee?' he asked, spooning instant into a mug, and when I nodded he went through the sugar and milk ritual. 'Well, you're easy,' he said when I declined them both.

You have no idea, I almost quipped, but it was there in my head and bizarrely he seemed to hear my thoughts, because he grinned and my stomach folded over on itself. Never, *never* had a first attraction been more intense and I could tell, I could just taste and breathe and sense, that the feeling was mutual, that it would be absolutely appropriate if he walked over now and kissed my face off.

Of course he didn't.

He sat opposite me at the table, a slow smile on his gorgeous mouth, and stared for a moment and I stared back—it was almost as if we *recognised* each other.

Thank you, Yasmin. Thank you thank you thank you thank you...

'Sorry about the glasses. Nic said they'd give you a fright,' he teased. 'I'll put in my contacts soon.'

Bloody Nicole.

His flight had been long, he replied on being asked, but he'd liked Singapore Airport.

We chatted about flying for a while and gave each

other a few horror stories and then I glanced at the clock and got up and pulled some bacon out of the fridge.

He made toast (which I don't eat) and more coffee while I cooked. I splurged carb-wise (for me) and added mushrooms and tomatoes. He was so bloody easy to talk to. He was sorry to hear I hadn't been well and said I really hadn't had to send Roz to pick him up, but it was appreciated.

Then I had a teeny panic that maybe he would be working in Emergency too and would haul up my notes (that's the sort of thing I would do if I fancied someone and had access).

'It's a busy place, Emergency,' I said.

He pulled a face. 'I avoid it as much as I can.'

'Because you're a consultant?' I checked, and he laughed.

'Not for another week.'

He looked too young for such a senior position and I told him so and he laughed again and said, yes, that he was. 'But psychiatry's one of those specialities where you can get on quickly, there's a real dearth.' I didn't hear anything else for a moment, for the great whooshing sound in my ears. He Was A Psychiatrist?

I was sitting opposite a psychiatrist?

I could think of nothing worse.

A psychiatrist.

Didn't they have half-rimmed glasses and patches on their elbows and start every sentence with *Perhaps what you're trying to say is...*?

I was horrified.

I would have preferred him to be a proctologist.

Oh, God, I should have been far more specific with my list.

Still, he was here now—and it was too late to worry because, psychiatrist or not, I fancied him rotten.

'Do you do hypnosis?'

'Sorry?'

'In your work?' I was cheering up suddenly. With my own resident hypnotist, there was no end to what I could achieve.

'Occasionally,' Hugh said. 'Why?'

'I'm just interested in it,' I said airily, then I realised the time and pictured Claire's face if I was late again. I toyed with ringing Roz to ask her to ring in sick for me, but I knew I mustn't. 'I'd better get going.'

'You work at the paper?' Hugh checked, as I (unusually for me) cleared and rinsed my plate. 'What do you do?'

Normally, when trying to impress, I lie. Well, not an outright lie, but I say something vague that hints I'm a journalist, but somehow I knew that he knew. After all, he'd clearly spoken to Nicole and would have spent time in the car with Roz.

'I work on the classifieds.' I rolled my eyes to show how mind-numbingly boring it was. 'With Roz.'

'That's right, she was saying.'

'It was only supposed to be for a year or two,' I admitted. 'Actually, I'm thinking of going to university.' It wasn't a lie: I had sent off for the forms.

'To study what?'

'Music.'

I didn't want to go to work; I so didn't want to go. I wanted to stay and talk, but I had no choice.

I smiled and headed out to the living room and sorted out my bag, lipstick, water bottle, keys, that sort of thing, and then he appeared again.

'Thanks a lot for letting me stay,' he said. 'It really is appreciated. I know Nic said you were looking forward to some time on your own. (Begrudgingly, in my head I thanked her.) It's just till I get my bearings. You'll hardly see me.'

I rather hoped that I would.

'Here.' He handed me a bag, which contained a box, which contained a bottle of a really, really expensive perfume that suddenly became my lifelong favourite. 'It's nice meeting you, Alice.'

I flew to work.

I swear I don't remember a traffic light or anything.

The cosmos had aligned.

Finally, *finally*, my ship was coming in.

Alice Watson.

I smiled as I drove to work and smelt my newly sprayed wrist.

Dr and Mrs Hugh Watson.

Or Drs Hugh and Alice Watson. (My fantasies had moved to epic proportions by the end of my shift. As I waded in my bag and took the shine off my nose before driving home—I had decided that I would never work, I would study full time, DMus sounded good to me.)

It was all about manifesting, right?

Thirteen

I loved our mornings together.

We'd chat over coffee. I'd make an omelette some-times, and we'd share it.

We read each other's horoscopes and sometimes I could feel him watching me, but when I turned around or looked up, he just carried on talking.

But, most of all, I *loved* our evenings.

About a week later I'd just got home and had had one of *those* days. I'd been jittery at work because, that morn-ing, he'd left his wallet on the kitchen bench and I'd had a little peek and seen a picture of Gemma. I had felt as if Hugh and I were on the brink of something, but when I saw that photo—well, she was gorgeous. Tiny, dainty, blonde, like a little pretty elf, sort of gamine—just fuck-ing gorgeous. Roz wasn't on, so there was no one I could really talk to, not that I'd admitted to her that I fancied him. I was pretty sure that Roz liked him for herself.

Anyway, I got back and even though I'd been stress-ing all day it was just so nice to step in the flat and sense him. The air tasted different that evening; I felt I was home. You know, that 'honey, I'm home' thing you see on television, that's how it felt—because he was pleased to see me and I was pleased to be home.

To him.

He opened a bottle of wine—we were watching some quiz show and, it sounds silly, we were competing against each other. There was an imaginary buzzer on the coffee table and our hands kept meeting.

We were flirting.

Real, innocent flirting and we were laughing too, but then The Elf rang and Hugh took it in his room.

He was gone for ages. I could hear his low voice, but not what he was saying, though I could tell it was tense and, call me barking, but I had this sense it was to do with me. Not that he was discussing me. I can't explain it. I felt I was to do with his unease and when he came out the frivolity of before was gone and I was sure I was right.

'What are you up to tomorrow?' I asked, all light and breezy, because he was cramming in some sightseeing before he started his job.

'I might look at some flats.'

'Nic's not back for ages.' I tried to keep my voice light.

I could see the gold flecks in his green eyes and something that had been shifting shifted again. We were having a very ordinary conversation but there was a vital undertone that I wasn't sure if I was imagining.

'There's no rush.'

He just looked at me.

Still I stared.

'Nicole said Gemma was coming out...' See how maturely and sensibly I approached it. I kept my voice light, as if we were discussing whether he was looking for a flat for them both, but there was another conversation taking place.

'Nic just assumed…' He looked uncomfortable. 'Nic's family are great and everything, but they don't…' He was gauging my loyalties and I knew where they lay.

'I don't discuss everything with Nicole.'

'Gemma and I have been having some problems.' I didn't jump in, I didn't fill the gap, I just sat there. 'Eight years is a long time…' Hugh said, and I could only nod— eight weeks was my all-time record. 'I came here to sort out my head.' I opened my mouth to make a little light comment about a busman's holiday, but for once I didn't mess up and stayed silent. 'I didn't come here for anything other than to sort out where Gemma and I are going.' And then he said it.

Confirmed it.

'I think it might be better if I moved out.'

And do you know what I did? For the first time I was thinking of someone other than me, because, instead of making a joke, instead of telling him to stay, after a moment's thought, I nodded.

'What are you on tomorrow?' It was his turn to be all casual.

'I've got a day off,' I said. 'I'm supposed to be doing a course but it was cancelled.' This, I will admit, was a complete and utter lie. Yes, I know I'm broke and I don't have any sick days left, but I was confused—I was confused, because I wanted him to stay though I knew he ought to go, but I wanted my chance as well. The universe had sent him to me, but I had to be proactive, I had to do my bit too.

So, yes, I lied.

His eyes never left my face. 'Do you want to do something tomorrow?'

'I'm not flat-hunting!' In hindsight that was inadvertently brilliant, because I sounded more decisive than needy (which I felt). I was decisive, though, because if he thought I was going to choose a nice bedroom and bathroom for bloody Gemma to enjoy with him…

'We could just go out,' Hugh said, and I nodded and I was nervous because I had the feeling tomorrow was a test. 'What do you like doing?'

We knew so little about each other.

Now, I don't really think going out on the pull, or getting pissed and reading horoscopes or spending hours on YouTube were the answers that he wanted. I felt myself colour up a bit, because what *did* I like doing?

It was like an application form where you had to list your hobbies.

What do I do on my days off?

What should I put?

No way was I going swimming, not with my hair, and anyway I don't know if I can swim—it's been years, decades, in fact. I nearly said hockey because I liked watching that in the Olympics, but would he be a fanatic and I'd find myself padded up and chasing a ball? My dangerous mind even flicked to the luge…

Oh, God, what *do* I like doing?

My eyes darted to what was behind him. 'The piano.' I swallowed, because I was precariously close to saying archery. 'And reading,' I added, because everyone puts that—I just hoped he wouldn't ask what.

But he must have liked my answers, because he didn't

say he'd let me know in the next couple of weeks, he just smiled and said he'd think of something for us to do.

I lay in bed all night, fretting as to what.

Fourteen

Hugh hired bikes!

You know that saying: 'It's like riding a bike, you never forget'?

I'd never learnt in the first place.

I never got past training wheels.

'You've got limited upper-body strength?' He stopped and looked at me.

I had been explaining to him as I wobbled along and tried to stay up that I really had no centre of balance. I mean *really* had no centre of balance. And when we decided, fairly quickly, that a bike ride along the Yarra, perhaps, after all, wasn't the best activity (he'd kept insisting I'd be fine once I was on, that you never forget) I threw in too my other disability. I told him about my limited upper-body strength, just in case he took me to an indoor rock-climbing centre next. I'd honestly forgotten he was a doctor, and he seemed worried, like I'd had a mini-stroke in the past or had mild cerebral palsy or something.

'God, Alice, I'm sorry—you should have said. What happened?'

And then I had had to tell him that it was a self-diagnosis. 'Well, I could never get up the ropes at the gym at school.' We were pushing our bikes back. 'I can't blow-dry the back of my hair...' He started laughing.

Not like Lisa who was laughing at me—he was just laughing and so was I. We got a full refund because we'd only been on our bikes ten minutes, but I hadn't failed. If anything, we were getting on better.

And better.

We went to St Kilda to the lovely bitty shops and I found these miniature Russian dolls. They were tiny, made of tin or something, the biggest no bigger than my thumbnail. Every time we opened them, there was another tiny one, and then another, all reds and yellows and greens.

They were divine.

We were facing each other, looking down at the palm of my hand, and our heads touched.

If I put my hand up now, I can feel where our heads touched.

I remember that moment.

I remember it a lot.

Our heads connected for a second and it was alchemic; it was as if our minds kissed hello.

I just have to touch my head, just there at that very spot and I can, whenever I want to, relive that moment.

So many times I do.

'Get them,' Hugh said, and I would have, except that little bit of tin cost more than a hundred dollars, and though that usually wouldn't have stopped me, I wasn't about to have my card declined in front of him.

I put them back.

'Nope.' I gave him a smile. 'Gotta stop the impulse spending.'

We had lunch.

Out on the pavement and I can't remember what we ate, I just remember being happy. Actually, I can remember: I had Caesar salad because it was the lowest carb thing I could find. We drank water and I *do* remember not giving it a thought.

I was just thirsty.

And happy.

He went to the loo and I chatted to a girl at the next table, just chatted away. Hugh was gone for ages and I was glad I hadn't demanded Dan from the universe, because I would have been worried about how long he was taking.

Do I go on about the universe too much? I don't know, but what I do know is that something *was* looking out for me, helping me to be my best, not to fuck this up as I usually do. You see, we walked on the beach; we went for another coffee and by that time it was evening and we went home and he gave me a present.

Those Russian dolls.

I held them in my palm, and it was the nicest thing he could have done for me.

They are absolutely my favourite thing and I've just stopped to look at them now. I've just stopped to take them apart and then put them all back together again and I can still feel the wonder I felt on that day.

He was the only man who had bought something for

me, I mean *something* truly special. Something beautiful, something thoughtful, something just for me.

And I hadn't even slept with him.

I would have.

It would have been the natural conclusion to our lovely day and he'd have probably loathed himself because of Gemma and thought a bit less of me in the morning, but, whether you believe it or not, I *am* sure that I was being looked after.

'Where is he?' Hugh had gone for Thai and I thought he had forgotten his key, but it was Roz standing there when I opened the door. Her face was bright red, her eyes piggy from crying and she was armed with a bottle of bourbon and some wine.

'He's gone to get some take-away.' I was tired suddenly—I didn't want misery's company tonight. I know that usually I'd have been delighted she'd popped over and I didn't want to do to Roz what Nicole and Dan and so many others had done to me—but Hugh and I were so new and so fragile and today was so important. But I could tell she'd been crying.

'I thought you had Lizzie staying.' I took the wine. 'What's this?'

'It's good for you,' Roz said. 'It's organic and tannin-free *and* it's the same alcohol content—just in case that's what you're allergic to.'

'So where's Lizzie?' I asked, knowing it was the real reason she was here.

I was weary from it, but I sat and listened as Roz blubbered her way through the story.

'Two days!' Roz sobbed. 'We couldn't even last two

days—she's supposed to be staying with me for the holidays and she's already back at her dad's.'

'What was the argument about?' I still didn't get it, I mean, Roz, well, she's just so kind and nice I couldn't actually imagine her arguing with anyone.

'She hates me for breaking up the marriage. She only came because she wanted me to spend money on her—which I did. I took her shopping but she left me in a coffee bar and said she'd meet me in a couple of hours and then we got home and...' Roz was crying so hard she couldn't finish for a moment. 'She said she was ashamed to be seen with me, that she hated me.'

Lizzie needed a good slap if you asked me, not that I said that, but I did tell Roz she needed to stand up to her more.

'I tried that.' Roz gulped her bourbon. 'I told her that she wasn't to speak to me like that, that if she couldn't respect me in my own home then she could go back to her father's. And now she has...'

I'd just got her to the gulping stage when Hugh came back. We shared a quick yikes look as he saw me sitting on the sofa cuddling a blubbering Roz, and he was just about to retreat when Roz saw him.

'Don't go on my account, Hugh,' she gulped. 'Stay and have drink; we were going to watch a movie.'

Actually, no, we weren't! Roz always brings the same two movies in the hope I'll watch them—*Run Fat Boy Run* and *Meet The Fockers*—honestly, I swear I will talk to her one day.

And they would have sat unwatched, as they had for the past few months, except Hugh's eyes lit up when he saw the two DVDs on the coffee table that just turned out to be his favourites.

'Are you sure I won't be interrupting?' Hugh checked.

'Please,' I mouthed, and he gave a half-smile. 'Roz has had a row with her daughter,' I explained, as he served up the curry.

'Lizzie?' Hugh said and I was surprised that he knew. 'I'm sorry to hear that, Roz—sixteen's a shit age.'

'Tell me about it.'

'Grab a glass,' I said. 'It's organic and tannin free.'

'I'll stick with my duty free.'

Okay, the movie was funny. They were *both* funny and it was kind of like the old days, not quite a full house but three of us, not in any rush, and I finished off the disgusting organic, preservative-free wine (actually, it wasn't that bad—I just felt it ought to be). We were working our way down Hugh's duty free when Roz suggested I play the piano, as she often does when she's had a drink.

'Play,' Roz urged, as I tinkered around, and I sensed Hugh's interest. Was I going to break into 'Chopsticks' or 'Row, Row, Row Your Boat' and disappoint?

Normally, when it's people other than Roz, I play something silly, the oldies but goodies. When it's just Roz, though, well, she's so encouraging that I try other things. I like Mika and I try to work out his songs by ear, and even though Hugh was there, unbelievably that was what I did.

I started playing 'Grace Kelly'. I love the beginning: there's this restless energy to it that makes my stomach go tight.

He's like musical cocaine to me—there's a rush that

comes with the sounds he makes. The range of his voice makes me quiver. Well, I played the intro and then I looked at Roz and she was grinning and so I played it again and then...

Even though Hugh was there, we did what we do when it's just us.

Roz got to be Grace Kelly, while I played and sang.

It sounds silly, but I just hammer that song.

I feel like I am galloping at breakneck speed along the beach.

Maybe I was showing off at first. Maybe I was flirting and showing Hugh a different side, but only for a few seconds—you can't be lost in music *and* show off. When you are lost, it is so exhilarating that there isn't room for anything else.

Roz could shatter a glass at a hundred paces but she was singing now as if she'd hadn't been crying, as if she didn't have a care in the world, and I was just flying—all the colours were vivid as I sang them. My voice is good and I was on a high as I sang. When it ended, Roz got off the stool, as dizzy and as euphoric as if she was getting off the waltzers at the fair. I fiddled around for a bit and with Roz urging me on I played a couple of pieces from my exam repertoire. I forgot about Roz and, for the first time since I'd found him in my kitchen that morning, I completely forgot about Hugh.

The piano does that to me.

When I was a teenager, I used to love the mornings that Mum and Bonny were both on early shifts and I'd have the house to myself for an hour before school. I could just play uninterrupted for an extra precious hour.

I'd have played from the moment I got in from school

till Mum told me to go to bed if I could have got away with it, that was how much I needed it—but now, rather than sustaining me, it drains me.

After half an hour I'd had enough and I would have, which is rare for me, been quite happy to go to bed. I felt depleted, but Roz was still begging for diversion from her fight with Lizzie and she suggested we play spin the bottle, which was just stupid, but we were all a bit pissed and Roz can really nag.

It was our own version and there was a lot of daring at first.

A tequila shot or three and then Roz dared Hugh to take off his top. She was giggling like a schoolgirl around him. I'm sure she fancies him—but he just laughed and did it.

And then it was my turn and I wasn't sure if my bra was ready for inspection so when the bottle spun my way instead of saying *Dare* I said *Truth*.

'How old were you when you lost it?' Roz asked.

I could feel them stare at me, knew they were waiting for me to wriggle out of it, but I didn't. I told the truth.

'Seventeen.'

'And?'

'I've answered the question.' I spun the bottle and it landed on Roz. 'How old were you?'

'Seventeen,' Roz said.

'And?' Hugh asked, but Roz used my line. 'I answered the question.' She spun again and it landed on me.

'And?' Roz asked.

'He was just a guy.' I didn't like this game. 'Someone…'

'And what was it like?'

'Nice, I guess.' My face was bright red. 'It was on his living-room floor...' I spun the bottle really fast and it landed on Hugh.

'How old were you?' Roz asked, and for the first time I saw Hugh blush.

'Twenty.' Hugh winced. 'As you can imagine, there was a lot of wrist action—you try being ginger with glasses.' For a second our eyes caught and I realised that neither of us were enjoying this. Only Roz was like a dog with a bone.

'What's your darkest secret?' Roz asked when the bottle landed on me.

The answer was easy.

'My credit cards.'

I was lying, apparently.

The bottle said that I was lying because it wobbled, and I laughed and did the right thing and had another shot of tequila, but I hated this game.

I fucking hated this game.

I just wanted to go to bed.

Except when I got there I couldn't sleep.

I never can when I've played the piano—I mean really played—because it reminds me how much I miss it. I know I've got a piano and I can play it as often as I like, but I miss stretching myself, I miss learning. It should have been my career and instead I was stuck in poxy classifieds with my brain shrinking by the hour as I took down details of births, marriages and deaths and typed up funeral notices.

'People will always die.' Roz had grinned when I'd told her my concerns about work. 'Anyway, you won't always be there. You're too smart, Alice.' Always she nagged me—she was thirty-four, and if she could do it then so could I.

Ah, but Roz had a massive divorce settlement.

I had massive debts.

And anyway I could never imagine taking lessons again.

I could hear Roz snoring from the sofa. My stomach was hurting, cramping actually, and I know I sound like I've got Münchausen syndrome or something, what with my mad dash to Emergency and everything, but I'm as healthy as an ox really—well, apart from my limited upper-body strength. Really I've only been to hospital five times in my entire life, three of them for my breathing. I have a lot of sick days from work but that's only because they're there. But I do struggle with my periods. My first one I had a seizure! That was another trip in an ambulance.

As if getting your first period in the middle of cookery lesson isn't bad enough. I went to the school nurse and she gave me this massive pad. Well, I wore it, but at lunchtime me and my friend Louise went to town and into the chemist for tampons. I felt all pale and shaky and I can't remember anything other than that, but according to Louise I screamed and then had a convulsion and wet my pants right in the middle of Boots. It happened occasionally with a first period apparently, the doctor had explained to my frantic mother. It didn't mean I was epileptic, so long as I didn't have another one, which I didn't. My mum was really nice to me around my periods after that and always watched out for me a bit more.

She was a bit obsessed with them, actually.

I got up to the bathroom but I didn't have my period.

This had been happening a lot lately, so I rummaged in the cupboard for some tampons (I'd rather risk toxic shock syndrome than wear a pad—see, I don't have Münchausen syndrome). But as I went to throw away the wrapper, I changed my mind. It seemed different with Hugh here, so I bunched the wrapper in my hand and tossed it in my bedroom bin.

Still I couldn't sleep.

Roz and her bloody questions.

I hated that stupid game; I wished we'd never played it, wished I'd gone to bed when I intended to as I was never going to get to sleep now, because every time I closed my eyes, I remembered.

Fifteen

His hand was inside my bra and I was still playing, though I don't know how.

I was still playing and his palms were soft and warm on my skin.

'God, Alice,' he breathed, his head burrowing under my hair and kissing my neck. 'What the hell are you doing to me?' I didn't know. I was still playing the bloody tune, chord after chord. I could feel one hand move to my knee and I opened my legs, felt it climbing up, and for a minute I thought I'd wet myself, my panties were soaked. I could see his fingers creeping inside, saw him push my knickers, saw the red flare of my bush and I hated my pubic hair, hated it, but I wasn't looking at it now. Stunned I looked at where his finger was stroking. I didn't even know I had a clitoris but there it was— sticking out like a tiny penis—and it was so exquisitely tender. I wanted to push his hand off, it hurt it was so raw, but at the same time I liked it. My bum was sort of shaking on the seat. I could see my knees opening and trembling, but my eyes were on his fingers, watching with morbid fascination as he slipped them deep inside me, the palm of his hand now on my clitoris.

'Stay there.'

I could feel his cock on my back, his other hand wasn't on my breast now, but I knew where it was, knew he was stroking himself, and I felt sick, excited but sick. For a second I thought of Celeste and knew it was wrong, but then something else took over. I felt it; it was exciting; I felt myself all warm down below, and I didn't think about Celeste but instead all the girls who had teased me for being a nerd, and how Louise would hate that I'd done it first if she knew.

'Alice.' His mouth was off the back of my neck and then he turned me around on the piano stool and I stared at his cock. He was stroking it up and down and I heard the crash of the keys as I leant backward.

'I won't put it in.' He was kneeling right between my legs now, stroking it against me, right against me. There was a trickle of silver running down, and he was making deep, breathy noises. His eyes were all sort of glazed, and all I could think was that I was doing this to him—that he really wanted me, that I must somehow be beautiful. He was right at my entrance now, my knickers the barrier, and he was pushing, stroking against them, just a little way in, and I wanted it all.

'We mustn't.' For a second he stopped, and I thought it must have been something I'd done, that maybe I wasn't sexy enough, pretty enough, that my boobs weren't as big as Celeste's.

I pulled down my knickers.

And he pushed his fingers inside, he was sliding them in and out, and his thumb was on my clitoris. My legs were apart and he was kneeling up. His hands weren't doing it to me now, instead he was stroking his cock against me, and I wanted it in. I wanted him to take me there, I wanted to watch, I wanted to see it. It was the most scary, beautiful thing. He pulled me down to the floor and I remember bumping my head on the stool. I remember crying out a bit, because it hurt, but he didn't say anything, didn't check if I was okay.

We were on the floor—I can remember his legs in between mine, his mouth on my tits, and he bit me so hard I cried out, but he wasn't listening. I could see his erection and I was scared. His jeans were down. This bloody angry thing was aimed at me and I wanted it to stop, but I wanted it to go on—knew that to lose it to a teacher meant I was sexy. He was heavy on me, his full weight on me, his knees pushing my thighs apart. One hand pushed and parted at my bush and sort of guided his cock, then he was in me and I knew the first time hurt, but this *really* hurt. He wasn't kissing me, he was just grinding inside me and it hurt so much I thought I was going to be sick. It was like every bit of hatred he possessed was being served up inside me. Every row he'd had with Celeste was being terminated with each painful thrust.

'You got your period again?' I can still see Mum delivering my laundry to my room. 'We should go and see Dr Hanson if it happens again.'

I bled for two days. I was so fucking torn I bled for

two days. But all I could think about was when I'd see him again.

All I could think about was what he was thinking of me.

Sixteen

God, I needed a drink.

I could hear Roz coughing on the sofa as I padded past. Walking into the kitchen, just about to flick the light on, I realised that it already was on. I jumped out of my skin as I saw him at the kitchen table, chatting into his mobile phone.

'Sorry.' I went to go, but he'd ended the call.

'For what?'

'I didn't realise you were here…on the phone…' My heart was still hammering in my chest. All I wanted was a drink, but I couldn't now, couldn't because it was two a.m. and what the hell would he think? 'I just wanted a drink.'

I headed to the tap and poured myself a glass of water, as if that was what I had meant to do. It was nice, actually. I gulped it down in one go and I filled the glass again.

'It's the middle of the day in England.' He walked over to the fridge and pulled out a beer, and I didn't get it. I didn't get why it was okay for him to have a beer and not me. At least I couldn't unless he suggested it. 'Want one?'

I shook my head, gave a casual shrug as if I was doing him a favour. 'I'll have a small wine with you.'

There weren't any clean glasses left so I found a mug, which was good, because hopefully he didn't see how far I filled it.

'Have you been crying?'

'No.'

Had I been? I could feel the damp on my face, eyes that felt swollen when I blinked, and I realised then that I must have been. That I must look a right bloody sight.

Bloody Roz—why did she have to have come? We were all awkward again.

'Jesus!' It was the first time I'd heard him snap, but when his phone bleeped a text he hissed the word out and he turned the phone off. 'We're supposed to be taking a break and she texts or rings every five fucking minutes.' Embarrassed, he sort of gave a half-smile of apology.

'Why *are* you taking a break?' I took a large gulp of wine.

'To work out what we want—well, I know what Gemma wants…' he took a gulp of beer '…and given we've been going out eight years, it's fair enough, I guess.'

'Marriage?'

'Yup.'

'And that's not for you?'

'I'm not against it. I just…' He gave a helpless shrug. 'You're not seeing anyone?' he checked, because it was already complicated.

'Not at the moment.' (I didn't tell him not for about a year.)

'Have you ever been serious about anyone?'

'I'm not serious about anything!' It was one of the lines I used regularly, made me sound sort of happily single, I thought, but Hugh didn't smile.

'I don't know about that.' He frowned at my swollen eyes. 'You're okay?'

'I'm fine.'

'Because if you want to talk…'

'Then I'll book in for a consultation.' I stood up and filled up my mug. I didn't care at that moment what he bloody thought—unconsciousness was my only aim. ''Night.'

He was standing too.

'Alice…'

I didn't want to talk, so I didn't. I just ignored him and walked to my room, but then I'd forgotten my mug of wine so I turned back for it, but I got Hugh instead.

I sort of landed on his chest and just stood there, because he didn't let me past. He held me, and I didn't cry, but I was crying inside. My head felt like a war zone; I didn't want to go to bed and think, I wanted to close my eyes and just forget.

Forget.

And his mouth let me do that. He kissed me, and the weight of his mouth was sheer relief. It was a slow, lazy kiss and his fingers were in my hair and his tongue stroking mine and it felt so good to forget.

Just so very good.

Seventeen

I was horribly untogether when I woke up the next day. Roz was still crashed on the sofa and even though I didn't have to be in to work till twelve I had somewhere I needed to be.

Two paracetamol didn't make a dent in my headache, add to that cramping pain even though I *still* didn't have my period, and my stomach was jumping as bit by bit I recalled the events of the previous night.

Truth or dare.

Me crying in the kitchen.

I grabbed a skirt and top and some clean undies and then staggered to the bathroom. I put on a cap and had a shower and spent ages on my make-up, trying to transform the cadaver in the mirror into a healthy, glowing thing who hadn't made a complete fool of herself and wasn't jangling with a hangover.

And then I remembered.

We'd kissed.

I doubled over in embarrassment and thank God the

tap was running because otherwise he'd have thought I had Tourette's I was cursing so much.

Had I kissed him or had he kissed me first?

Shit!

I had no idea how to face him.

Had he had to peel me off him?

I turned off the tap and it all sounded quiet outside so I dashed to the kitchen. My handbag was there and I punched out a couple of Valium, the last two actually, washing them down with a very gratefully received glass of water as I boiled the kettle.

There was one benefit of feeling and looking like death, a cramping uterus and 10 mg of Valium on an empty stomach, I was still so pale fifteen minutes later that I didn't blush when he walked in the kitchen. I was trying to find my keys and purse to put in my bag so I could beat a hasty retreat.

In fact, the only person blushing was Hugh.

'I'm sorry.' He came right out and said it. 'If I was out of line last night, if I forced myself on you...' I didn't really hear the rest. There was a roaring sound of relief in my ears as he went on about being a bit confused about Gemma, how he'd never come here with the intention of meeting someone, how he'd had a bit to drink and, well, look, he liked me and...

A martyred look I'd perfected came to the fore then.

'It's fine. We'd both had too much to drink.'

'Look,' Hugh said. 'I'm going away for a couple of days, it's been planned...'

'That will be nice,' I said, sure he was lying.

'Just for a couple of days, catching up with some

friends of Gemma's and mine, and I...' His voice trailed off for a moment. 'Look, about Gemma...'

'Hugh!' I glanced up from trying to wedge my purse into my bag. 'It's no big deal.'

'But it is.' There was this note in his voice that made me start. 'And I haven't had too much to drink now.'

And he kissed me again. A different kiss, a kiss that was deep and slow and *deliberate*, a grown-up kiss that meant business.

'We'll talk when I get back.' I wanted to count each fleck in his eyes. I gazed at each one in turn, as his mouth patiently waited, while his arms held me. And then selfishness won—because I kissed him. Because, whether or not I was good enough, or good *for* him, still I wanted him. I got a glimpse, almost as if I were floating outside my body and watching couples the world over kissing each other goodbye at breakfast, a sort of vision of a normality that I really ached for. The picture had never seemed right before, the picture had only ever had me in it, and a man, just a man, but I could see it clearly now, because this picture contained Hugh.

'I'm going to talk to Gemma.'

And I almost floated out—I mean, for the first time in my life I was winning, and then a little white box fell out of my overloaded bag and I felt my throat squeeze closed as Hugh bent down and picked it up.

'Valium?' I could see that shrewd psychiatric brain tighten a fraction as he weighed me up.

'Yeah.' I rolled my eyes. 'Remember I wasn't well before you came? I had an allergic reaction.'

'And they gave you Valium?'

'And steroids. It was pretty scary...' I shrugged. 'I've

got to have some tests to find out what I'm allergic to. I just got worked up when I couldn't breathe—I haven't taken any.'

I dropped the white packet he was holding back in my bag; fully knowing the blister pack was empty.

Fully knowing that I had to do something about it—a week in and I was down to zero.

Which was why, even though I was on a late at the paper today, I was up at eight to get to the doctor's by nine.

Dr Kelsey is, I suppose, my family doctor. Well, she's Bonny's doctor and when I got flu when I first arrived in Melbourne, Bonny took me to her. She's a nice lady, and worth the trek for certain things. It took me living here for a year though to work out that I didn't *have* to see her. Doctors are a bit like McDonald's here: there are massive bulk-billing clinics, and you can walk into any one and see any doctor. I did that for things like a sore throat or when I needed a sick note for work, but for this I figured I had more standing with Dr Kelsey and she would know I wasn't after drugs or anything. Well, I'd never asked for any before and I also wanted to talk to her about the horrible cramping.

She was lovely—as I said, she's a nice lady—except she didn't want to give me Valium, and she suggested I go on the Pill, but wouldn't give me a script for contraceptives without doing a smear.

I had tried to lie and say I had my period, but I'd already put my foot in it by saying that I'd had cramping with no bleeding, so I had to sit and go through the Valium thing knowing what was coming next.

'You're not sure that it was a panic attack?' She peered

over her glasses at me. 'But you want me to prescribe Valium?'

'They've helped.' I swallowed. I didn't want it to be a panic attack. I had been sent home with twenty from the hospital and I'd used them all. I don't know how they worked. I wasn't even sure that they did, but this morning I had been jangling with nerves and hangover and I had taken my last, and by the time Hugh had joined me in the kitchen I had felt better.

Had been able to chat to him normally.

As if I was normal—which I was, of course.

'I have been feeling anxious lately,' I grudgingly admitted, and I was back in the kitchen suddenly, standing over us, watching us kiss. Then I was peering into the bathroom, to that pale unmade-up face and the chaos behind the locked door, aware suddenly of the sheer effort that had gone into that small moment, that it was getting harder and harder somehow to *be* normal. I looked at Dr Kelsey's face, could see her waiting for me to continue, only I truly didn't know what to say. 'I tried talking to a psychologist but it didn't help.'

'Who did you see?'

So I told her about Lisa and the pointless hour we had spent. 'The hospital said that if I came to see you...they wrote a letter.' I was rummaging in my bag, trying to find the blasted thing, but I couldn't. 'I had a letter!' I could hear the note of desperation in my voice and I tried to check it. My hands were shaking as I pulled apart the contents of my bag.

'Alice,' Dr Kelsey said, 'I believe you. I've been your doctor for years now and I know you don't make a habit of asking for this type of thing.' She scanned through my notes. 'Let's get the Pap smear done and then we'll have a little chat.'

Joy and double joy.

I hate having Pap smears. I had one with Dr Kelsey six years ago but she asked too many questions. My last two have been at one of those lovely anonymous places, but I've been putting this one off, and Dr Kelsey isn't taking any excuses.

'Just relax, Alice. Let your knees flop.'

I can't. My legs are shaking and I can't let them flop, but eventually I do just enough, and I lie there with my eyes screwed closed and her idle chatter does nothing to soothe me—I just want it over.

Every cervix tells a story—I'd read it in one of the magazines. I hated anyone looking. I mean, I was careful and everything. I always used condoms. I was so paranoid about getting pregnant and, given the transient nature of my lovers, no matter how pissed I was I always made them dress for the occasion.

Dr Kelsey asked the same questions—had I had any problems, any procedures or pregnancies?—just as she had done last time. She asked about my medical history in the UK and I answered as I had done last time—nothing. I scaled down the number of sexual partners because, well, given they always wore condoms, she really didn't need to know, and anyway this last year there'd been hardly anyone.

Well, anyone down there.

'Okay, all done!'

I dressed behind the curtains as she tapped on the computer and chatted away to me as I walked over and sat down.

'I don't like to prescribe Valium without counselling. I'll give you a script but I want to see you again soon.' I could feel a flood of relief as she started typing up my script. 'But I'm not going to give you any more without you seeing Lisa again.'

'Can you recommend anyone else?' I asked.

'She's excellent,' Dr Kelsey said.

'She's expensive,' I attempted as Dr Kelsey typed up a very long letter. I was trying to peek but the screen was angled so that I couldn't really see.

'We'll put you on a mental health plan,' Dr Kelsey said (bloody cheek!). 'You'll get a decent rebate. I'll get the receptionist to make you an appointment, but I'm not giving you any more till I've heard back from Lisa. Okay?'

'Fine,' I said, because she didn't really give me much choice.

Lisa had a cancellation for the day after tomorrow, Saturday morning as it turned out—and because Dr Kelsey was at the desk I nodded and said that would be fine and then I stepped out onto the street and went to the chemist.

Fifty-five mg and no repeats.

I was relieved, of course, to get them, but instead of the euphoria of before I knew that these would only last me a few days.

I opened my purse to pay and there it was, tucked inside, the letter from the hospital.

It was almost as comforting as paying for my pack of Valium.

Eighteen

When I went back for my next lesson, neither Gus nor Celeste were home. I'd had my hair straightened again. I was nervous but looking forward to seeing him, sort of. There was no answer at the door and, even though Gus had mixed up my lesson times once before, this time I knew it was no mistake.

I also knew I couldn't tell Mum.

That she would ring him and ask for an explanation.

And when, on the next Thursday, it happened again, I knew that Gus didn't want to see me. I rang him, but he just hung up. So for the next few weeks I practised hard on my own, and took the money from Mum. I did go to his house once or twice, but in the end I would just spend the evening sitting in the park.

I never worried at first that I might be pregnant—I was just consumed with wanting to see him. I knew how hard it must be for him, I mean, he had a wife and a baby on the way and was moving back to Australia soon, but I couldn't believe it could just end like that. He had told me I was beautiful and sexy. I knew for a fact that he wasn't happy with Celeste—if I could just see him again then it would all be okay.

He was all I thought about.

I practised on the piano all the time. It helped me to think of him, to remember, and I liked remembering, so I practised some more.

I should have been worried, of course, when my period didn't come, but I was sort of numb from worrying and I told Mum that I'd run out of tampons and she bought me some more. I remember flushing them one by one down the loo unused over the next couple of days so that she could see the packet getting smaller, and I felt safe—I'd got away with it.

Nineteen

Even though he was away, even though I normally hated spending a night on my own, I was quite enjoying this one.

In a wretched, maudlin, suicidal way.

I'd got my credit-card statements and two phone calls from recovery agencies, so I'd turned down the phone and was letting it go straight to the answering-machine. The period Dr Kelsey had said was imminent had arrived by the time I'd got home from the doctor's surgery, and even by the next night it was still sending my uterus into spasm. Still, the Valium combined with wine was helping. I had my little Russian dolls all out beside me. I was reading a New Age book, but I was tired of all the affirmations and crap about loving my inner child, so I'd given up. I lay on the bed, tackling the never-ending problem that was my bikini line with a pair of tweezers, tossing up whether I'd get the Brazilian keratin treatment or get my pubes lasered away when my ship came in, and watching for maybe the fiftieth time *The Holiday*.

I love that movie—not the Kate Winslet and the other

guy bits, but Jude and Cameron. I want to be her. I want to lie with kids who think I'm a princess, staring up at the sparkles, or look sexy as I swig out of a wine bottle. I want to have sex like that and wake up and he's still sexy even in his glasses.

Like Hugh.

I paused and rewound—watched Jude all bumbling and so lovely he made my toes curl and had a giggle to myself, and then I heard the bedroom door open.

'Alice?'

I felt as if I'd been caught.

I *had* been caught.

Lying on top of the bed, drinking wine, eating chocolate and wearing a pair of knickers and a vest top. Thankfully the face mask was off, the tweezers down and the nails were painted, but this was so not how I wanted to be seen.

This was my night in.

And I was supposed to be out.

'Hey.' He sat on the edge of the bed as I turned over my book so he wouldn't think my life needed healing (he was a psychiatrist after all). 'What are you watching?'

'Just a movie.' I flicked the pause button again, didn't want him to know that I was home alone and watching a romantic comedy. I'd far rather have been found watching a documentary or reading something highbrow. 'How come you're back?'

'I think jet lag hit.' He shrugged; he was wearing his glasses and he looked a bit tense. 'Well, that's what I said to them—they're nice and everything, but they're friends of Gemma's. It just got…' He gave another shrug. 'It's complicated. People want answers and I don't want to give them. Probably because I don't know them. Look, about before, Alice...'

'Forget it,' I said, and I was being very grown up, because even though I fancied him rotten, even though I hated Gemma with a passion, I didn't want to mess with his head, I mean, we were talking an eight-year relationship.

I just never imagined what would come next.

'I can't forget about it.' Hugh sat on the edge of the bed. 'I've got a headache from trying not to think about it—the thing is, I don't want to forget about it.'

Thank God the main light was off because my face was burning. I didn't say anything, I didn't really understand what Hugh was saying, so he clarified a touch.

'When I asked Gemma for a break—I meant from each other. I never thought I might meet someone else while I was here. I have to tell her.'

My eyes jerked to his and he just stared; he stared at me and I looked back. And what I saw was so unfamiliar that it was scary. I could see his want, his desire, his affection for me, see what I had never actually seen in a man's eyes before, and I didn't know what to do with it.

I just didn't know how to respond, so I turned my eyes back to the screen.

I stared unseeing at a frozen image on the screen and I wanted to pause my life. If there had been a button I could push, I think I would have done it then.

You see—I had wished for this. I had demanded it, in fact, had read that book and put in my order for the perfect man, and here he was. The only thing was, I liked him.

Which should be a given, except I *really* liked him and that also meant, I guess, that I cared for him.

This gorgeous, talented, educated, sexy man was sitting on my bed and weighing up tossing in eight years on one kiss.

One kiss, for God's sake—hell, he should be shagging his way through the next ten months, not agonising over a kiss.

I snog anyone. A few drinks and I snog. That's what I do.

He didn't know me and that's what worried me most. How would he feel if he did?

'So, what happened to your night out?' he asked. (I had lied and said I had plans.)

'Oh, I just didn't feel like it,' I said airily.

'What are you watching?'

I had no choice but to tell him because he was already reading the cover of the DVD. Then he asked if he could watch too and sort of sprawled on the bed beside me. I guess I could have said no, only it would have seemed stupid. I mean, if it was Roz or Dan or anyone else, I would have been begging them to stay, but it was Hugh, and I felt uncomfortable.

Especially at this bit.

I always get embarrassed watching kisses on screen—even on my own. I can feel this sort of knot in my stomach. At the movies too. As if everyone in the cinema is watching my reaction, watching me blush, as I watch them make out.

As if.

Lying on the bed next to Hugh, as Cameron and Jude's tongues mingled I was exquisitely uncomfortable, because I knew Hugh was sort of watching my reaction.

Because I could sense his.

Knew without looking that he was turned on.

I pulled up my knees, the cramping in my stomach at odds with the fire in my groin.

'Are you okay?'

'I've got my period.' Better to be honest, I decided, better to just say it. Better that he knew that this wasn't going anywhere.

'Do you want some paracetamol?'

'Wine will do.' I didn't swig out of the bottle, I'm no Cameron Diaz, but I took a *very* grateful slug of my glass and lay back on my pillow as he went to top it up. The bottle was empty and he padded out to the kitchen. I lay there, not so innocent.

You see, I am an over-thinker.

I just am. As I said, I don't mind stupid people, I just get irritated at stupid people who pretend to be clever.

Hugh *isn't* stupid.

Hugh, I knew, had been a touch worried when he'd found those Valium.

Well, since then I'd had the script dispensed and had replaced those empty blister packs. They were now lying in the same white box he had seen that morning, near the top of my handbag.

Okay, I had left them, intending him to find them when he came home from his trip, but when he walked back into the bedroom with a bit more of a spring in his step, I guessed he had been rummaging in my bag just now.

I didn't blame him for snooping.

I'd have done the same.

Clever, you see.

'So, what are you allergic to?' (Told you he looked.)

'No idea...' I shrugged, but my blasé demeanour lasted about point seven of a second as I felt his lips on my shoulder. 'They thought it was hazelnuts. When I was seven Dad took us to a pub and then...' I couldn't really continue. His tongue was in my clavicle.

'Then?' He paused for oxygen, but not for long. His fingers were pulling the strap of my top and his lips were nudging my skin.

'Well...' I was doing my best to speak normally, except Cameron and Jude had stopped talking and Hugh was kissing this bit of skin near my neck and I was finding it really hard to speak let alone think back twenty years ago. 'Bonny started screaming and my dad came running. I couldn't breathe.'

'Poor little Alice,' Hugh said, and then we kissed. We were just legs and arms and mouths and tongues. We kissed and then we'd stop and smile and then dive back for another one. We kissed for ages, like two teenagers. We just lay on the bed and kissed and all I can say was that it was delicious.

'I've got my period,' I said again a little while later. I was on my back; he was on his side and one leg was over me.

'Is that why you stayed home?'

'Mmm.' He hadn't got my message. His hand went to my stomach, massaging the ball of tension that was my uterus. At least now I had a reason to be stuck home on a Friday night and I relaxed a touch.

I watched his hand, his fingers still stroking my skin and then digging in a bit, sort of kneading. My knees were still up and he pushed them down.

'Relax.'

'I can't,' I admitted, because I couldn't. I had my shagging period and he was in bed next to me with this massive erection pressing out of his jeans.

My phone bleeped—I have never in my life been so grateful for the distraction. I leant over and frowned as the name Marcus appeared on screen and then remembered that an hour or so ago I'd succumbed to an advert and texted to find out the name of my ideal lover, hoping it would be Hugh.

'Just Roz.' I turned off the phone.

'It's so good she's got you.' Hugh sort of pulled me in as I rolled back on the bed. 'She's really struggling.'

'Tell me about it,' I groaned.

'You're a good friend,' Hugh said, his lips diving back to my clavicle. 'Fuck, imagine coming out at thirty-four...'

'What?' I sort of pushed him back. I pushed him away a fraction, my lips so ready to correct him, so nearly there, and then I checked myself. I lay in his arms on my bed and about fifteen hundred sentences that I'd heard in the last few months all seemed to crunch into some sort of line. The writing appeared on the wall, and I was the bloody idiot who hadn't seen it.

'You don't know?' He frowned down at me. I could see the blaze of confusion—that his PC, Valium-free lover might not be quite as she appeared—and I knew I had to come up with something quickly.

'Of course I know.' His lips were there, tense, confused and pulling away, but I kissed them. Hugh pulled back and my mind whirred into sudden action. 'I'm amazed she told you...she's really shy about it...' I was sort of showering his face with kisses. 'It's good that she's started to say it.'

And I got away with it.

His face was lowering onto mine and he was kissing me, his tongue stroking deep in my mouth. It was a deep kiss that made me curl inside, made me want to bring my knees back up, only he was sort of lying half on top of me, a lovely heavy weight gently pinning. Then his tongue was at the tip of mine, circling it and then sucking it into his mouth. I pulled back.

'I can't do anything.'

He frowned, frowned as if he didn't get it. God, maybe he was one of those guys who didn't care and would just whip out my tampon. I hoped he didn't want a bloody blow job, or worse.

'You can do *this*.' His tongue licked my lips, and from anyone else it would have been disgusting, but it was the single most erotic thing he could have done. He was licking my lips and then sucking my bottom one and my knees were pressing to come up but for other reasons now. He stopped. 'Alice…' His eyes held mine, lobbed the ball squarely into my court. 'Do you want me to go?'

'No.' I flailed at my boldness. 'But I can't…'

'Can't what?' He was kissing me again and he was so goddamned sexy, just this scent of DKNY and this deep, slow kiss that smothered the protests in my mind. He slid out of his jeans and lay next to me.

He had on his hipsters and I could see the bulge pressing into my thigh and his finger was still stroking my stomach. Then his hand slipped down, stroking my clitoris and I was mortified. I mean I had my period, but all he was doing was stroking it and sort of pressing himself into me.

When the movie was over he turned off the telly and turned off the lights. He took the bottle away and I lay there staring at the black ceiling, wondering what was going to happen. I rolled onto my side as he went to the loo.

And then he was back.

I'd told him sex wasn't on the agenda, yet I could feel his arousal as he spooned in behind me.

I could feel the small, idle circles he was drawing on my stomach, I could feel his breath on my neck when his other hand moved my hair.

The room was hot—I wanted to get up and open a window. I could feel the sheen of sweat on my body, could feel it on my scalp and neck, could feel my hair coiling at the nape, and then I felt his lips pressing into the back of my neck. They parted and he was kissing me deeper and his hand was still on my stomach.

I couldn't breathe. I ignored his mouth that was sucking and nibbling at my shoulder because I could feel his fingers, that idle stroking moving down, and I had my period, except his hand wasn't urgent, just a lazy spiral, a never-ending circle on my stomach. I knew he had bruised my shoulder. I sort of wriggled away because for a second it hurt and then I wriggled back and felt him pressed into me.

I really couldn't breathe. Like those fucking self-help tapes. I couldn't remember how to breathe, because his hand was moving lower and his groin was pressing harder.

I was so tense. I can't describe how tense I was. I

knew that it wouldn't stay like this. That soon I'd be on my back, with my knickers round one ankle, but his hand never moved. It just stayed on my lower stomach, making these strange, backward circles as I waited for his erection to nudge. It was there. I could feel it hard. In fact, I was now pressing against it, but he never moved, bar his hands, bar this lovely, lovely circle, bar me as I moved a touch against him.

I pressed harder and so did he.

And then I turned towards him, my legs wrapping around him. I was pushing myself against him, rubbing myself against him and kissing him. I could feel the contractions in my stomach, and a sort of choking sound that came from me. I knew he was going to come, but he didn't. I knew he would stop kissing me, and moving the same as me, and pressing hard into me, but still he didn't. I was coming and he wasn't, I was pressing into him and he was rubbing so hard against me, but he wasn't coming. My mouth was open and his lips were drinking from mine and his hand pressed me in and I was coming. I waited for the spill, for something, for nothing, he just kissed me.

'Better?'

My pain had gone.

Then he pulled me into the crook of his arm and after not too long started to snore.

Seemingly not romantic.

Except I had come.

And he hadn't.

After too many lovers to mention, for the first time I'd had an orgasm.

That elusive thing I had faked and sometimes,

occasionally, almost glimpsed had been borne to me at the age of twenty-seven—not that Hugh could have known this was my first.

A calmness spread through me, a peace I had never known. All my muscles felt like water and my mind felt quiet. Better than Valium, better than wine, there was a numbing effect as I lay there.

A peaceful calm where I could almost feel myself floating out of my body as I lay with him holding me.

It was a strange detachment, where I could stand at a distance and watch without fear.

Twenty

'You need to eat.' Mum plonked down a steaming plate of pork sausages, mashed potatoes and onions, and I felt my stomach curl.

'For fuck's sake!' Bonny said as Mum went out. 'Just eat it, would you? She thinks you've got anorexia.'

Which cheered me up a bit. I mean, everyone knows that pregnant women put on weight. In my case it was falling off me. I couldn't eat, and if I did I was sick, and of course Mum had noticed.

Mum liked us to be slim. There was no problem with Eleanor, she hardly ate and if she forgot and went crazy and had an extra peanut or something she just took a laxative or threw it up. Bonny, Mum was always telling off, because…er…Bonny was a mini-Mum—and if she carried on eating the way she did, well, she'd be a full-grown Mum soon. And me—well, I'm tall, but not naturally skinny. I have large hips and a thick waist but, as I said, all that had slimmed down nicely. The only thing that hadn't slimmed down was the boobs.

I could feel Lex watching me as I ate my dinner,

could see the worry in his eyes as I forced down a bit of mashed potato and gravy. I knew he felt as guilty as hell, because we could all hear Mum blowing her nose in the kitchen and trying to pretend she wasn't crying. Now that the wedding was over, there was no denying it—in a few weeks Lex's project would be over and he was taking Bonny to live in Australia. No doubt he probably thought I was on a hunger strike.

Well, I wasn't. I just wanted to be sick.

Again!

'Excuse me.' I fled upstairs and just made it to the bathroom, flushing the loo as I puked (Eleanor had taught me well) to drown out the noise. There was no relief, though. I didn't feel better when I'd been sick, and the thought of going back downstairs to face those sausages had my stomach heaving again.

Rather shakily I stood up and saw my reflection in the mirror. I was as white as a sheet but, worse than that, I could, for the first time, see the fear in my eyes.

I was worried; of course I was worried, but I told myself that the bleeding after sex hadn't been because Gus had hurt me, it had been my period after all. And I'd just missed one, what with my exams and Gus being mean and everything. I knew I couldn't be pregnant because, well, I simply couldn't be—I had my A levels coming up; I was going to university.

My stomach was cramping. It felt as if I were getting my period, it really did. My period was due, in fact (long overdue, actually, but it had been a month since the last lie) only every time I checked, nothing had happened.

I splashed my face and rinsed out my mouth and

headed outside, but there was Lex standing on the landing and I knew he was waiting for me.

'What's going on, Alice?'

'Nothing.' The good bit about being a moody teenager is that there was no expectation that I'd engage in conversation so I just brushed past, but Lex caught my wrist.

'Alice, don't give me that crap—I heard you throwing up.'

'Oh, so I'm anorexic now,' I snarled, 'because I don't want some greasy fat sausages.'

'I'm not worried about anorexia!' He stared right at me. 'I've got four sisters, Alice, I'm not stupid.'

Tell him. There was a voice in my head that kept telling me to *tell him.* That he would understand, that he could sort this out. Only if I told him it was real, if I told him, I knew what would come—and anyway it might all be for nothing. I could feel my stomach cramping and I was sure, *sure* that my period was about to come. Maybe it just had, my boobs were tender, I had all the signs.

'Alice, you can talk to me.'

'I can't.' I was crying. I hadn't cried since it happened, and I didn't want to start now, but there were big fat tears rolling down my cheeks and my nose was running.

'Alice, you *can* talk to me…'

'I'm…' I opened my mouth, the words were there, the truth a second away, 'I'm worried what Mum will say.'

'Alice!' Mum was calling, and I saw Lex close his eyes in frustration. She sounded so normal, so fucking oblivious. I couldn't do it. I just couldn't make myself say it. 'Alice!' She was standing at the bottom of the stairs and calling up. 'Your dinner's getting cold.'

'Coming!' I managed, and when I knew she'd gone I knew the moment had too. I could feel Lex waiting for me to continue, knew that he wasn't going to go away until he got to the bottom of this.

Or thought that he had.

'I don't feel well.' I sniffed back my snot and when that didn't work I wiped my nose with the back of my hand. 'I've got the worst period ever and you know what she's like—she makes such a fuss since I had that seizure.'

'You've got your period?' I could hear the doubt in his voice.

'Really badly. I just get it like that sometimes and I don't want her fussing.' I could see the relief whooshing over his features. 'I just want to go to bed, but I know I ought to do some piano practice…'

'Go to bed, Alice.' He led me to my bedroom door. 'Go and lie down and I'll talk to your mum.'

He must have, because fifteen or so minutes later Mum came in my room, with two paracetamol and some tea and toast and a big hot-water bottle.

'I'm not going to make a fuss.' She sat on the bed and smiled at my pale, tear-streaked face. 'You should have told me.'

'I didn't want to worry you.'

'Well, I do worry,' Mum said. 'That's my job.' Which didn't make me feel better.

'Look—I know you struggle with your periods, but why don't we make an appointment with the doctor and see about you going on the Pill? That should help.'

'No!' The last thing I wanted was a doctor poking me

and asking questions and I started crying again. 'I don't want to go on the Pill.'

'I know, pet.' She was sort of kneading my shoulder with her hand. 'But just because you're on the Pill—well, it doesn't mean it's for that. You can go on it for medical reasons. You'll still be a good girl…'

It was hopeless, fucking hopeless.

How could I tell her?

How could I tell her?

'We'll just leave it for now,' Mum said, and I took my paracetamol and ate my tea and toast as Mum watched. Then I lay back on the pillow with the hot bottle on me and hoped it would make *something* happen, that this awful cramping meant something.

'You rest, darling,' Mum said. 'Take the day off tomorrow. I have to go into town, but you can have a nice lazy day and hopefully you'll feel better.' She stood up. 'I'm going to the corner shop to get some cigarettes—do you fancy some chocolate?'

I shook my head.

'Is there anything I can get you?'

And I knew then what to say.

'Some tampons.'

Twenty-One

'Hey.'

I couldn't quite look him in the eye, so instead I glanced at the clock and sort of jolted when I realised the time.

'I've got to get going.'

'It's Saturday,' Hugh reminded me, pulling me back in.

'I've got plans.'

'Sorry.' He was immediately apologetic. I mean, it was Saturday, of course I had plans. I went for a shower—well, I didn't shower, I didn't want the steam messing up my hair, so I had a wash in the sink and afterwards I did my hair and make-up and dressed in record time.

He'd made me coffee, and toast too, but I just had the coffee.

'I don't know if you've got plans for tonight,' Hugh said, 'but maybe we could go out...'

'I'd love to,' I said, because on any other Saturday night of the fifty-two on offer I would have dropped everything, dropped anyone, if I could go out with him, but I had promised my sister a night out.

Now, you should be able to dump your sister for a man like Hugh.

Most sisters would completely understand that a hot date had come up.

Their sister wasn't Bonny.

And Lex had told me to make a special effort.

'I just can't—sorry.'

'Don't be sorry,' Hugh said. 'I'll have to come up with something.'

'Something?' I wrinkled my nose (the trouble with Botox) and my heart almost stopped as he pulled me towards his full, sexy mouth. 'I'll think of somewhere nice to go on Sunday, just us…if you like.'

I did like—very much.

I was rewarded for my accidental coolness with a long, slow kiss and the promise of a date on Sunday night. There was a certain spring in my step as I walked along the street to my bloody appointment with Lisa and a thought occurred to me—I had done what all the glossies had been telling me to. Had looked all in demand and mysterious. It hadn't been my intention, I just hadn't had time to come up with a good lie.

I *was* being looked after.

Twenty-Two

Orange.

Lisa's colour choice for a Saturday morning was orange.

Not russet, not amber, not sienna, nor peach.

From her lips to her toenails she glowed *orange* and dangling between those horrible breasts was an orange beaded necklace that she'd tied into a knot.

Do you know, it was like Big Tits had read a 'what not to wear' book and missed the *not*!

I sat there staring in morbid fascination at her choice of clothing as she read Dr Kelsey's long letter. I had been dying to peek, but Dr Kelsey had sealed the envelope and put her practice stamp over the seal and stapled her business card to the envelope.

Oh, I'd tried holding it up to the light and everything. I was dying to know what had been said about me—if my cervix had been mentioned, if she liked me.

'So what brings Alice here this morning?'

Here we bloody go.

There was a minute's silence. I guess I was supposed

to admit now that I was having panic attacks, given I'd had another one, but as the silence dragged on I got angry.

'I think I've been misdiagnosed.' I watched her eyebrows raise a fraction. 'I'm having some difficulty with breathing and everyone is insisting that I'm having anxiety attacks, or panic attacks.' I was on a roll. 'I haven't had a chest X-ray. I haven't had blood tests. I'm just told to come to a psychologist.'

'But the Valium helps?'

'Of course it helps—I'm stressed because there's something physically wrong and everyone's ignoring that. I'm fine. I'm in a new relationship—'

'Oh!' she interrupted. 'When did that happen?'

'It's early days,' I said. 'But it's nice.' I warmed at the memory of last night, of his kiss this morning, at the promise of tomorrow. 'He's staying at the flat.'

I watched a frown flicker over her face as she glanced at my notes.

'Hugh?'

'Yes.'

'He's only just arrived.' I gave a tight shrug at her innuendo. 'And you're in a *relationship*.'

'The point is,' I said, cheeks flaming, 'that I really don't think I am having panic attacks. I was asleep when it happened. How can I be panicking when I'm asleep?'

She folded up the letter before answering.

'There are several types of panic attacks, Alice. There are cued or situationally bound attacks, which are set off by a trigger. Then there are predisposed attacks. They don't always occur when the trigger is present, though the situation you find yourself in makes one more likely.'

WTF?

'Then there are spontaneous attacks, with no warning, even when you are sleeping.'

Well, there was no trigger, except…I found myself frowning as I recalled Hugh's words.

God, I had been so busy enjoying Hugh, I'd not had time to think about what he had told me.

Roz.

Roz!

'I've just found out…I mean *just* found out that one of my close girlfriends is gay.' She cocked her head to the side. 'She was there both times,' I explained. 'I mean, she's thirty-four and divorced and has a kid and everything. I had no idea.'

'Are you homophobic?'

'Of course I'm not!' I was appalled. 'My best friend happens to be gay.' (Okay, yes, normally I *do* hate it when people say that, but in my case it happens to be true.) 'I'm the *least* homophobic person I know.' (Okay, I do have issues with Dan being gay, but that's because I fancy him rotten and it's not bloody fair.) 'It's just…' I flailed for an explanation. 'She should have told me.'

'Perhaps she felt she couldn't.'

'Well, she should have. I mean, we go out together, people probably think we're a couple.' I was appalled, just appalled. My face was burning as I sat there and realisation hit—no wonder I hadn't been pulling lately. 'People might think that I'm gay.'

'And that worries you?' Lisa said. 'What other people think?'

I could not stand this.

Adrenaline coursed through my muscles and I wanted to shoot out of the stupid middle seat and walk right out.

She pissed me off.

What did she know? She was just some fat housewife who had a psychology degree—she probably got it online, or she studied years ago when things were different. She had no idea what it was like out there and, PC or not, hitting the bars with a screaming lezza could not be helping my chances.

She just sat and watched me, judged me, thought she knew me…

And then a worrying thought struck—maybe she was gay.

Oh, God, maybe I'd offended her, maybe Day-Glo orange was a… But, no, she'd been wearing green.

Red and yellow and blue and green, purple and orange and blue.

She dressed like a fucking rainbow.

She was making a statement.

'I'm not gay, Alice.' She broke into my thoughts, read them actually—yikes. 'Even if I were gay, even if it appalled you, it still wouldn't offend me, because this counselling session is about you.'

Well, we chatted about Roz for a bit and she rather quickly (carelessly perhaps) dismissed my theory that my subconscious had been telling me there was something amiss with Roz.

'Tell me about Bonny.'

'Bonny?' What the hell did Bonny have to do with all this? We were supposed to be talking about me!

And I really didn't know what to say about Bonny—I mean, where do I start?

Bonny and Lex, as you know, married and moved to Australia. Well, their eldest, Conner, was popped into crèche while Bonny accepted a promotion as Nurse Unit Manager. And then after a few years, tears and IVF, Declan happened. And naturally he was popped happily into crèche too—only her figure didn't snap back so quickly this time. In fact, it never snapped back because exactly one year after Declan's birth along came Hamish and Angus, the twins. Bonny gave up work to become a full-time, completely disillusioned, utterly useless housewife.

She never got out, so Lex had paid for Bonny and me to go to a hotel and have beauty treatments and champagne and *everything*.

And it was just a bit late to back out.

And, anyway, I owed them rather a lot of money, which Bonny was politely not mentioning, though I'm sure she wouldn't hesitate to if I pulled out now. (Now do you see why I couldn't cancel her for Hugh?)

Not that I told Lisa all that.

'She's a housewife, she's got four children, and she used to be a nurse.'

'Like your mum?'

'I suppose.'

'And do you see her a lot?'

'A lot,' I said, to show her I had normal, healthy, family relationships. 'In fact, I'm going out with her tonight. Lex, her husband, is treating us to a night out in a luxury hotel, for Bonny's birthday.'

It annoyed me that she wrote something down; it really annoyed me that she didn't smile or say, 'That's nice.' Instead she frowned.

'What?' I demanded to her smug, self-knowing face.

'Nothing,' Lisa said, jotting away on her pad. 'Do you ever look after the children? With four children, a night in a hotel with her husband...'

'Lex wants her to have a night out with me!' Stupid cow, I felt like saying, what did she know? 'Bonny hardly gets out; she's really low at the moment...' I swallowed hard, and I swear if she said 'like your mum was' I would not have been responsible for my actions, so instead I breathed it out and said in a much calmer voice, 'I get on great with Bonny. That's why we're going out...there's nothing wrong with their marriage.'

'I never said there was.'

'Well, you implied,' I said. 'And you're wrong. Lex and Bonny...' I didn't finish. I was sick of her, sick of her writing her little notes and drawing some deep and meaningful conclusion from every innocuous comment.

What the fuck did Bonny and Lex have to do with all this?

And then, when I just sat there, when we were only half an hour in and clearly getting nowhere, she closed her pad. 'Have you thought of a life coach?'

I shrugged.

'Only it's different from psychology—it's about moving forward, instead of examining yourself, examining the past.'

'You think that would be better for me?' I liked that idea, actually. Someone to remind me to do things, someone to force me into action, to achieve.

'No.' She stared at me.

'Why not?'

So she told me.

'You're very controlled, Alice. You always look nice, you have your routines, you're very ordered.'

'Routines?' What the hell was she talking about? I yearned for routines and I certainly wasn't ordered—she should take a look at the flat.

'Your keys always go into the same place in your bag. You check your make-up before you leave, you—'

'I'm just neat,' I said tartly.

She said nothing, because she had no idea.

Controlled and ordered indeed.

She should see me after a few wines.

She should have seen me last night with Hugh.

She had no idea what she was talking about.

'You never take a sweet,' Lisa said. 'I mean you look at them often, only you never take one.'

'I thought they were for the children,' I said.

'They're for anyone.' She smiled. 'Help yourself.'

'I don't want one.'

'That's fine.'

'No,' I argued. 'Clearly it's not. God!' I shrilled out the word but she just sat there. 'You'll be writing down "Eating disorder" now because I don't take one of your sweets.'

'I'm not writing anything, Alice. You asked for my opinion, my observation, as to why I think you need to be here, and I'm giving it.'

'And if I eat a sweet, will you change your opinion?' I challenged. 'If I suddenly cram the whole jar in my mouth, will you strike off that I'm controlled?'

'Strike off?' She frowned. 'I'm not taking notes now.'

'But you will.' Did she think I was stupid? 'Well, will it change it?' I stared at the jar. I stared at a week's allowance of carbs, and if it just shut her up, I would have swallowed them all.

'I'll have a word with the receptionist.' Lisa smiled. 'Maybe you should come weekly for now.'

'Weekly?' I laughed; I just sat there and laughed. 'I have to see you weekly now because I didn't eat a stupid sweet.'

'You don't have to see me at all, Alice, that's entirely up to you.' She stood up, took me out to Reception and had a word with her happy receptionist who, lucky me, found a slot for next Thursday.

Well, I wasn't going.

I just wouldn't turn up.

I got to my car and I was furious, so bloody furious that I unzipped my bag and punched a couple of tablets out of the blister pack—so much for psychology. *And* I stuck two fingers up at her window just in case she was watching.

Stupid fat cow!

Twenty-Three

'Where the hell were you?'

Bonny fell on my neck as I climbed out of the car. I was ten minutes late—but then again she didn't get out much.

I walked into her house, which was brimming with strollers and Portacots and babies and toddlers, and there in the middle was Lex.

I am assured it's normal to have a crush on your brother-in-law. I mean, biologically, Bonny and I have the same genes—we are probably destined to be attracted to the same sort of bloke.

'Hi, Alice!'

'Hi, Lex.'

It was a bit uncomfortable. We always were, but this was different, I could sort of feel there had been a row.

Another one.

The trouble was, as much as I had defended them to Lisa, I was worried.

Bonny was huge. She started off as the perfect mother, jogging each morning before work, mashing organic

pumpkin and insisting the crèche feed Conner her prepared meals. Now the place was littered with fast food.
There were kids and toys and nappies and mess and
dishes and plates and bottles everywhere.

It's as if their house (that looked fine from the outside) had been built on landfill, and it was spewing up
through the floorboards.

Mind you, I could understand Bonny's lethargy, because frankly I wouldn't have known where to start.

And then there was Lex.

Lying in front of the telly, feeding a baby (not sure
which one), unshaven, pissed off with his lot and terribly, terribly sexy.

I had this terrible conflict of feelings because I love
Bonny so, but frankly, if I were Lex, I'd be pissed off
with her too.

Bonny should be an anagram for lethargic.

She hadn't worked a nursing shift since she'd found
out about the twins.

Her house was a pigsty.

Her clothes were a mess, covered in baby sick, and her
hair was just a lank, greasy mess that she had scraped
back into a ponytail.

I wanted to shake her.

I swear sometimes I wanted to shake her.

'Where's his dummy?' Lex stood up and stared at the
pile of magazines that hid the coffee table. His trackpants
were too big, thanks to my sister's meticulous washing,
his T-shirt too small thanks to the same—and he was
like a bull, this gorgeous, sexy man. I wanted to shake
Bonny, who was clipping her toenails somewhere in the
corner of the living room.

'Where he dropped it last,' Bonny said in this sarcastic voice, without even looking up.

Look, I get it. I get that she *is* working. I get that four children *are* a lot of work, but—what the fuck does she do?

Lex was making up bottles, loading the washing machine and working 80 hours a week, and on his precious weekend off he was looking after the kids and paying for us to go away.

And it was Lex, when she finally emerged half an hour later, in black pants that were way too tight and a black blouse that could have used a good iron, wearing a splash of red lipstick that was way too much for an unmade-up face, who pulled her into his arms, telling her to have a good time.

'He doesn't get it.' Bonny stared out of the taxi window. 'It's easy for him. I've sterilised the bottles, and made sure there are loads of nappies and...'

'He's a nice guy, Bonny.'

'Yeah, a nice guy who bought me a year's gym membership for my birthday.' I saw a flash of tears in her eyes and I felt a glimmer of guilt, because when I was coming up with gift ideas, if I'd had the money, I'd have bought her a gym membership—not just for her weight, but for the crèche, for the fun, for her to get away from the house and the playgroups and to be herself again. Then I felt a bubble of panic—true panic because Lex and Bonny can't be in trouble.

I honestly couldn't stand it if Lex and Bonny were in trouble.

They can't be.

They just can't.

He'd booked us into the Langham—a stunning hotel on the river—so nice that we actually sat down at a lovely polished desk to check in. Bonny handed over her gold Amex, courtesy of Lex. I truly don't know why she has to be so down on him.

Still, her spirits lifted when we got to the room. It had two windows, city and river views, two massive beds and one bottle of champagne chilling in a bucket, which Bonny soon dealt with. She pulled another bottle from her case and shoved it in the ice—and then she smiled and so did I.

You see, when she's being Bonny, she's probably the funniest person I know.

Half a bottle of champagne (each) later, we were in our swimming costumes, wrapped in fluffy white dressing gowns and heading down to the spa for our beauty treatments. Our appointments weren't till three so we sat in a vast spa, where, unfortunately, champagne glasses weren't allowed. I knew she felt awkward, peeling off her dressing gown, and though I looked away, I could see why. She had put on loads of weight, I mean loads. Bonny has always been curvy, but she has a confidence that could carry it, that makes it look fantastic. Or rather she'd had this confidence—she didn't any more.

'I must go on a diet.' She closed her eyes in relief as the water covered her body. I didn't know what to say, so I said nothing—just lay in the lovely water, feeling it splash over my body. Apart from a couple of serious swimmers in the lap pool, we had the place to ourselves. 'Can you imagine going to the gym looking like this?'

'I can't imagine going to the gym, full stop,' I said,

relieved that Bonny opened her eyes and giggled, but then her face was serious.

'He'll have an affair. I mean, look at him, Alice—and he travels all the time. I know the girls hang on his every word. He'll leave me. I'll be stuck here away from Mum…'

'He won't.' I sounded assured but my own panic was rising. 'He loves you,' I insisted.

'How can he when I'm such a miserable cow? I don't know what's wrong… I mean, I just smooch around all day, hating that he's at work and I'm stuck home. I'm like Mum, aren't I?'

'You're nothing like Mum,' I said, because, though I loved my mum, she really had given up—whereas Bonny, sometimes when she smiles, sometimes when she puts on eyeliner and lipstick and puts on her Pink CD and sashays around the living room, shaking her boobs and bum, she's the sexiest woman I know. And from the smile on Lex's face when the old Bonny occasionally surfaces, she's still the sexiest woman he knows too. 'Anyway, Lex is nothing like Dad.'

Lisa had been right, I conceded, there did not need to be a trigger, because as I lay in the lovely warm water, seemingly relaxed, seemingly without a care, tiny fragments of pictures were joining up, like bees collecting into a swarm, a mass moving and darkening. I sat up suddenly then, opened my eyes and looked out of the floor-to-ceiling windows, stared at the spectacular Melbourne skyline and felt the panic subside. After thirty minutes or so we were called in for our treatments.

I hate massages—honestly—and I knew Bonny was looking forward to stripping off and being pounded about as much as me, but we'd had a look at the price list and it was so expensive it would have been just wrong to wag off.

So I lay there, head down, having my expensive spray tan pummelled off me, and murmuring 'Lovely' when she wafted oils under my nose and made me choose which one I preferred.

They all smelt the same, but I said the second one.

I just desperately wanted it over.

Still, it would be worth it for Hugh—the masseuse had promised my skin would feel like silk afterwards, and really, as much as I was having fun with Bonny, it was such lousy timing. I mean, it was all very well playing it cool, but it was Saturday night, for God's sake. It was all so new and so... I mean, I hadn't even told Bonny. I didn't know what to tell Bonny and it seemed a shame to rub things in her face when she was clearly so worried about Lex.

They *had* to be fine.

I couldn't stand it if they broke up—I honestly didn't think I could stand it.

Would he tell her?

I felt my head tighten.

What if he told her?

What if he threw it back at her?

'Are you okay?' the masseuse asked.

'Fine.'

'Only you suddenly tensed.'

'I'm fine,' I insisted, wishing her two-hundred-dollar-an-hour hands actually worked, wishing the poxy smell of lavender actually soothed. But as I lay there head down, trying to will my muscles to relax, trying not to answer my own questions, I felt as if a light bulb was exploding in my head.

Twenty-Four

The second time I asked Mum to buy tampons I knew I had to do something about it—knew I had to find out.

I had gone to a chemist on the way back from school, and face burning, trying not to look at the shop assistant, I had bought a test along with hair serum, shampoo and conditioner and some make-up. I spent a fortune trying to cover up the test in the basket, but of course she saw it and asked if I would like to speak with the pharmacist.

I mumbled something about it not being for me and dashed out with my purchases. I went to the loos in the shopping centre and dipped the little stick into my stream of wee and, all this crap about waiting two minutes, it took ten seconds and there was this thick purple cross. No matter which way I turned it or read the instructions, it meant that I was pregnant.

I rang Gus.

'Just stop pestering me, Alice.'

'I'm pregnant.' He'd been about to hang up when I blurted out the words and I felt the fear and anger and shock and disgust in his silence.

'Please meet me—Mum thinks I've got a lesson—seven at the park. If not, I'll come to the house.'

'Stay away from Celeste.'

'Then meet me, Gus. I don't know what to do.'

I knew when he saw me again it would be okay.

I knew, because that was the reason he'd felt he had to stay away.

Yes, Celeste was pregnant, but these things happened. Dad had fallen in love with someone else and had left us for her, and, yes, it had hurt, but these things happened.

Celeste would get over it.

I went to the hairdresser's and got a blow-dry. I put on jeans, then changed my mind and put on a skirt because it would be easier if Gus wanted to do it again, and I rubbed my skin in Bonny's body lotion.

'Where are you going all done up?' Mum asked as I headed out of the door.

'My piano lesson.' My face was on fire. 'Gus said to dress as I would for my exam.'

'Well, less make-up,' Mum said, and so I wiped off the lipstick and then got to the corner and took out the stupid velvet bow and added more lipstick and undid my blouse.

I waited for ever on the park bench. I knew that he'd come and he did.

I didn't know what to expect. I knew what I hoped for, for him to take me in his arms, to tell me we would sort something out—that Celeste and he were over, something, anything, I don't know, but he had to have an answer.

He gave me nothing.

'You'll have to sort it out.' He didn't even look at me. 'I so don't need this.'

'You think I need this? I've got my exams...'

'I leave for Australia on Friday, Alice.' Only then did he look at me, dark, angry and accusing. 'We have to leave now or it will be too late for Celeste to fly...'

'I'm having your baby.'

'You!' He just stared aghast. 'You with a baby? You stupid fucking cow—how would you cope with a baby? You'll have to get rid of it.'

'I can't...' I begged. I didn't know, I didn't know what to do, who to speak to, our old family doctor, how could I? I just didn't know. Yes, there were numbers in the phone book but every time I rang them I froze and hung up.

'Just sort it out, Alice.' His face was white, like putty. 'I don't even know it's mine.'

'There's only been you!' I had snot pouring down my nose, I was crying and sobbing. 'You know that...'

'We had a shag on the floor—you led me on,' he raged. 'Don't tell me I'm the only one.' He was savage then, told me I'd never cope with a baby.

Only he said it a bit harsher than that.

That it was unthinkable—me as a mother.

He even laughed at that.

An abortion would be kinder to the baby.

You get the gist.

I could give it nothing.

I *was* nothing.

And then I watched him leave. I just stood there and watched him leave.

And if he could walk away, if he could deny its existence, then so could I.

And so I did.

In the background I knew that I was—I even made
plans. I had always dressed neatly, but I started to wear
big sloppy T-shirts long before I had a bump, so that
people were used to it for when I did. I also, even though
I was studying for my exams, went for an interview for
a job in a burger place, even though Mum was furious,
but I knew I would get bigger, and that gave me a good
reason to be putting on weight and a good reason to be
out of the house.

So, yes, I sort of knew, but I hoped it would go away,
that I'd wake up and I'd be bleeding, or that it would just
die and be absorbed. I never let myself actually think
that I'd have it and what I'd do with it if I did.

I simply refused to think.

Twenty-Five

The massage took longer than expected, and by the time we got to the hair and beauty salon we were way over our appointment times. I had my hair washed and sat watching my finger- and toenails turning the most glorious shade of coral—and having my eyebrows waxed and eyelashes and brows dyed. Then make-up was applied as the hairdresser dried Bonny's hair, and then it was her turn to go and get the finishing touches as I slid into the seat.

The hairdresser rubbed some serum into it. I was really feeling nice and relaxed and then the hairdresser picked up and attached that stupid diffuser thing and I stopped her. 'No, I want it straight.'

She frowned down. 'There's too much product in it for it to be straight.' She'd weighted it down with thick waxy product. I hadn't been paying attention and realised that she'd been intending to leave it curly.

'There isn't really time…' She was waving the diffuser over me and I wanted to rip it out of her hands.

'Make time!' I glared. If I've learnt one thing in this

life, don't pretend you're happy with a hairdresser when you're not. Kick and scream and cry if you have to—and I was about to—she could shagging well wash the product out and start again. I didn't care if my make-up was done and it was already six p.m. I was not going out with curly hair.

But then Bonny chimed up, 'It looks great, Alice, and anyway we don't have time.'

It was no big deal to her, she didn't realise I never went curly, and I wouldn't have that night, but Bonny was laughing as she chatted to the beautician. Bonny was actually laughing and having fun and we had a table booked in an hour. I couldn't bring her down. I had tears in my eyes as I stared at my fuzzy hair.

'It looks fantastic!' the hairdresser said firmly. 'Look.' She was pulling the long ringlets out through her fingers, arranging them around my face—and she'd actually done a bloody good job, it was just that I hated it so.

I hated it.

And even if I could put up with it for tonight, for Bonny's sake, I couldn't stand the thought of Hugh seeing me like this tomorrow.

He was going out, I remembered, going cycling or something—I'd ring Karan perhaps and tell her—ooh, I could tell her the goss about Roz. It was Bonny's night, so I didn't make a fuss that for the first time in ten years I would be out in public with curly hair. In fact, when we got back to our room and Bonny opened another bottle of champagne I cheered up immensely and gave her her present.

'You shouldn't have!'

'Don't be daft.' I was nervous as she unwrapped the

parcel. I'd put loads of thought into this present and it had cost way more than I'd intended but, hell, it was for Bonny. And the thought of her coming out on the town in those shagging black pants. Well, I'd read every how-to-look-good book and had come up with the perfect dress for her.

Embarrassed, when I'd asked her her size a couple of weeks ago, she'd confessed to being a size sixteen, so naturally I'd bought a size eighteen, and when Bonny frowned at the label I hurriedly assured her that the assistant had told me that this designer's sizes came in tiny.

Well, as she unfurled the dress I saw her blink a couple of times.

It was black, but it had a really low neckline and was sort of ruched, and belted in at the waist. The best I can describe it is like a German beer *fraulein*, and then it tapered in a bit at the skirt and then there were all these sort of ruffles.

Like a gypsy German beer *fraulein*.

And I have to congratulate Trinny and Susannah and Gok, because when Bonny slipped it on, with her hair done, and ringlets gleaming, she looked fantastic.

I'd bought her some fishnets and she put them on too, and, yes, she was huge, but I felt drab beside her.

And Lisa was right, I realised as I watched her swirl in the mirror.

She should be doing this in front of Lex.

Still, Lex or no Lex, we had a brilliant night—we actually got chatted up by two Qantas pilots. It was so much fun, too much fun actually, 'cos for a moment there I seriously thought Bonny was going too far. She was flirting and just *reckless*. I know I can be reckless, but I don't have Lex at home.

And Lex was paying for this too, I thought angrily as I saw one of them pressing his leg against her. They were bloody sober, of course, but Bonny was roaring drunk and I felt a sort of panic for her, she had a desperate look in her eyes that unsettled me.

The other one was buying me drinks and normally, well, I don't know, 'cos normally I'm not in such a lovely hotel with pilots buying me drinks, but a couple of weeks ago I'd have been in his room by now. Maybe not, given I was with Bonny—but there was Hugh and there was Lex and for the first time in my life I felt like the grown-up.

It was a relief when he texted me.

Hi.
Hi.
Are you having a good time?
Yep. You?
Call me.
Can't. Too noisy.

I clicked off, but I wanted to call. I'd played it cool, too cool with him, and I made my excuses and dashed to the loos. They were very nice loos too, with fluffy towels and a place to sit, and I rang him. I could see my strawberry blonde curls and I didn't like them, but I sort of did…

'Sorry about that,' I said.

'No problems. I shouldn't have called.'

'I'm glad you did.'

'So what are you doing?'

'Getting chatted up by two pilots.' I laughed then blinked, because I heard his silence, knew he was worried, and it felt sort of nice. It had only been a few days and yet it was way more than that. 'Well, I'm trying to get my sister safely to bed before she does something she regrets.'

'How about tomorrow we go for dinner?' Hugh said. 'Just us.'

'Okay.' I was sort of glowing inside.

'You choose where.'

'No, you choose,' I said, and it was a date.

I was sort of glowing as I walked back—but I couldn't find Bonny. I did a bit of a frantic search, then dashed back to the loos and then back to our table. The pilots had gone and I caught sight of myself in a mirror again, my curls bobbing, my face worried, and that swarm of bees was chasing me again, only this time they caught me.

As I searched for Bonny, they surrounded me.

Each memory a sting.

Because it hadn't been the hazelnut torte—Dad had told Bonny and me to sit quietly while he went downstairs for a drink. Margo, the landlady, had brought us in cake and cream, but I took a bite and I didn't like it. I wanted ice cream like Dad had promised and I went to find him. Normally if I stood on the stairs one of the bar staff would see and get him for me.

Only I never made it to the stairs. I could hear something down the hall, a low voice that sounded like Dad, and I walked down the corridor, saw Dad and Margo kissing against the wall, her skirt round her waist and Dad pushing at her. I knew I shouldn't have seen it. I

ran back to the room, and saw Bonny's panicked face
at my expression—and I knew I couldn't tell her, knew
I couldn't talk about it, must never mention it. She was
crying and calling for Daddy, for someone to please
come, Alice couldn't breathe…

There was a whoosh of relief as I saw Bonny walking
towards me, the bees dispersing and the panic fading.
Lisa had just unsettled me. Of course things were okay.

'Where were you?'

'Looking for you,' Bonny said. 'Where the hell did
you go?'

'To the loo.'

'I've just been to the loo and you weren't there.'

It was a mix-up, a stupid mix-up. I told myself that—
then told myself again as we drained our drinks and
headed to the lifts.

I chose not to mention that her lipstick was smeared
all over her face.

Chose not to tell Bonny that she shouldn't worry—she
was nothing like Mum.

Instead, she was her father's daughter.

Twenty-Six

'So you're not actually living together,' Big Tits said as my stomach tightened. 'He's just staying at your flat...'

It was my fifth visit.

My fourth week with Hugh and my life was brilliant.

Well, not brilliant.

I was seriously broke and I couldn't even ask Roz for a loan because, well, we were hardly talking, or rather I was hardly talking to her.

Karan hadn't reacted the way I thought she would when I told her the gossip about Roz—in fact, she'd made me feel a bit small. She told me that Roz was a good friend and that she needed me now. Then she'd added twenty dollars to the bill, saying it was because it was a Sunday, but I knew she thought I was being mean.

I wasn't, though.

She should have told me.

At work I couldn't look at her without blushing and her eyes filled up with tears and she looked away.

At home she kept texting me.
Over and over.

I should have told you.
I didnt know how. (Roz can't do apostrophes on
her phone.)
Im sorry.
Im so sorry.
Talk to me Alice.

I just couldn't.

Dr Kelsey had reluctantly, extremely reluctantly, given me another script, which had already run out. But if there was one thing going swimmingly it was a certain Dr Hugh Watson. The universe had aligned for me there. Nicole had emailed (the house phone was permanently turned down by now) to say that she was staying in the UK for an extra two weeks and Hugh and I were delighted.

We were in our little bubble of love and we wanted no one to pierce it.

Bonny tried. She kept calling and she warned me to be careful, told me that I was getting my hopes up and it was way too soon to be serious. And Lisa clearly didn't see it as a good thing either.

'He's your friend's cousin?' Big Tits checked her notes. 'How long has he been in Australia?'

'A month now.'

'And you're sleeping with him.' I could hear the implication—knew she thought he was using me, but she had no idea, no idea at all.

God, I didn't need to justify myself to her.

Except that was what I found myself doing.

You see, I had told her a bit about my rather vast sexual history, or rather she wormed it out of me, but Hugh was nothing like any of them.

Nothing.

She just refused to separate him from them and there was no point being there, I realised as she droned on and on—Dr Kelsey wasn't going to give me another script anyway. I didn't actually need another—I was fine. The only problem I had now was her and, I glanced at the clock, in twenty minutes she would be out of my life.

For ever.

And maybe she sensed it, because she let me have it.

'This is not a relationship, Alice.'

'You have to set boundaries, Alice.'

I was paying two dollars a minute to hear this!

'Just because a man takes you for dinner, or asks you to dance,' Big Tits persisted, 'it doesn't mean you have to sleep with him.'

Christ, what planet did she live on? She was stuck in the 1950s—in a world where a guy walked up and asked you to dance.

'So he should,' was her response when I told her the same. 'You deserve more,' she insisted to my rigid face. Next she'd have him pinning orchids on my chest.

'Why should they expect to have sex with you?' Big Tits demanded. 'Why would you let them?'

I hated this consultation—hated it the most, sitting there with her telling me I should bestow my favours on men who were worthy, on men who would respect me. 'You deserve better, Alice!'

'I know that now.' I was having great trouble keeping

my voice even. 'Hugh's not like that. We're serious about each other.'

'Is he serious about Gemma too?'

I could have slapped her.

'You've only been seeing him for four weeks. You slept with him the first week you met!'

'No, I didn't.'

'Sorry.' She flicked through her notes as my face burnt with shame, as she reduced the one good thing in my life to a meaningless shag. 'The second.'

Fuck you.

I didn't have the guts to say it, though. I just stared at her sixty-year-old creped chest and *how* I hated her for not understanding. Then I picked up my bag and walked out as the bubbly receptionist called me back to pay.

'I'll send a cheque,' I called over my shoulder, and then I got into the car park and I tried to breathe. I tried to get the keys in the ignition, and then I jerked out of the car park and nearly hit a kid on his bike.

And *how* I hated her for not understanding.

Twenty-Seven

They were wrong. All of them.

And when I got home to Hugh, he proved them wrong.

'Come.' Hugh was shoving clothes in his case. 'It will be fun.'

'I could have done with a bit of notice.' I gave a nervous laugh.

'I didn't know I'd be crazy about you then.'

He was going to some psychiatric convention that was being held in Coogee—a beachside place about ten kilometres out of Sydney. Three nights away with Hugh. God, I was tempted, but I hadn't prepared. Okay, I was waxed and ready, but the thought of stripping off on Bondi bloody beach—where Hugh wanted to go—and displaying my body to the beautiful locals had me breaking out in a sweat. And what about my hair? I had a blow-dry booked for nine a.m. tomorrow. Three days of surf and sand and Hugh might just work out that my straight hair actually wasn't straight at all.

'Won't they mind?'

Just go, Alice, my head was screaming, *just grab a*

few clothes and go. He'd offered to pay for my flight, there was no reason *not* to go, yet the thought of being alone with him for three days had me in a tailspin.

'Why would they mind?' Hugh shrugged. He was tapping on his laptop, had pulled up the Qantas page and there was a flight available. 'Loads of people will be bringing their partners.'

I stilled inside. I just stood there and froze, the word 'partner' sideswiping me. Oh, I knew he didn't actually mean I was his partner—but that single word had me slightly in his fold, that elusive word that had never once been used to describe me. A good friend, a shag buddy, a date, a casual date, a mistress once. I had been many things, worn many hats, but I had never been the one who a guy asked to come away with him. In fact, I had never been away with a guy before, unless you counted Dan. My head was buzzing with the implication, with the excitement and also fear, this fear that once he saw me, the real me, then he wouldn't want me any more, and three days was a long time to keep up the dazzling façade.

But that word had turned the key. I was nodding, he was clicking on the computer, and suddenly we were confirmed.

I was off on holiday, with my partner.

A bit more notice *would* have been nice. Still, Nicole's stuff had been moved into a cupboard to make way for Hugh's and was in little cases and drawers all neatly washed and folded.

Can you believe she had a holiday drawer? I kid you not. She had a drawer of little bikinis and sarongs and sunblock lotion and lip balm. How ironic was it that

Nicole, the least spontaneous person in the world, was one of the few women who could spin off at two minutes' notice—and best of all Hugh had no idea what her wardrobe consisted of.

I didn't take *everything*. I packed my own underwear, hair serum and heavy-duty sunblock and of course my straighteners, but just as I was shoving my hairdryer with a motor that could power a Harley into my travel case, Hugh pulled it out. 'There will be a hairdryer at the hotel.'

'My hair's so thick and curly, though…' I could feel my cheeks go pink, I sort of felt I had to warn him in advance. 'It takes for ever to dry.'

'Curly?' Hugh picked up a strand of my mirror-smooth hair. 'You?'

'Yep.' Somehow I managed a nonchalant shrug and there was no major debate, no Hugh suddenly trying to get a refund on his ticket, but he hadn't seen it in all its ringleted glory.

I could feel a little bubble of panic inside, growing and fizzing and multiplying. I wanted to take something, but I had nothing.

There were two for emergencies that I kept in the bathroom, but I had taken them this morning (well, so would you if you had an appointment with Big Tits). I couldn't face him seeing my hair with nothing. It sounds stupid, but it was a massive deal for me and I didn't want to spoil the weekend by stressing about my hair.

It had to be perfect.

I had to be perfect.

'I've just got to pop out.'

'We can get whatever you need there…'

'No.' I shook my head. 'I was supposed to be catching up with Dan for lunch tomorrow. He'll be put out if I cancel—I'll just go over for coffee.'

'Well, be back by two.'

I didn't even need the note from the hospital. The doctor just listened. I'd actually learnt a thing or three from Big Tits about what to say, and from Dr Kelsey I'd learned what not to say. This doctor was usually my sore throat doctor when I needed a sick note for work. Well, he briefly checked my boring medial history and nodded approvingly when I said I was thinking of going to a psychologist, and he gave me a script. I paid for my consultation and read it as I headed to a (different) chemist. 'Diazepam 10 mg x 50 x 3 repeats.'

Which was one hundred and fifty tablets and, given they were double the strength of the others, well, it was like having three hundred. Finally I could relax.

I smiled as paid for the script.

I was going to Coogee.

Everything was beautiful.

Within a couple of hours I was sitting at Melbourne International Airport. My heart was fluttering with nerves, but happy nerves—especially when he came back with two large gin and tonics which, combined with the Valium I'd just dashed down in the loo and a glass of champagne on the one-hour flight, had me floating all the way to Sydney.

Hugh was entranced with Sydney. There is huge rivalry between Melbourne and Sydney—you can only like one, but not the other, but I didn't buy it.

Melbourne is a brilliant place to live.

Sydney too if you're loaded.

Melbourne has sport and art and history.

Sydney, though, well, there is no harbour more beautiful in the world.

None.

And that's from a (not born and bred) Melburnian.

And if you like beaches, well, Sydney's your gal.

Hugh was like a child in a sweet shop. As the plane descended he was nose to the window, staring at the Pacific Ocean and the glittering harbour with the Opera House standing proud.

'We have to go there!'

'We will.' His enthusiasm was infectious. We swept through Baggage, it was already waiting, as was a taxi. It was so easy, and so hard to believe that just a few hours ago I'd been gearing myself to a weekend alone.

And now we were here, a short drive to heaven.

Coogee Beach was stunning, a golden expanse with sandstone rocks either side and crashing waves and our hotel room had glorious views.

Apart from a couple of dinners, I had never been *out* with Hugh—does that make sense? I guess we were too busy in our love bubble to socialise just yet. I knew he was gorgeous, red hair and all. I knew the impact that he had on me, but I just hadn't anticipated the effect he had on others.

As soon as we got there we had to go down to a champagne cocktail reception. I pulled on a slinky black dress and did my make-up in record time as he put on a suit. I was still floating from the Valium and gin and champagne—and, call it self-preservation, instead of champagne I took a glass of orange juice. I was nervous, of course, meeting his colleagues and their partners, but it was relatively painless. Hugh chatted easily to everyone and so did I. I was drunk on lust and atmosphere and the effect of Hugh, because everyone seemed to like him. I went outside for a cigarette and was delighted to find that most psychiatrists and their partners smoked like trains.

I did remember to say thank you, just as Yasmin had said I should. I stared up at the glittering stars and beyond to the universe that had brought me my dearest wish and I thanked them, or whoever it was who dealt with these things, for delivering him to me. My good manners were rewarded because, as the waiter came by and I was toying with having just one glass of champagne, a hand snaked around my waist.

'Bed.'

'It's only nine o'clock.'

'Business is done—it's time for pleasure.'

Twenty-Eight

I couldn't breathe.

I shot out of bed and pulled on my dressing gown to cover me and then I went downstairs.

I could see the light on under the door and I burst into the kitchen.

Mum was ironing. She'd taken in ironing to pay for my music tuition and with Bonny's wedding still needing to be paid off, she was busy, and worried and stressed.

'Mum…' I didn't know how to start it, what to say, I mean what did I say? Not that I got a chance. 'You know when we spoke about me going out with guys—'

'I don't even want to hear about it, Alice,' she interrupted my pathetic attempt to tell her. 'You've got plenty of time for all that.'

'The thing is…'

'Alice.' Mum held up the iron. 'Why do you think I'm standing here at one a.m. ironing?'

I just stood there.

'I have a shift tomorrow that starts at seven-thirty, so tell me why the hell do you think I'm ironing?'

Still I stood there.

'So you never have to.'

And she went on and on about how this was the most vital time of my life, how everything was pinned on the next few months, how she never wanted me to be in her position. I was to forget about boys. I was to forget about everything apart from my exams. It was bad enough that I insisted on working at a burger bar. I was to buckle down with my music practice and she didn't want to hear any arguments.

It was hopeless, so I just stood there staring at her.

Should I have said it? Should I have just blurted out the words—*I'm pregnant*?

And then what?

She'd understand?

It really was hopeless.

So I met up with Dad.

I don't blame Dad for leaving Mum—he married this fun-loving, sexy, sparkly thing (because she was pregnant, I'd heard him say in a row) and she just gave up when she had kids. Every picture tells a story and our photo album and the collection of pictures on the mantelpiece tell Mum and Dad's. He got better looking as he got older; Mum got bigger and cared less. He had an affair when I was about five or six. I had just started school and I can remember the rows. He left for a while and Mum lost some weight and made an effort and they got back together again but it soon started to slide, or rather Mum did. When I was fifteen Dad moved out for good with—cliché upon cliché—Lucy, his young, blonde, thin and beautiful junior assistant.

Everyone said Dad was a complete bastard—everyone

except me. Bonny is Mum's favourite and I guess I'm Dad's and we could always talk. So I rang him up and he sounded delighted to hear from me, though he wasn't keen on going to the Nag's Head. He suggested a pub I'd never been to, but I got the bus and met him.

'Hey there, baby girl.' He grinned when I walked in, and when he went to get me a Coke he offered to slip in a Bacardi. It was a treat and made me feel grown-up, but today I said no. I knew it was bad for...well, I didn't think much further than that.

'I hope you're not looking for money!' He grinned. 'Things are a bit tight at the moment, what with the wedding and everything...'

Ah, the wedding—he wasn't talking about Bonny's because Lex and Mum had paid for that—no, he and Lucy were getting married in a few weeks in the Caribbean. My mother was furious—that he couldn't afford to pay for his own daughter's wedding, but was going to the Caribbean for his.

'Why are you having such an expensive wedding, Dad?'

'It's not for me, Alice.' He shook his head. 'Lucy's put up with a lot. I mean she's had to go without while I've supported three kids and...well...' Drone, drone, drone.

You know, the trouble with divorce is you don't know who to believe. See, if you listen to Mum, then Dad never gives her anything, or hardly anything, and even then only occasionally. That's why she has to work so many jobs—that's why she's so skint. And if you listen to Dad, well, according to him, he pays Mum more than he has to. That said, Eleanor is married and Bonny was eighteen when he went, but Dad says he gives Mum a lot of help with me and that she got a brilliant divorce settlement—well, she got the house.

But if you listen to Mum she got the bloody mortgage too.

'Lucy deserves a decent wedding, and...' He glanced down at my glass. 'Do you want another drink?'

I didn't but I nodded. For the first time in weeks I didn't even feel sick, just calmer, and safer too. I could talk to Dad. I watched as he chatted to the barmaid—he was born flirting, my dad. He looks like Bonny, and she's a wild flirt too—and there he was chatting away to the barmaid and then glancing over to me, but he gave me a bright smile and brought over my drink. As he sat down I took a deep breath and braced myself to tell him.

Dad spoke first, though.

'It's good you called because actually I've got something to tell you, Alice.' I watched him swallow and sensed he was nervous, and I was too, because I didn't want to hear about him, or his latest drama or scandal, and there always was one where Dad was concerned. For once I wanted to talk about me and my problems, not listen to his.

'Lucy's pregnant.'

I could feel tears in my eyes as I took a gulp of my drink—he'd put in a Bacardi. 'I don't want you telling your mum yet—you know what she's like. I just want to keep it quiet till after the wedding but, well, now you can see why Lucy needs a holiday.'

Mum was going to freak.

That was my first thought.

Mum would go off when she found out about this.

And then I thought about me, or rather how the hell could I tell him? How could I tell any of them?

It was at that point I realised I couldn't.

Twenty-Nine

It just got better. He had to go to a seminar in the morning, and I could have dozed and sat on the balcony, but I knew, because he'd said what time he'd finish, that he'd want to go to the beach. It was a humid day. I wouldn't even make it to the water's edge without my hair starting to curl.

I also had visions of my mum sitting dressed from head to toe and miserable at the poolside as my dad, splashing in the water with his daughters, urged her to join in.

I didn't want to be that.

So, when Hugh left, instead of dozing or lounging about, I showered, and redid what the woman at the beauty centre on Bonny's birthday had done. I squeezed my hair dry with a towel and spread a palm full of Curls Rock through it that I had bought that day. I sat for close to an hour then I got up. I took a Valium as I saw my hair coil into ringlets, but instead of panicking I read Hugh's trashy blockbuster and waited it out. At one, I ran my fingers through it as the hairdresser had done and twisted some curls into better shape and then I sat again with my heart in my mouth.

And I waited.

He was going to see me with curly hair.

He didn't really look at me as he careered into the room. I sat cringing inside as he pulled off his suit and pulled on board shorts. He was chatting away, desperate to get out into the sun...

And then he turned around.

'Jesus, Alice...' He stood and I swallowed. I sat there, no doubt purple from head to foot, but I was pretending to read my book—pretending that I often looked like this, that I was used to this, that this was my holiday hair.

He loved it.

In fact, we didn't get to the beach till four...

Thirty

It never moved when I played.

The world moved on. Gus had left, my exams drew closer. Lex's company gave him an extension, which meant he had a few more weeks, but it wasn't a relief.

Bonny just unleashed her fears more.

She didn't want to leave Mum.

She didn't want to go.

Lex tried to help. He bought Bonny and Mum a week in France at the end of May with his bonus money, as something to look forward to, except Bonny refused to look forward.

She wanted to stay right where she was.

The house was chaos. Dad was now married, and Mum was ironing like some Chinese laundry slave. I was handing out toys and asking people if they wanted fries and doing school and just getting on, I guess.

My solace was practice.

I still hated the lessons.

I had my music teacher from school and the usual scurf-ridden vegan as an extra and I still sang in the choir but I couldn't manage to get to choir practice.

I was studying for English Lit and hated *Macbeth*—I hated it all.

I just loved to play.

And you must have liked to listen because you never once moved when I did.

You were still and quiet as my fingers stroked that ebony. You let me be and I just flew.

Music drenched me.

I heard it, I played it, I felt it.

It calmed and excited.

I stared at my fingers sometimes, heard the sound that poured out, and couldn't really believe that it came from within me.

I was so lucky—I could read music—I just could, and some were stressing about that, but it was obvious to me.

Yes, I hated the lessons and the theory but I did them, because then I got the reward.

I got to play.

I got to watch my fingers and hear it.

And sometimes it happened.

It.

This sound that came if I let it.

A sound that came from somewhere and was delivered through me and then moved beyond.

A place where I could go and I know you went there too, because not once, not one single time as I sat at the piano, did I feel you move.

You allowed me to forget.

Thirty-One

I can say, without doubt, it was the best weekend of my life.

It wasn't just that there was no phone, no mail.

It wasn't just the brilliant sex.

It was more than I can begin to explain.

Idyllic?

No, because that sounds like it was a dream and it wasn't—it was real and it was fun and it was us.

Perfect?

Yes, but it was more real than perfect—it didn't have to be perfect to be perfect, so I don't choose that word either.

It was us.

Us.

Not Hugh.

Not Alice.

But this new person (I don't think I can explain it, but I am trying) we became when we were together.

Or maybe not a person—a *version* of us when we joined up.

A better version of Hugh and of Alice.

That's the best I can do.

Together we were a better version.

I was.

Certainly.

I listened, I actually listened when he told me about Gemma. My hackles didn't rise at the threat either. He loved her; they had been together for ages.

Lived together.

He had declined marriage—it wasn't necessary, he said.

Then she had started talking about babies.

He knew they were in trouble because, yes, he had always wanted one day to have kids, but that meant for ever and he was wondering if he could do for ever with her.

If that was *it*.

And then a temporary position had come up in Glasgow—a junior consultant's position for six months—and he had jumped. He hadn't been sure it was bad enough to end it, but neither had he been sure it was good enough for life, but the offer had been withdrawn and then this maternity leave position had come up in Australia.

Ten months to sort his shit out—to decide what he wanted with Gemma.

But he had met me.

And he was starting to wonder if this was actually *it*.

We talked and we learnt and we grew.

I popped a few pills, but really (comparatively) not that many. We had some drinks, but it felt normal rather than necessary.

And we laughed so many times.

I laughed.

If I close my eyes this second, I can see me, waist high in the waves with Hugh, bracing myself to body surf and then falling and then rising out of the ocean. My hair is everywhere, salt water coming out of my nose. I'm gagging and choking and then laughing. He is holding my shoulder as I cough and then laugh and then he is laughing too.

I could never forget it.

I remember it, the same way I remember to breathe— sometimes it hurts to breathe, sometimes I have to think to do it, sometimes it happens naturally, but still I do it, just as for ever I will remember that moment.

If I get to be old, when I'm mad and can't remember my name and there is nothing else left, I will be content if all I have is that memory.

I never want to lose it.

Me, waist high in the waves with Hugh, bracing myself to body surf and then falling and then rising out of the ocean. My hair is everywhere, salt water coming out of my nose. I'm gagging and choking and then laughing. He is holding my shoulder as I cough and then laugh and then he is laughing too.

Sorry to repeat, but it's what I do with it.

It's my one clean, perfect memory.

Thirty-Two

Planes don't just crash.

Planes don't just fall out of the sky for no reason.

Even if it seems instant (and I hope for those souls it happens to that it is) there is generally a moment.

Where it drops.

Where it veers.

Where that bell pings too many times.

The oxygen masks fall down.

The captain says something.

I watch the shows and it says the same thing over and over—that there was a series of incidents.

Errors made.

It can be callous acts unnoticed, or pay cuts that left bags unchecked, or lack of experience that meant a four-inch bolt should have been six inches. Then there's computer errors and fatigue and fuel wastage and taking off on reduced thrust to save costs…and the more the crash investigators look, the more it seems obvious, the more it seems blazingly clear this was going to happen.

We tut and shake our heads and are furious on those souls' behalf (while mightily relieved it's not us).

We console ourselves that they will learn from this.

That flying will now be safer.

That the same mistakes will not be made.

But they are.

Over and over they are.

And that's just flying.

I'm talking about living and that's more complicated than aviation.

So, of course, *of course*, there were signs and warnings.

You read this and it's obvious, it's so obvious I should have seen them.

Guess what?

I could.

I had set the timer, knew the bomb was about to go off, but I had changed my mind and I wanted to somehow defuse it.

That weekend, I thought I had.

I *almost* thought I had.

I can't tell you Hugh's story.

I do not know when the warning light pinged on for him—I don't know what happened to alert him, I just know something did.

I wasn't expecting it.

As I said, we were, for want of a word, close to perfect.

There was nothing major (apart from euphoria) and nothing trivial (well, I found out I like Earl Grey tea).

We were ticking all boxes after my perfect memory and then we got back to our towels and our place on the beach and his phone must have got sand in it 'cos it wasn't working.

He didn't freak or curse or anything really. He sat down on his towel and turned it on and off and then pulled it out of its case and blew into the little thingy that joins it to the charger in case there was sand in there.

And he could surely do that at the hotel.

The knot was starting in my stomach and I wanted to go back to the hotel.

And he was sitting on the sand, blowing into a phone, and I really wanted to go back to the hotel.

Or rather my make-up bag, which was in the bathroom.

So, finally, *finally* we headed back and I was happy to leave him sitting on the bed playing with the phone, except he followed me into the shower. I really wasn't in the mood and neither was he because he went back to his beloved phone. I got to my make-up bag and the tiny glitch was over.

But Hugh was minus a phone—I just didn't see it coming, didn't realise that there was so much riding on that four-inch bolt that should have been six.

We were getting the red-eye in the morning at 05.50 hours and we both had to be at work at nine, Hugh preferably by eight (or seven if he could possibly make it).

We made good time. We were in the flat before eight and as I walked in I could see the phone in the hall blinking rapidly.

Hugh didn't notice.

He downed a coffee.

Brushed his teeth.

Kissed me.

'Can I ask a favour?'

'Sure.' I was a bit unsettled. The bloody answering-machine

was like a strobe light flashing and I imagined all the debt messages.

'Can you buy me a phone in your lunch break?' He quickly kissed my frown. 'Just a cheap one—any one...'

'Sure.'

He went then and, I have to say, the little break had left me calmer because I was brave enough to check my messages, to see what they were threatening now.

There were none from the credit-card people, which should have cheered me up, but it didn't.

There were about ten from Gemma.

She couldn't get him on his mobile: she needed to talk to him.

Could he just pick up the phone?
Hugh, please pick up the phone.
Hugh, don't do this.

It was then that my warning light pinged on.
I just can't believe how quickly it happened after that.
How something so good rapidly turned so very bad.

Thirty-Three

I would have got his phone in my lunch break except I had an unexpected appointment.

'I just didn't get the grades that were expected.'

'By who?'

'By anyone.'

I had sworn I wouldn't go back, and I still hated her with a passion, but I sat in Big Tits' office, because…

I don't know.

It didn't help: it was making things worse.

I knew, though, that I was looking for answers.

But I didn't give her the questions.

I wanted to talk about Hugh.

I wanted to fix it before it unravelled.

Because of my tantrum the previous week, I had to pay for my last session and pay up front for this one.

It would be worth it for some insight into Hugh, I told myself.

Not that she'd let me talk about him.

Instead, she kept asking about me.

'Did you expect better grades?'

'Not really.' I shrugged. 'I mean, I can play the piano, but I'm not brilliant…' I struggled to explain. 'It was a difficult time. Bonny was emigrating, Dad's girlfriend was pregnant.'

'So you didn't expect good grades?'

I didn't answer.

'So who did?' Big Tits said. 'You said you didn't get the grades that were *expected*.'

For fuck's sake.

'I didn't get the grades I had aimed for.' No bloody wonder kids topped themselves—ten years on and I had to explain why I had flunked my music A-level. 'I wasn't sure what to do—I could maybe have scraped into university on the second round, I was hoping to be a music teacher, but I was tempted to take the exams again…' *To be all that I could be.* I didn't say that bit, I heard it. I heard my voice say it to me and I wanted to cry. I wanted to fold up in two on the chair and cry and to say it.

To be all that I could be.

And I hadn't been.

'What did your mum want, Alice?' Her voice was for once gentle, kind even, but I remembered then I hated her. I wanted to talk about Hugh.

'Alice. What did your mum want? What did she say about your results?'

'Mum wasn't actually that bothered…' That halted her. 'She was worried because Bonny and Lex were struggling. Bonny was homesick, Lex had been arrested…' I saw her lips purse, as if Lex was some sort of scum. 'He's nothing like that,' I rapidly explained, 'that was why it was such a shock, it was completely out of character. He got in a fight at some pub, but the charges were dropped. Of course, Bonny was upset and she was threatening to come home…'

She didn't fill the silence.

'I can't remember who, if it was Bonny or me or Lex, but it seemed a good idea for me to take a gap year—and to come to Australia and cheer Bonny up while I worked out what I do.'

'What did you do?' Big Tits asked.

'I came to Australia and I got a job.'

I moved into the youth hostel and I got pissed and partied.

I didn't have to come home and I didn't have to answer to anyone, so I did it some more.

I got a job, which meant I could party harder, so I did.

And I had friends and I got a flat and I partied some more and then the friends moved on and so I got some more. I partied and I got drunk and then when they moved on I partied harder.

I didn't say it, of course, but my answer was the most honest I had ever given Big Tits.

'Pretty much what I'm doing now.'

Not that she appreciated my honesty—she asked about Eleanor and I could not think of much to say. She asked about dad's daughter Charlotte, who is nearly ten now and I've only seen her a couple of times so there wasn't much to say about her either.

'Alice.' Lisa gave me a tired smile. 'Being a psychologist isn't like being a car mechanic.'

My head hurt.

'It's not like a car, where it doesn't matter if you have no idea what's going on under the bonnet.

'You can't drop yourself off and have me fix you.

'I need to know things.

'I need you to help me to understand you.'

'And then you'll fix me?' My eyes darted with hope and then she shook her head.

'Then I can help you to help yourself.'

Which I took as a no.

Thirty-Four

I really didn't want to visit Olivia—I hate hospitals, and the only thing the maternity ward reminds me of is both my sisters' rapid descent into PND.

I can remember both Bonny and Eleanor—eyes pleading with me to get this baby off their tit as various relatives snapped away with their cameras.

Still, Roz had organised the envelope and she was on my team so it was only right that I come along—and we'd been given an extra hour's lunch break so I had no excuse.

Roz is so girly in some ways: she burst into tears when she walked into the four-bedded ward. I was rather more restrained (we still were hardly talking) and handed Olivia her present.

'Are you better?'

It had been Olivia's leaving do I had collapsed at, and I said I was fine now as she opened her present and Roz cradled the monkey.

I am not being horrible.

This baby was covered in hair. Its hairline stopped

at its mono-brow and it had this down all over its body. And Olivia—who had always been sort of sassy and sexy and had bawled her eyes out when she found out she was pregnant and had even gone for an abortion—was suddenly like the Virgin Mary, taking the sobbing baby from Roz and offering it her breast.

I have never seen a nipple so big.

I thought she would drown the baby. I could see milk dripping and this huge, dark brown nipple being thrust down its throat and, worse, Roz was helping. She was shoving the baby's face into this vast white pillow of a breast and telling Olivia she was doing great.

I felt like I'd landed in the Ukraine. I just didn't understand anything they were talking about and, worse, she stopped feeding it and Roz brought the monkey over for me to hold. I'd missed breakfast and now lunch, and with the hospital smell and everything I also felt a bit sick, and then I looked up and there was Hugh.

I had seen him leave for work this morning but he looked different now that he was here. He had a couple of pagers in his jeans pocket and a big lanyard round his neck with his photo on.

Roz was delighted to see him.

So too was Olivia—I couldn't believe that she knew his name.

I felt rigid. I was holding this very ugly baby and Hugh was assessing me. I knew that—I got that—because Roz was laughing and Olivia was chatting and I just sat there holding the monkey and not knowing what to do. I mean, he was my boyfriend and I was the only one in the room who didn't know how to react.

Thankfully Roz was still in clucky mode and scooped up the babe and I headed out into the corridor with him.

'What are you doing here?' It was a reasonable question—he was a psychiatrist, this was Maternity. I had this false grin plastered on and I still felt sick. The smell of hospitals always makes me feel like that.

'I do a ward round here each day.'

Of course he did—I mean, I'd heard of PND and all that—it was just…I never got the multi-faceted nature of his job. I just thought he was stuck with the loons, or that the occasional private patient lay on his couch and told him about their problems. It unnerved me that he walked amongst the normal.

And Olivia knew his name.

Was she having problems?

He suggested lunch and took me to the canteen where he bought me a club sandwich. He asked if I'd managed to get his phone—er, when? I pointed out, given that I was here. I saw him watching as I ate the chicken, cheese and avocado but left the bread.

We had sex that night but something shifted.

I don't know what.

But something changed.

It just did.

Thirty-Five

'Alice, get up!' It was way past the third and final call, but I was so tired I didn't care.

I'd crammed in two hours piano and a three-hour shift at the burger bar and had fallen into bed at about eleven, just too tired to be careful.

Normally I dressed and undressed in the bathroom—there was no such thing as privacy in this place. Bonny was always wandering in to borrow something. Mum didn't think she needed to knock. So for bed I had these massive flannelette pyjamas, which thankfully were fashionable at the time if you wore them with big fluffy boots.

I hated them but they did the job.

Still, last night I had been beyond tired and had just peeled off the disgusting burger bar uniform and fallen into bed in my bra and knickers.

'Alice, I won't tell you again… I've got to go soon…' She pulled off the duvet. My hand went to grab it, to stop her, to cover myself, but it was too late.

I was lying there flat on my back, naked except

for my bra and knickers, and my mum was standing over me.

'I'm going to work—you need to get up!'

And I thought I'd been caught—I thought, *she's surely seen.* I mean, she was standing there in her nurse's uniform. *She's a nurse, for God's sake, and I'm lying here practically naked.* But then this was Mum we were talking about. She didn't look to the side, or up and down, *she didn't look*, she just headed to the wardrobe and started pulling out my school uniform as I pulled the duvet back over me.

'I want you up and dressed before I leave.'

How could she not have seen?

My hand slid down to my stomach, to the hard mound that was there. It was not soft, not a slight roundness, and I pulled my hand away. I didn't even wash, I just pulled on my uniform and then found my jumper and put that on and went downstairs.

'What have you got a jumper on for?'

'I feel cold.'

She put a hand to my forehead but I pushed it off.

'You might be getting a cold. You do look a bit pale.'

Stupid bloody cow.

Stupid blind cow!

'I'll be home about four.' She was making the lunches, and I poured myself a mug of tea as she chatted away.

'I thought you had to be there at seven?'

'I'm in Outpatients, I don't have to be there till eight-thirty,' Mum said. 'Prenatal.'

Lucky them, then…to have such an observant, clued-in nurse looking after them.

I just stared into my mug. I almost said it. I don't even

think I was nervous at that point. I just wanted to say it, and watch her reaction.

But I sat in silence.

Thirty-Six

'Sorry, your card's been declined.'

I could feel the impatient line behind me suddenly curious; feel my face burning with colour as I rummaged in my purse to pull out another card.

Except I knew that one had already been stopped.

'Oh.' Attempting a casual shrug, I put down the phone I had been getting for Hugh. 'My pay mustn't have gone in.'

Flaming, embarrassed, I fled out of the shop, grateful that Roz hadn't been there to see my shame. I'd finally agreed to have lunch with her, but first I had to get his phone and Roz stayed outside to cram in a few fags.

She wanted to talk.

Wanted to go back to how it was.

I couldn't.

'Did you get it?'

'Nope.' I shook my head. 'They didn't have the one he wanted.'

'The guy needs a phone,' Roz insisted, heading back towards the shop. 'Come on, we've still got time.'

'He can get it himself!' I snapped, marching in the opposite direction. 'I've got better things to do with my lunch break than look for phones for Hugh. I'm busy too.'

Thirty-Seven

You weren't moving tonight.

Always you were still when I practised, then I would have a bath and you would move.

I dropped my hairbrush.

I'd read that if you brushed your conditioner through to the ends your hair would thank you within a week.

As it dropped into the water and hit the enamel you moved.

I felt it, I saw it.

I smiled.

Thirty-Eight

Even if it was awkward, even if she had lied, it had been so nice to have Roz in my life that I decided that I would cancel the bad and try to accept the good.

That we'd be friends again, just take it slowly.

But she's like a puppy with a new toy.

After four weeks of near silence from me, when I started to come round, she should have slotted into my life a little more discreetly, in my opinion. But the day after we went out for lunch and my card was declined, almost as soon as I let her back in, she was knocking on the door.

She had forms Hugh had asked for.

Tax forms.

He had been setting up the phone that I had finally got for him.

I had no money, but Nic's rent had pinged into my account and, yes, I should have paid the rent, but Roz was right. He needed a phone and he paid me back anyway, so it wasn't a big deal.

Well, Roz came in and they spoke a mumbo-jumbo

language as I escaped to the bathroom. I walked past the perpetually flashing light on the answering-machine. I had a bigger problem than debt collectors—this one was small and blonde and wanted to speak to Hugh, was begging, in fact, for him to pick up.

Hitting 'Delete' was bliss.

I had a new doctor.

I still had loads of Valium but I knew it ran out, so I had gone to someone else and she had given me some Kalmas.

Lovely, they were.

Like a glass of wine.

Not quite as good as Valium, but very, very nice.

They worked within twenty minutes and she had given me one hundred and twenty.

One to be taken as prescribed.

I took three and then I headed back out.

They were watching the news and Roz was making him laugh.

Then a news story came on about some woman who hadn't known she was pregnant and had flushed it down the loo.

'For God's sake,' Roz said, 'how could she not know? How can she say she didn't know?'

And I gave a half-laugh, topped up my wine and carried on watching the news. But my face was burning, just as it did during a love scene at the movies when I felt as if the whole cinema was watching me and gauging my reaction, just as it did when Dr Kelsey asked all those questions.

I couldn't hear the scratch of Hugh's pen any more and I was sure he was watching me.

I just felt as if he knew.

And Roz was wrong. That woman didn't know. Well, of course she did, but she didn't. I could see how it happened, I knew how it happened.

Because it had happened to me.

Thirty-Nine

I didn't even pretend to kiss her back as Mum gave me a kiss on the cheek. She didn't notice me flinch as her lips brushed my skin. She picked up her basket and waddled off to work.

I don't think I was scared at that moment.

I was certainly angry—but I didn't know why.

And maybe I'm slow, maybe I'm thick. I don't expect anyone to believe me, because even now I can't believe it myself, but until that point I didn't *really* know.

I mean, I'd had a test ages ago.

I had a bump.

I hadn't had a period in months.

I was deliberately, actively, covering my body, making up stories, hiding at every turn.

So, as Roz and everyone else says—every time some poor cow flushes a baby down the loo, or it turns up in a rubbish dump, or she arrives in Emergency with abdo pain and gives birth, or pops a foetus into her hand luggage and tries to head from home—*she must have known.*

No.

No.

No.

She didn't know.

She *couldn't* know.

Because when she did, *then* it was real.

She *didn't* know.

And as for me—well, I only really found out that morning.

Even though there was no one home, just in case, I wedged a chair against the door and took off my school uniform.

I took off my jumper and then my tie and shirt, and then I fiddled with the elastic band and safety pins that allowed a big enough gap in my skirt, and took it off. I took off my bra and pants and stood there and looked at myself in the mirror.

I moved in close and I couldn't see my head, just my torso.

I was pregnant.

I stared at my breasts. They were big and had veins, but it was the areolas that held my attention. They were huge, and my nipples were thick and swollen...

And then, only then, did I stare at my stomach. I had a white, almost silver line down the middle. I could see my hip bones, but above that there was a firm mound. I didn't touch it; I just stared at my torso in the mirror, my head chopped off. I stared at a pregnant torso and then I stepped back and there I was. There was my head on a pregnant woman's body.

And was that the moment that separated me from the

others—the one where I grew up and made decisions and took responsibility?

No.

I pulled on my uniform and raced down the stairs, because I didn't want to miss my bus. I didn't actually have to go in—it was a study day—but I wanted to practise my piece and the teachers were available.

Even before I got to the bottom step, I wasn't pregnant again.

I swear, even before I got to the bottom step, I didn't know that I was...

Forty

There had been a house fire on the outskirts of Melbourne.

Roz was stapling up forms at the table.

Hugh had come to the sofa and was sitting next to me. I was relieved that the news bulletin about the baby was over and we sat watching, hearing that a husband and three kids were dead, and then you saw the poor wife dashing down the street and being held back.

'God...' I turned my head in the direction of Roz, who was behind me. 'We're going to have a great week at work with that lot.'

And as my head turned back to the television, I saw Hugh was staring at me agape.

'Four people are dead, Alice.' He stopped himself then, he didn't say 'You selfish, self-absorbed bitch,' but I know he thought it.

It wasn't a great night.

Roz went home for a row of her own, because Lizzie texted and said she was on the train and could her mum pick her up? Then Hugh got called into work and I took some Kalmas and lay in the dark and waited, wondering if he'd come back and if he did, if he'd sleep in Nicole's room.

But, no, he came in at three and his body was cold as he slid into bed. He pulled me in to him and he kissed my cheek and my shoulder and then he did a really nice thing, he pulled up the duvet and tucked it in around me. He cuddled me so hard, but it wasn't for sex.

He thought I was asleep and he really cuddled me.

Apart from the Russian dolls, it was, on reflection, the nicest thing ever done for me. Okay, nicer than the Russian dolls, except it was sad too.

He kissed my cheek.

Then I realised I wasn't even pretending to be asleep.

I can't explain it.

My body was limp, my eyes were closed, as in sleep, and my mind for once was fairly quiet. It was like I was hovering over the bed and watching him holding me.

He was stroking my hair, but I could see it rather than feel it.

He was tucked into me and I was the cold one now and he kept me warm.

I know he was awake for a long time.

I know he was thinking.

I know we had, by then, moved into injury time.

I didn't want it to end; I didn't want it to happen.

But it was, of course, inevitable.

Forty-One

I hated being by myself.

I'd been really looking forward to having the house to myself while Mum and Bonny were in France. It sounds babyish, but at seventeen, very nearly eighteen, I'd never actually spent a night on my own.

Well, Mum rarely went out and if she did, say, she had a nightshift, there was always Bonny, or sometimes Eleanor would come over with the kids. But this was the first time I had the house completely to myself for a whole night and I found out that I didn't like it one bit.

It was Sunday night and a week till my music practical exam, but on Friday Bonny and Lex left for Australia and I didn't know what I was dreading the most.

Both.

I didn't want it to be next week, I didn't want her to be gone, so I tried not to think about it.

Mum rang in the evening—it sounded like they were having fun. I heard Bonny laughing in the background and I lay on the bed and spoke to Mum for a bit, said that everything was great. Then I headed to my piano and practised for hours—played and played and tried to get it right. It was fantastic. I hadn't got it completely right, and I accepted that could never happen. You never actually do with music—unless you're brilliant and write a masterpiece—and I doubt you could repeat it every time. In fact, I doubt it could ever be repeated again.

It's perfect energy.

I'm close to heaven.

I'm alone with my music.

I just glimpsed it.

I will never hit perfect, because it isn't about hitting G or F or hand rollovers—it's how you hit the notes, how the fingers hit the notes. More than that, it's the emotion that floods sometimes through your fingers.

You do the lessons.

You practise.

You practise more and more.

And you can play and play and spend a lifetime trying to re-create the sound that is heaven.

And you'll never quite get there.

But if you practise, and then you let it come, you get to glimpse it.

It *almost* aligns.

A sound that lasts longer than you can hear it, a sound that carries on long after it is lost to us. It vibrates up to heaven: it has to, because it is real, it existed and you made it.

It *has* to go somewhere.

It's energy and energy can't die.

It can't.

I think I learnt that in physics.

I couldn't stand the emotion of my real life.

I could not bear to examine it.

I poured it out here on a secondhand piano that had just been tuned, but needed it again.

It was never going to be perfect.

I never could get it completely right.

I understood that.

I got close though.

I glimpsed it.

I had energy and it coursed through me that night.

I felt so close to the music; it was all coming together and I kept playing and playing till the neighbours banged on the wall, and given it was after midnight I really had no choice but to stop. Anyway, I was tired now. My back was hurting from sitting so long on the piano stool.

The energy had gone.

I tried to do some theory but I couldn't concentrate.

There was nothing on the television, just news and someone selling a foundation that came with a brush set and a religious show. I flicked back to the make-up, not that I was watching it. Even though I had it on loud, I could hear every noise, every creak. I paced around. I couldn't *think* of going upstairs to bed. It was nearly two a.m. and I couldn't think about sleep. The blinds weren't closed in the kitchen and I was sure there was someone in the garden, so instead of going to check I closed the blinds.

I filled a mug with some wine and hoped it would make me sleep. Then I remembered that I couldn't drink, so I tipped it down the sink and wished it was seven a.m. and morning, and that I wasn't on my own, that Lex was back...

But then I didn't want to be on my own with him, because he asked too many questions.

Maybe I should tell him?

He'd hate me; he'd hate me so much because Bonny wouldn't go.

I knew that she was looking for an excuse, any excuse not to go, and this would give her one.

Maybe I could go with them.

My brain lurched with new possibility. I headed for the kitchen. Surely I could have some wine.

What seventeen-year-old wouldn't while their mum was away?

It wasn't as if I was throwing a wild party. Maybe I could go to Australia after the exams. I filled my mug as for the first time I saw an option. They could have it.

It.

I shouldn't drink; I shouldn't be drinking. I was pregnant and I shouldn't be drinking.

It was like worlds colliding. I threw the mug into the sink and it broke—and I felt like it was my brain cracking...

I never thought about it.

I never let myself think about it.

But I was thinking about it all the time.

It was like a noise in the background I was trying to ignore, but it just kept getting louder and louder and it was three a.m. now and it was screaming and I couldn't turn it off.

I wanted to drink the whole cask.

I wanted it to stop, to just go the fuck away.

I hated Gus. I was on my knees, and I cried so hard

that I threw up. I hated him; I hated that Celeste would have his baby now.

I hoped it was ugly.

I hoped it screamed and never slept and that Celeste was a fat ugly cow and that he hated his life and would choose me.

Me and my baby.

My baby!

It was like all the cracks joined up—all the thoughts I hadn't had, or had ignored, just formed one big thought.

I felt like I'd come out of a coma. I could see my puke on the kitchen floor and I cleaned it up. I was frozen cold and numb, but not numb enough, because my mind was clear and the noise had stopped.

I *was* pregnant and I had to do something.

I lay on the sofa and pulled a throw rug over me but I was still cold and I didn't care.

I pushed my hand on my tummy.

I felt nothing.

I pushed my fingers in.

I felt a stab of fear that I had left it too late, but then I got my reward, a flutter beneath my fingers. I rolled on my back and I watched my tummy move.

You danced for me.

I saw ripples in my tummy like waves rolling in.

I couldn't catch them but I was awash with them.

There was an energy inside me—that energy was you.

I didn't care what Gus said, I *was* good enough.

Or I would be good enough.

I would try to be good enough for you.

I was already a mother.

I think I loved you.
I would ring someone, or could I talk to Eleanor?
Maybe I *would* go to Australia…

Forty-Two

I slept for two, maybe three hours, but then I woke up. I was the coldest I had ever been and I could smell sick in my hair. My back was killing me from all the piano practice and sleeping on the sofa.

It was May, almost June, but I put on the central heating and because it was light now and the house seemed normal I went upstairs and ran a bath. I wanted to get warm and it helped my back as well. I lay there for ages, topping up the water, and I was scared but surprisingly calm.

I could hear the traffic in the street and the world waking up and carrying on. I stared down at my stomach, my belly button was flat and big and it looked weird. I touched it, then I touched my stomach. I put both hands on it. It felt tight and hard and I wanted you to kick for me. I hated the bath usually, because that was when you moved, but you didn't now.

There was no hot water left when I tried to top up again, so I pulled myself out and felt this sting in my back…and suddenly I wanted to be sick again. I pulled my wet hair off my face and was sick in the sink. I was shivering and cold, even though my skin was red from the hot bath. I wrapped a towel around my shoulders and dried myself with another one. I just wanted to put on my robe and crawl into bed and then the towel was wet, a different wet, a gush of wet and I knew what was happening and I was back to being scared.

I could hear someone humming and I knew it was me. I wanted to kneel down, but I knew if I did...well, I knew that I couldn't. I just hummed for a minute or so, leant over the sink and hummed and shivered. I caught sight of my face—it was blotchy and red from last night's tears and my hair was a mess, all wet and curly. And I was having you.

I pulled on my robe—I had to get to a phone.

Or not?

I could just have it here.

I could just kneel down like I wanted to, like my body was telling me to do. I could just crouch down and soon it would all go away and no one would ever have to know.

Forty-Three

'Let's ring in sick…'

I was spooned against him, eyes stuck like a stamp to an envelope, trying to peel them open, and hit the snooze button for the second time as Hugh dropped the bombshell.

Had I suggested it, it wouldn't have been a bombshell—I had suggested it every morning lately and often followed through—but for Hugh to say it was a first.

He scooped me closer, the arm that was under me dredging me over the bed, sucking me towards him like a tsunami had struck.

'We can't.'

'We can,' Hugh said. 'Let's go out for the day. Just for a drive, we can find somewhere nice for lunch.'

'I can't.'

'We can talk.'

He wanted to talk.

I knew that.

He kept trying to talk to me.

'I have to go to work.'

I climbed out of bed and so too did Hugh.

He followed me into the bathroom.

'Do you mind?'

I closed the door; I couldn't even pee in private in this place.

I waited till the loo flushed, just in case he was outside, and then I went in the cupboard and took a couple of Kalmas.

I could feel his eyes on me as I walked into the kitchen.

'Better?' he said, and handed me a coffee, but I swear he sneered.

'I just can't take a day off right now,' I explained, but he just looked at me. I shook my head as if he didn't get it, and then left for work.

All morning the row unsettled me—okay, it wasn't a row, but I had seen the dispproval in his eyes.

By lunchtime I'd talked myself out if it.

Everything was fine, I convinced myself.

'Do you want to go out tomorrow night?' Roz put a massive take-out latte in front of me as I peeled off my headphones for a moment's break and she waited for me to say no again.

'Okay.'

I could see she was surprised—Roz had been badgering me for weeks—but suddenly I could use a night out and it had nothing to do with Hugh being on call over the weekend and staying at the hospital. I genuinely wanted Roz.

'Are you all right?'

I nodded.

'Only you're really pale.'

'I just got the grandparents.' The death certificates were in and relatives of the victims of the house fire had been ringing all morning; it was pretty grim going.

'I just had an aunty,' Roz said, and grimaced.

I clipped back my headphones, took a massive swig of latte and took the next call.

'I can't send a fax,' said the voice on the other end.

'Hello.'

'The man said I should send a fax, but I can't.'

'Okay.'

'I'm sorry if I keep crying. They are my babies.'

'That's okay.' Roz had turned to go, but I grabbed her wrist. 'Tell me what you want to say.'

'Mum!' I frantically mouthed at Roz.

'Shit!' she mouthed back. And she couldn't hold my hand because I was typing, so she held my shoulder instead.

'Mark—

'We had a dream.

'We had so many dreams.

'Our children make them real.'

'Make?' I checked.

'Made,' she answered.

It took an hour—she kept crying. She refused to let anyone do it for her—she wanted to do this herself, she said.

So I sat there, as the woman I had seen being held back on the television news tried to sum up her three children in a few lines.

I had to read it back to her over and over.

I had to be professional and detached, and kind too.
I had to listen to her grief and somehow not compare
it to mine.

Forty-Four

'Hey, Alice.' I was standing at the top of the stairs as Lex came in. I had my robe on, and I was as wet with sweat as if I'd just come out of the bath. 'It's like a bloody sauna in here.'

He was so tired he looked grey. I knew he just wanted to fall into bed and I felt sorry for him. In my selfish world, there was this thought for another person and I felt so sorry for him.

So sorry for what he'd come home to.

'I'm having it.'

He was fiddling with the heater control, not looking at me. I saw him still, watched him turn around so slowly—or maybe it was quick, but it seemed so slow. I saw every flicker on his face as he turned around, realisation descending. He blinked and I swear I heard the bat of his lashes, saw the dread as he opened his eyes and looked at me.

'Lex…'

I was humming again. He was going for the phone, but it wasn't there and I remembered it was in the bedroom from when Mum rang last night but I couldn't move to get it. I was holding onto the banister and making this funny noise.

He was racing around, trying to find it and patting his pockets for his mobile, and then he raced outside.

I followed him to the car.

He was trying to find his phone and he looked at the traffic. I could see him judging it—the hospital was about five minutes' drive away.

'When are you due?' Lex—lovely, lovely Lex, who never got angry, who never was anything but nice— turned and swore. 'Alice, when are you fucking due?'

'I don't know.'

There was a sign. Emergency was closer but he turned for the arrow that said Maternity.

No.

I wanted Accident and Emergency.

I wanted quick—to be dealt with, not Maternity.

But we were pulling up.

I felt normal as I walked through the sliding doors; I felt normal, except for the frizzy hair and disgusting dressing gown.

Except for the fact it was seven-thirty a.m.—and I was here.

I wanted to go home.

'Did you ring ahead?' There was a bored voice coming from behind a desk. 'Who's she under?'

'I don't know,' I could hear Lex snap, knew he was going to lose it soon. 'She's having a baby.'

'Is she booked in here?

'Can I see her card?'

'I didn't even know she was pregnant!' He was about

to crack, but I didn't really notice. The humming was back. I was leaning on the desk and I think she guessed I was about to throw up or kneel down and make a mess of the blue carpet because she pushed a bell—and there was a woman.

Her bottom lip was too big. I swear, if she had chosen to, she could have stretched it right over her forehead.

It was all I could look at and then the pain stopped but I didn't go back to normal this time.

She was practical; she took me to a little annexe just off Reception and asked my name. She asked when I was due, if I was seeing a doctor there, but I didn't answer and Lex couldn't answer either. He was just a mountain of panic, pacing the room and shouting at me to tell her. She put her hand on my stomach and I couldn't stand anyone near me.

'Get off me!' I shouted at her, at Lex, at everyone. 'Just leave me alone.'

And then *she* came over.

'Hi, Deb, do you need a hand?' She had a jacket on and a basket and she was clearly on her way out. Her shift was over but she stopped.

There was chaos. Lex was shouting at the receptionist to get a doctor, Big Lip was telling Lex that he wasn't helping and to calm down…and she just stood there and put her arm around me.

'I'm Fi.'

That was all I heard.

Well, I heard her saying she was taking me to Birthing Suite Two but it sounded different.

I heard her asking Lex to wait outside and telling Big Lip that she would take it from here.

But I didn't really hear it.

And then I stared at the room I was in and felt her arm around me.

'I'm going to take care of you.'

'You're going home.' I shivered.

'No.' She took her jacket off and put her basket down.

And I wished she were my mum, or Bonny, or Eleanor.

I wished she could have been there sooner.

My back was hurting and I wanted to run away again, but she held me tighter and I didn't tell her to fuck off when she put her hand on my tummy.

'How long have you known?'

'I don't know.' She rocked with me through it. 'It was just once…'

'You've only had sex once?'

'Once.'

'When, Alice—do you remember when?'

I'd never forget.

The pain was gone and she took me to the bed and I lay down without asking. She shook her head at the doctor who looked around the door and I let her put something up my nose.

'I'm going to listen to the baby's heart.' She pushed a white thing over my stomach and I heard a swoosh, swoosh that told me it was alive, and then I watched her put on gloves and she didn't have to ask, I guess I knew what to do.

I lifted my knees and she was so gentle and kind and I cannot tell you.

I mean, even I knew it was urgent.

I knew.

I had known.

I knew the doctor was outside but I would rather have smashed myself through the window than have him do this to me at that moment—for him to confirm, to judge, to assess and not understand.

Fi gave me a minute.

I had listened to my baby's heartbeat and then her hand was inside me and she touched you; she felt your head and confirmed that you existed.

I'd only just learnt.

And then she let him in.

I held her eyes as she cuddled me and he confirmed her findings.

I just lay there as he mumbled about dates and effaced and hypertension and waters broken and SFD—with his hand still up me.

And then when he stopped and was putting in a drip Fi translated his words for me.

It was too soon and too small and they couldn't stop it.

My baby would be born, Fi said, and if it survived birth then it would die.

'Do everything.'

I didn't care then—I didn't care about anyone. I begged and I pleaded and I knew I had been careless. I knew I had wished you away, but I had changed my mind now.

But it was too late.

'I don't want Lex in.'

'Is he the father?'

'No!' God, poor Lex, he was the good guy, pacing outside, and Gus was in oblivion.

He was gone.
I was here.
And I had to—*had to*—do this right.

Forty-Five

I hadn't eaten all day and I suppose I should have been starving, but I wasn't.

I pushed my trolley around the supermarket and tried not to think of that poor woman who had lost her kids. I loaded my trolley with ready-made chicken Kiev and mashed potato and baby peas for two—although Hugh would devour them in one.

I had a trolley because I was going to get some wine and some Bourbon for Roz too.

I got paid on Tuesday.

The rent could wait.

Christ—I suddenly remembered I had sworn not to drink tonight and that I was trying to prove a point to Hugh.

I sauntered with not much enthusiasm to the chocolate aisle.

The one night I really needed a drink and I'd sworn not to have one. I could sort of sense Hugh frowning when I poured a drink lately. I had a cask in the kitchen cupboard that I topped up my two glasses a night from, but to show him I didn't have a problem I was determined not to have any tonight.

But given the day I'd had, I could really use one.

Chocolate would have to suffice.

The short kid in a blazer had more manners than me—he stepped back when our hands both reached for the last bar of Lindt.

'It's Mum's birthday,' he said. 'It's her favourite.'

'Yeah, right.' I grinned, because ten-year-olds did that—tripped the guilt switch. He didn't realise that I didn't have one. I just put it in my trolley.

'Luke…' Even before he continued, even before his father spoke again, I recognised the voice. He might just as well have been shouting '*Celeste*' as he emerged from the fast-food aisle.

His face froze when he saw me.

In the years I'd been here, despite my frantic searching at first, despite a few phone calls where I'd hung up when he'd answered, despite driving past what I thought was his house (it turned out it wasn't when I plucked up the courage to knock), I'd never seen Gus.

He hadn't aged well—maybe later it would give me a surge of satisfaction to recall his receding hairline and the beginnings of a paunch over his jeans.

He certainly didn't dress well—he looked like nothing.

Nondescript.

Without the past, I wouldn't have given this man a glance.

Wouldn't have stared into his trolley and seen the nappies and chaos and the one-litre home-brand ice cream.

I saw fear on his face.

Real fear.

But it didn't make me feel triumphant.

I just stood there, staring, till he had no choice but to speak.

'Alice.'

'Gus.'

'What are you doing here?'

'I live here,' I said. 'I have for years now.'

He sort of nodded to the top of my head and then steered the trolley away, walking off at high speed, but I wasn't watching him.

I was watching Luke.

Who looked just like his dad.

Forty-Six

I needn't have worried about an alcohol-free night. The shock of seeing Gus didn't propel me to Liquor Land. Instead I had enough trouble just getting my trolley to the checkout. I dragged my shopping home and up the steps. And as I got in the door, just as I was thinking, shit, I need a drink, and wondering if there was any in the cask, and if I could have a quick one before Hugh got home, I realised Hugh was home.

What was more he was halfway down a bottle of wine himself.

'Hi.' His face was grim. I remembered this morning's disaster and that he was probably still annoyed with me. He looked up, and he looked shocking, but he gave me a sort of smile.

'Hi.'

I went over and kissed him, which is quite touchy-feely for me, but I wanted to. He sort of gripped me back, and I smelt him.

I wanted to burrow in his neck.

I wanted to tell him just how shit today had been.

'Here.' He poured me a glass—see? The perfect guy.

'You hungry?' I asked.

'Nope.'

Which was good, because the thought of chicken Kiev, mashed potatoes and baby peas was making my stomach curdle. 'I'm sorry about this morning.'

I saw him frown, like he was trying to even recall this morning.

'I wish I'd taken your advice actually and rung in sick.' I gave him a sort of wobbly smile. 'I had a shit day.'

'They happen.' He looked over to me. 'I discharged a twenty-eight-year-old yesterday—he suicided last night...'

I could never win.

I realised that I could never win, with anybody.

My shit day could never be as bad as theirs.

I don't know how love dies.

But that night it finally did.

I lay curled up.

I had seen Gus.

I had seen his son too.

I had listened to that poor woman on the phone.

I could feel Hugh beside me—and I knew I should roll over, should comfort him, but I wanted to be comforted too.

And it was very grown up—I mean, to be in bed and just lie there—but I needed a cuddle and so too did Hugh, but for some reason we were on stalemate.

I heard the answering-machine click in the hall.

I could almost hear the captain's warning.

Forty-Seven

'I don't know how to tell people.' Roz was staring into her glass and I sat there wondering how the hell I didn't see it—when it's so obvious now.

'How long have you known?' I asked, because I'm curious. I mean, am I going to wake up one day and find I don't like willies any more?

'Always,' Roz said, and then she shook her head. 'I didn't want to know—I can't explain it. I didn't want to be a lesbian.' I did my very best not to look around and shush her but my cheeks were on fire. 'Andrew was nice, I thought...' I just didn't understand and Roz couldn't explain.

'I thought you liked Hugh?'

'I do,' Roz said. 'I wanted him for you.'

And if you think that conversation was awkward, well, there was worse to come, because there was something that made me feel sick, something I had to know.

'What about me?'

Roz frowned.

'I mean, do you...?'

She shook her head. 'God, Alice, no! No.' She grabbed my hand. 'No! Not at all. Never once.'

And two seconds before I would have pulled my hand back, I don't know why and I don't know how, but it was Roz again and it was me. Not quite the same, but not all different.

'Why not?' I was actually a touch offended that she sounded so appalled at the very thought. 'Why don't you fancy me?'

We laughed—well, not belly-laughed, but we did have a little laugh and then, I'm not sure how, the conversation turned to other things. Roz often got teary, but she was more worried than teary tonight.

'She hates me.' Roz took a slug of Bourbon as we sat on our first girls' night out in ages, but neither of us was in the mood to party. 'My own daughter hates me. God, I've messed that kid up—maybe I should have waited to leave.'

I really didn't know what to say—because privately I was now on Lizzie's side. I love Roz and everything (not that way), but imagine at fifteen that you discovered your mother was gay—I'd have died. I honestly would have died. And now at sixteen, nearly seventeen, Lizzie was dressing like a tart and sleeping with everyone, just to prove to the world that she wasn't like her mother, and, frankly…I took a slug of my wine…I'd have done the very same.

'She'll come around,' I said instead. 'You just have to give it time.'

'I guess…' Roz gave a worried nod. 'I mean, what's the worst thing that can happen?' Roz stared at me for answers. 'She gets pregnant like I did—well, I coped.

Or she gets herpes or… I just hope to God she's using something.'

'Talk to her.'

'She won't listen. Every time I try to, all she wants to do is to take the opportunity to tell me how much she hates me. I don't know what to do with her. I think she's cutting herself…'

I pulled a face—that was so off.

'Sorry.' Roz blew out a breath. 'You said you had a problem…'

Had I?

That's right, I had. I kept forgetting things I'd told her—I was doing the same with Hugh.

'It doesn't matter…' I vaguely remembered telling her, yesterday on our coffee break, but I could hardly land my tiny stuff on Roz, and anyway, if I voiced it, it would be real and, I asked myself, what advice could Roz possibly give about men?

'Is it Hugh?' My tongue was on the roof of my mouth as she continued, 'He was a bit short with you the other night.'

I hated that she'd noticed, because I'd been trying not to notice. 'He's fine…' I shrugged. 'He just gets in a knot if I have more than half a glass of wine.' I waited for her to grin, but she didn't. 'He hates me smoking,' I added, because Roz smoked more than me, but she didn't shrug and she didn't grin, she just kept looking at me. 'Anyway, it's not that…'

'Then what?'

'Gemma's called a couple of times.'

'His girlfriend?'

'His ex-girlfriend,' I corrected.

'And what did she want?' Roz asked. 'What did Hugh say?'

'He doesn't know!' I saw a frown on Roz's face, and I didn't like the disapproval I could feel winging its way over.

'You can't stop him talking to her.'

'If I can I will.'

'Alice, if he finds out that you haven't told him…' I'd come to her for help, yet I didn't like what she was offering—and, again, what would she know?

'Look…' I stood up, swung up my bag '…you've got enough on your mind, with Lizzie and everything. Don't worry, I'll talk to Hugh.'

No, I bloody well wouldn't.

What I did, though, when I got home and there wasn't a red light flashing was take out a Post-it note and write 'Gemma called' and then I took out another one and wrote 'Gemma again—please call her back'. I placed them on the floor just under the side table where the phone sat.

And I was relieved later that I'd done it because, though Hugh was working that night and all weekend, he blasted through the door at six a.m. still wearing his lanyard and…er…not very happy.

'Has Gemma been ringing here?'

'I told you…' I started, but seeing his expression I got out of bed. 'I wrote you notes.' I was scrabbling on the little side table. Really, my acting skills were marvellous, because I picked up the notes from the floor. 'Here they are.' I watched him read them.

'You could have said.'

'And what? Should I have checked if you'd called her back? We always write phone messages on notes.'

I could see him swallowing, trying to believe me, to rationalise.

'I bought you a mobile,' I said. 'Why didn't she just call on that?'

'That was just for work. I'm on a crap plan—she doesn't even have the number. For Christ's sake, Alice, did you not think?'

'I think,' I shrilled, 'you're rather overly upset to have missed Gemma's call.'

'She called me last night at work from Singapore!'

'Singapore?'

'She doesn't want it to be over, she doesn't understand why I won't talk to her, so she's on her way here to talk to me.'

Oh, God. What had I done?

'My first weekend on call and I've had to ask someone to cover for me.'

Oh, God. Oh, God.

'I'm going to the airport...'

'When will you be back?'

He didn't answer. He was furious, I could tell, and I knew I deserved it, but I still denied it. I watched him check his wallet, and call for a taxi, and then I heard the slam of the door—and I did the only thing I could think of.

I took a Kalma.

Then another, and a few hours later, when he still hadn't called, I took a couple more.

It was the longest day.

Just unbearable.

Roz was out, so too was Dan.

I spun around the apartment, pacing. I checked my phone constantly. I checked the flight times from Singapore and she'd been in the country for hours. What the hell did they have to talk about? In the end Dan answered and I begged him to come over and hold vigil, and he was a good friend because he came, and by midnight, when there was still no Hugh, I gave up being brave. If I closed my eyes I could see Gemma's head thrashing on the pillow at their tender reunion.

I wanted to text him, to ring him, but Dan said to have another margarita instead.

'Don't look needy.'

'I feel needy…' Oh, God, it was three a.m. and he hadn't called. Dan was holding my mobile hostage.

'You will not call him!' He frogmarched me to bed and poured me another margarita. We had the jug with us, and he lay on the bed with me and ordered me to sleep—but I couldn't. I just lay in the darkness, itching for my phone, hating Hugh for not calling. I surely deserved that at least?

And then the front door slammed.

And he was home.

As the light flicked on in my room I climbed out of bed and I was beaming, but I saw the look of disgust on his face as he saw there was a guy in my bed.

'It's Dan!' I grinned, because for Christ's sake he was only on top of the bed—and he was gay. 'It's Dan!' I said again, as Dan got up and gave me a grim smile and left us to it.

I was doing my YMCA dance, but Hugh wasn't smiling. I was—he'd come home to me. Late—very late, perhaps—but he had come home.

He'd come back to me.

'You're pissed.'

'A bit,' I admitted.

'In bed with Dan.'

'I didn't sleep with him.' I was still grinning, 'You know we're just friends—as if I'd sleep with him...'

'Oh, but you would have...' There was disgust in his eyes as he scanned the room, the ashtray, the margarita jug, me half-dressed. 'If Dan had tried, do you know what, Alice? I reckon that you would have.'

'Hold on a minute.' I lurched towards him, because the margaritas had gone straight to my legs. 'You're the one who just spent the night with your ex.'

'She's flown ten thousand miles,' Hugh roared, 'and had you passed on the messages she wouldn't have had to—she's been ringing all week!'

'So it's my fault?' I demanded, grabbing his arm, but he shook me off. 'My fault your loopy ex can't stop ringing you? My fault your psycho ex hops on a plane to the other side of the world?'

'I can't do this...' Hugh shook his head. He was in his room and shoving stuff into his backpack. 'I can't do this any more, Alice. The one time I needed to come home and talk, the one time I needed to have a sensible conversation, what do I get?'

'You spent the night with your ex!'

It had surely been my right to call friends, my right to get pissed and feel sorry for myself, but Hugh refused to see it, and all I could see was that he was packing his bag, that he was leaving and I didn't want it to end.

'Don't walk out.'

'If I stay,' Hugh hissed through very taut lips, 'then I'll say something that we're both going to regret.'

'You're going to her, aren't you?'

'Alice.'

'You were always going to.' I let rip then. 'I'm your last fling—your last shag before you settle down. You were always using me.'

'Alice!' He shouted the word, his lips white. 'Shut up. This isn't about Gemma...'

'Then who?' I screamed. 'Everything was fine and then she turns up...'

'Everything was not fine.'

'Yes, it was!' I insisted. 'Look at Coogee—you said this was *it*, and now she's back, bloody Gemma...'

'This isn't about Gemma!'

We went back and forth, or rather he carried on packing his stuff as I ripped it back out and demanded he stay—demanded that we talk—and he said he'd been trying to talk, and then I said...

Something... (I can't remember—sorry...)

And he went to walk out.

And I was pulling at him and he was shaking me off.

And then it was Hugh's turn to let rip.

In hindsight, had I let him go when he first wanted to, we might have had a chance. He might have come back the next morning and we'd have spoken. But I hadn't let him go. I'd demanded that he stay, demanded that he talk.

Oh, my!

Did he talk.

'We have a name for people like you, Alice.'

We—it was a 'we' I didn't like: a sort of professional 'we' that I didn't want attached to my name. I wanted him to go now, but Hugh wasn't keeping quiet, Hugh wasn't holding back.

'FITH syndrome.'

I wasn't going to listen to this—I didn't want to argue; I didn't care what it meant. I walked back along the hall to the living room, only that didn't stop him.

'Fucked In The Head.'

And he told me how he'd come to his diagnosis and I just sat there. I sat there silent, stunned, as he packed—properly this time—not just a toothbrush or a change of socks—no, he put everything he could into his backpack, and the stuff left over into carrier bags.

And I hated him for turning this on me—he was making an excuse, blaming me, when really he was just looking for a reason to go back to her.

He was standing in the lounge looking at me, breathing so hard you'd think he'd been running, just standing there for the longest time.

'You need help, Alice.'

'Just go to Gemma!'

'Yeah, blame it on her, why don't you? Instead of taking a look at yourself.' He grabbed at my handbag and I moved to stop him. I pulled at his hands as he shook the contents out.

'Just go.'

'I am going.'

'Then go!' I was screaming. The neighbours were banging. But Hugh didn't care about that.

'I'm doing you a favour, you stupid bitch. For the last time ever, I'm doing you a favour!'

And he opened all the zips and took out the bottles, the blister packs and the prescriptions, the fags and the lighters. Then he went under the mattress and pulled out the credit-card bills, and I was grabbing at his arms and trying to stop him, but he shoved me off as easily as brushing off a fly. He stormed into the kitchen and turned on the waste disposal and tipped in my pills— only he didn't stop there. He took out the wine casks, and then he went to my make-up bag and found some laxatives. He tipped out my protein shakes and broke all the eggs for my omelettes, and turned the waste disposal on again. I stopped fighting him then. I just sat there.

'You know why I hate my job sometimes?' Hugh said, and I didn't look at him and didn't answer. 'Because I know where to look.'

And I knew as he closed the door that he wasn't just talking about my bag, or under the mattress, the sink, the cupboards... Hugh was talking about my mind.

I just sat there when he'd gone.

Hugh did know where to look, because he'd seen everything.

I couldn't have a drink.

I couldn't have a pill.

I couldn't even bloody kill myself as no doubt he'd hidden all the knives, so I just sat there in silence. I didn't even wonder if he had gone to Gemma, because I knew it didn't matter whether he had or not.

He had been preparing to leave anyway.

Just as they all did, just as anyone did when they got too close.

Or grew up.

Or got a life.

Or saw me.

I cried then—real tears this time. Cried so hard I was retching, I cried more than I ever have in my life.

Except once.

Forty-Eight

She was here.

That quickly.

It was a girl.

She was a girl.

A life.

And it ended.

She was as big as my hand, perhaps a little bit bigger, and they wrapped her up and brought her over and offered her to me. She wasn't dead—she was breathing, she was pink, more red than pink—she was alive and I couldn't stand it.

'Just take it out!' I could hear my voice. I was shouting. 'Take it out.'

So they did.

And as I tried to wrap my head around it—as I thought it was over—Fi pulled me back to the world.

'Sweetie, you need to hold your baby.'

I hated Fi. As she spoke on all I did was hate her. I don't remember what she said word for word but it took eight minutes—eight minutes of her telling me to do something that I didn't want to, to do the hardest thing imaginable.

'You deserve this time.'

Shut the fuck up.

'I will hold her for you if you want me to, but you need to have this time.'

I looked at the clock and it was only ten past eight.

An hour ago I had been in the bath…

Seventeen.

A day ago I had been worried about my music exam.

'This is the most important decision you can make. Some time in the future…'

Now I was a mum.

And my baby was going to die.

So I let Fi bring it in.

She was wrapped in a lemon brushed cotton baby rug.

Fi held her for me and explained things to me.

She held her till I was ready to look properly; she explained that the soft, colourless hair on her head had no pigment—and I was twisting inside. I was twisting and folding over on myself and twisting in pain, because even if I could guess its potential colour I would never ever get to see it.

And she showed me her eyebrows, these little translucent lines that I wanted to touch but my hands stayed closed.

And she showed me her fingers, but I pulled at the rug because I needed more of her and I saw tiny, tiny toes.

I touched her foot and it moved; she felt my touch, and then I touched each little toe.

And then I wanted more, so Fi passed her to me.

It was like catching air.

She weighed nothing as I took her in my hands, yet she felt like everything to me as I drew her in.

'Have you thought of a name?'

'No,' I said because I had tried so hard *not* to think of her—but now she consumed me, her skin, her tiny little hands. I wished I'd eaten better, wished I could feed her, wished I'd held on just a little bit longer and given her a tiny chance.

I thought she had stopped breathing. I felt a shudder of panic because she seemed so still and then she breathed again and so could I, but I knew for not much longer.

'She needs to be named,' Fi said gently, and because she had lived she would be registered and I was relieved to hear it.

'Lydia,' I said.

It's my middle name.

No matter how I held her—no matter how my body tried to warm her—she grew colder. I saw her colour change from red to pink, to this mottled colour like when you've sat too close to a fire—and I held her closer and she got paler and sometimes she didn't breathe for ages but I always knew there would be one more. I kind of knew that it wasn't over. So much so…that I knew when it was.

I wanted to kiss those lips, to literally give the kiss of life, but my kiss, I knew, was too fierce for that tiny mouth. I held my breath with my lips open and tasted your last breath and I didn't breathe out—but you didn't breathe in.

You were a whisper…

And I closed my eyes and I closed my mind and I tried to hear it.

They say that when you die, life rushes past you.

I disagree.

I think, if you are lucky, you get a glimpse at the truth.

I feel that I nearly died at seventeen with my daughter, or rather that I glimpsed it with her, because she was too fragile to do it alone. So for that moment I held her tiny fingers and I pressed my lips to her cool soft cheek and I whizzed to the white light with her.

I went beyond music.

I went beyond.

I saw time.

I saw my music practice timetable beside my piano.

My alarm clock.

My future.

My goals.

Mum's goals for me.

This race to get there that was life.

Fi's race to get home.

I saw my future if I could ever catch up.

Or my demise.

I could see the luxury I had in this moment—and all that had been denied you.

I sped through differences as you slipped away from me, through so many different scenarios.

Different father.

Different year.

Different mother.

But it was here and now and I was the mother you

had and then, though I tried to reclaim it, I knew that you had gone.

My lips were on your cheek and I never wanted to let go.

You did.

You were ready.

You were so fragile and tiny, but you know what? You were so much stronger than me—you were ready to go.

You left me.

Don't go.

Don't leave me.

I could taste my tears but they didn't matter because at least I could still feel you. There was a bit of your back that was still, not warm, but tepid. I don't know if it was from the way I'd held you, but there was still warmth there and I held it.

Don't leave me.

And then she had to go.

Fi, I mean—because you had gone already.

I felt it.

I felt the feeling I would feel, diluted a million times over in the years to come, but I felt it first today.

Saw Fi glance at the clock.

Heard the whisper from the day staff who came in to check we were okay, and who quietly questioned why Fi was still there—and I understood that she had to be back for her shift tonight.

I felt her leave before she said it.

'You can hold her for as long as you need.' I didn't hear the rest—I just knew that Fi had to go.

And so had you.

I knew I could sit in this bed; I could hold you; I could

rest here with Fi; I could stay till tomorrow, till next week, next month, next year, but nothing could change the fact your time had run out.

And the best, the absolute best, I could do for you was to end it now.

'Take her.'

'Sweetie.' Fi was uncomfortable, as if she'd speeded up the end—but it had already happened.

I *wanted* Fi to do this.

I didn't want to be on the next shift; I didn't want it to be anyone other than Fi who took you.

I wanted her to be the one to take my baby.

To take Lydia.

And so she did.

Forty-Nine

'No...' It was four in the morning and poor Roz woke to my sobbing. 'That's not it.'

'Alice?' I could hear the worry in her voice; hear her talking to someone about Alice not being able to breathe again. 'No, Roz, that's not the worst thing that can happen. The worst thing that can happen is if your kids can't talk to you.'

'Alice, what's going on? I'm coming over.'

But I was not listening, I was rambling on, trying to make her understand, that that wasn't it, that wasn't the Worst Thing That Can Happen. 'Because you can be gay or straight, or sleeping around, or pregnant or depressed, but if that's how you feel and you can't tell your parents, how can they help you?'

She was over in minutes.

With...wait for it...Karan too!

Even in my self-absorbed, totally devastated state, I did manage a flicker of—ohmygod so Karan's gay too.

Am I the only straight one?

How did I not see?

Her hot date hadn't been with Trevor, it had been with Karan.

So that was why Karan had been so shirty that Sunday she did my hair and I bitched about Roz.

All of that I thought for a second.

Then I got back to woe is me.

Fifty

'What did Bonny say?'

Lex had come into the room as they prepared to move me from the birthing suite to the ward. I didn't look at him; instead I looked at the wall.

'Bonny hasn't rung back. I've rung a few times—you know what she's like, she never has her phone.'

I had accepted that they knew now, had assumed he had told them. It had been hours, after all; then I glanced at the clock and saw that it was only eleven a.m. And it wasn't like now—there was no Twitter to record your farts, no texts to demand where you were. Or maybe there were, just not in this family.

Bonny never turned on her phone.

You had been born, lived and died and it was still only eleven a.m. and no one else knew.

'You don't have to tell her.' I didn't argue the point now, I just said it. I wasn't even scared of them knowing—there was just no point.

'You can't go through this alone, Alice.'

'So stay in England,' I said. 'Because if you tell

Bonny, that's what will happen, and you know what, Lex? It won't change a single thing.'

I was moved up to the ward.

Oh, the joy of the NHS.

I was on the maternity ward, though I did get a side room—not that it silenced the lusty cries of the other babies.

They almost could have been her—they just didn't quite hit the note.

My heart leapt each time I heard one.

But it was always too deep, or too soft. It sounded like Lydia as much as a G sounded like a G.

Every time it's different.

It was perfect music.

It just wasn't mine.

Where was she?

Where was that energy?

I don't think it's fair.

Not on me, I hasten to add, on those poor bloody babies, because they're all ten years old now and walking around not knowing that there had been a mad woman a few yards away who'd felt like taking a pillow from her hospital bed and shutting them the fuck up.

Permanently.

Oh, yes, I thought about it.

It was torture and the nurses thought they were being nice.

I hated Big Lip, who took me up and then gave a hand-over out of my earshot. I mean, what the fuck could she say had happened that I didn't know already?

I hated the awkwardness of the student midwife who

came in and took my temperature and checked my pad and had no idea what to say.

Then lunch came around.

Lunch.

I was an emergency admission so I got a cold lunch. I lay on my side and gazed at a club sandwich as a woman next door said lunch was late and she was putting in a complaint.

She had her baby.

I wanted to wee—and it would have been so much easier to let go, to lie there, to let someone change me.

I nearly did.

But I couldn't.

With massive effort I staggered to the toilet, but I got dizzy.

'You shouldn't have got up on your own. Why didn't you ring the bell?'

I've no idea who she was, but she found me on the loo and told me off.

Not nastily, she said she was worried, that I could have fainted. She told me off for getting up, for not ringing the bell, for not asking for help.

She shoved a flannel between my legs, wiped me, tucked in a pad and then pulled up my paper knickers.

She dealt with my bodily functions.

I dealt with breathing.

I hated that place.

I hated the social worker who called me Alex instead of Alice and made a lot of notes, despite the fact I said absolutely nothing.

Lex came in then.

He'd been crying, I could tell, and I hated what I'd done to him.

The funeral director could take care of everything, apparently.

I should, of course, have counselling.

Like that would change a thing.

They had already taken photos and they would make footprints and whenever I was ready I could make an appointment.

'I don't want my mum to know.' It was all I said to the social worker.

'You're eighteen soon, Alex,' she replied. 'That's your decision.'

'Her name's Alice,' Lex sneered. 'And can I suggest she's in no fit state to make any sort of decision?'

'I'm just telling her her options.' Her pager went off and she excused herself, and then Lex's phone rang and he stared at it for a long time before answering. I could hear Bonny's voice in the still, silent room, hear her cheerful and laughing for once, even asking why he'd rung so many times. I saw Lex's face screwing up as he braced himself to tell her.

What?

The drama was over.

I wasn't in labour.

There was no chance.

Hurry home, darling—we need to squeeze in a funeral before we head off.

'I just miss you.' He forced himself to smile so that the words would sound truer. 'But I'm glad you're having a good time.'

They chatted for a moment longer and then he clicked off the phone and walked out of the room.

The lie was born.

When I wanted to go home from the hospital at three p.m.—when I demanded to go home—they didn't try too hard to dissuade me. My placenta had been delivered intact, I had seen the social worker, and I had someone to take me—and the *paperwork* for her was taken care of. So I got to go.

I got to sit in the car with Lex.

Who silently drove.

I got to walk into my home.

And I saw the mug and the wine and I wanted to say that I hadn't had any but I just stood there.

'Go to bed.' He was picking bits of china out of the sink, throwing them in the bin. 'They said you should rest.'

'Lex…' I didn't know what to say, I didn't know how I felt, but unfortunately I wasn't numb enough not to notice the contempt in his eyes when he turned his face to me.

'Alice, please go to bed. I can't talk about it.'

'Lex…'

'I *can't* talk about it!' He stared at me. 'I can't even tell my wife, Alice. The worst fucking thing in my life and I can't share it with her.'

There was nothing I could say. I tried 'Sorry' but he didn't nod, he didn't accept, he just stared. So I went to go.

'Who was he?'

I carried on walking.

'Surely I deserve that?'

I kept on walking.

'Do you even know?'

I stopped at the bottom of the stairs—and realised that, yes, he did deserve that.

'Gus.'

I couldn't look at him so I didn't turn around.

'Your piano teacher?'

'He's not a teacher.'

'Yes, Alice.' His voice followed me up the stairs. 'He is. He's married, isn't he?' I could hear his feet behind me on the stairs. 'Wasn't he the one with the pregnant wife...?'

'Leave it, Lex.'

'Did he know?'

'I told him.' My teeth were chattering. 'He told me to sort it, said that he didn't know it was even his—but it was only that time. That was the only time I've...'

He stopped the barrage of questions then. He drooped, as if all anger and fight and fear had gone out of him. His face was putty-grey, his lips were white, and without another word I went to bed.

I lay there. I could hear Lex throwing up in the bathroom. And then I heard the poor bastard trying to sound upbeat when Bonny rang.

Fifty-One

'I'm sorry.' I stared up at the best friend I had ever had—a woman I'd treated like dirt when I'd found out her secret. The same woman who had raced round in the middle of the night to find out mine. 'I was so mean. I was so embarrassed that you were gay…'

'My own family hated me.' Roz gripped my hands. 'At least you kept talking to me, so talk to me now.'

And I did.

I told her; I sat as she held me and I told her—about the wedding and then about Gus and then about the baby. I told her my shame, how scared I had been, and she understood, because she had been seventeen and scared and pregnant too.

'You told someone, you got help. You did the right thing,' I said to her.

'And fucked up so many lives…'

It was Roz who cried and I felt like it was me. 'I didn't want to be gay,' she howled loud enough for the neighbours to hear. 'I couldn't tell her,' Roz said. 'Alice, I couldn't tell my mum either. She was a little bit relieved,

I think, that I was pregnant. I think she'd been worried that I wasn't girly enough, and then when she found out about Andrew, well...I think she was actually relieved. And Andrew did the decent thing. He said he'd marry me straight away. How could I turn around and say that I didn't want that—that I didn't fancy him, that the only reason I'd slept with him was to get rid of the rumours, to somehow prove to myself that I wasn't different?'

And we both cried some more.

'We were seventeen,' Roz said, 'and scared.'

We spoke all night; I thought we would never stop talking.

We spoke through till the next morning and then Roz put me to bed, and when I woke up that evening, when I stared at the devastation, quite simply I couldn't talk any more.

Roz took two days off work.

My phone rang a lot. Dan, Roz would say when she looked at it, but I didn't pick up, and a couple of times it was Bonny, but I didn't pick up for her either. I didn't once jump or lurch in hope that it was Hugh.

She answered the house phone too.

Told them all I was sick and that, yes, she would pass on the message, but I was unwell and would get back to them just as soon as I was able.

I lay in my bed and occasionally got up for the loo.

I wasn't hungry and I wasn't thirsty and I didn't want to talk any more—I felt like I was staring down a long cardboard roll and looking at my life and my past and watching it but not feeling it.

Of course Roz couldn't ring in sick for ever, and she

had an important class tonight. I knew soon I would be left alone—and for the first time I wanted to be.

I just wanted to lie there and close my eyes and sleep.

I didn't need a drink or a Valium; I didn't need anything. I had found the place I was seeking—I was finally completely numb.

'I have to go to uni just for a couple of hours.' She was hovering by the bed. 'Are you sure you'll be okay?'

I nodded.

'Bonny rang, I said you had the flu—do you want me to ask her to come over…?' Her voice trailed off. If Bonny saw me like this she'd freak.

'No.'

'Well, she's coming over anyway,' Roz said. 'Tomorrow, apparently.'

I could not face Bonny.

I could not, *could not* face her.

As Roz was on her way out, because my mobile must have died Dan rang the house phone, and I stared at the wall without blinking as I heard Roz's practical voice.

Hugh was gone.

Alice wasn't doing too well, apparently, then a pause.

'It's not Hugh she's upset about, Dan.'

Then another pause.

'It's not my place to say.'

And then, with mammoth effort, I blinked at what I heard next.

'I've been worried for a long time too.'

And then another pause.

'That would be good. I've got to go to work.'

And one final pause.

'Please.'

Fifty-Two

I wanted grief.

I wanted the curtains closed and everything to stop. But I had chosen silence so the world just carried on, unaware that it was without her.

'I'm the one emigrating.' Bonny sat on Dad's old chair and poked her tongue out at the stairs she'd come down after a row with Lex. 'What is his problem?'

'He's been here for two years,' Mum said. 'It's a lot to say goodbye to.'

Lex had already left his job, but today he'd put on a suit and tie and said he was going into the office.

'I'll come…' Bonny said. 'It will be nice to say goodbye.'

'There's no point,' Lex said, pulling on his jacket. 'I've just got to go in to sign some papers.'

'Well, we can have lunch after.'

'Just leave it, Bonny!' Lex snapped, and Bonny did a dramatic flounce off and stomped back up the stairs.

I was lying on the sofa, where I'd been for the last couple of days.

Mum thought I was depressed that Bonny was leaving.

Funny, the world didn't revolve around her.

She thought it did, of course.

Actually, had I had the energy to think about it, the minute Lex had more on his mind than worrying about Bonny's latest mood, almost the second he'd seemed less urgent to get her to Australia, said it might be okay to stay for another month, the moody cow perked right up—almost as if she realised she'd got her way and suddenly didn't want it.

Now she was hanging off his shirt and wanting to go to lunch.

'Alice,' Mum said. 'Lex is talking to you.'

I stared in his direction because I still couldn't look at him.

'I thought you wanted a lift into town…' His voice was almost steady. 'If you get dressed quickly I can drop you off.'

'No, thanks.'

'Are you sure?' Lex pushed. 'I can wait.'

'No.'

'Alice, you said…'

'Just leave her, Lex,' Mum soothed. 'She's upset about tomorrow, and with her exam and everything on Monday.'

He went and Bonny came downstairs and I stood up.

I went over to the window and saw Lex climb into the car. The traffic was thick so it took for ever for him to get out of the drive, and I wanted to run out, still in my dressing gown, to climb in the car and go with him.

'What is his fucking problem?' Bonny asked again,

throwing herself on the sofa. 'I'm the one who's emigrating!'

'I'm going to lie down.'

I closed the curtains in my bedroom and curled up on the bed.

There was a tiny pathetic trickle of milk that had come through this morning, as Fi had warned that it might, and my breasts hurt a bit now.

I was glad they did.

I knew where Lex was. I knew he had been giving me one last chance to go.

I wanted to scream and wail but I lay there in silence.

I had never been to a funeral.

I had no idea what happened at one.

And what happened at a funeral for a tiny baby?

Was it even a proper one?

Thank God for Lex.

The airport is just a blurry memory.

Heathrow, big and noisy, tears and taxis, Bonny guzzling gin and Lex looking grey. I dashed off to the loo and changed my pad and swallowed a few Nurofen and came back and Dad was there and so too was Lucy.

She stood back from the throng, nervous and shunned, tiny and dainty, but glowing and nursing her bump.

I know what your baby looks like, I wanted to blurt out, but I stared instead and felt her blush because I couldn't help staring at her. *I know that its eyes are like little golf balls and that it has no pigment yet and that the skin is thin and red and that it moves and, if it was born this very minute, it would breathe and gasp and then die.* She gave me an embarrassed smile and I looked away. But then I found myself staring again. *My baby died, you see.*

Eleanor was there with Noel and their two angelic kids.

Perfect Eleanor.

Who ate a bar of chocolate and a muffin and a BLT sandwich and then another bar of chocolate in the airport café as Noel frowned. Still he amused the kidlets for her when she disappeared to the toilet for twenty minutes and came back reeking of mints and no doubt minus a layer of tooth enamel.

There were a few aunts and uncles, and Mum in flat shoes with her ankles spilling out over the top and her stomach spilling out over her skirt. She hadn't bothered with make-up because she knew she'd be crying—but, hell, could she not have made *some* effort? I mean, her ex was there, with his stunning new wife, and Mum couldn't even do her skirt up.

We were just one of many families, crying, saying our goodbyes—a normal family, or so I thought.

It took me more than ten years to realise we were that, oh, so commonly bandied-around word, that the Jamesons might possibly be…

Dysfunctional.

Fifty-Three

'Get up.'

Nurse Dan was there within fifteen minutes, flinging open the curtains and opening the window. He pulled a face when the light hit and he saw mine.

'You're having a shower.'

I didn't want to get up. The duvet was too heavy to lift anyway.

I didn't want to wash.

It's my nervous breakdown and I'll lie if I want to.

Except Dan didn't believe in nervous breakdowns.

He didn't know what was wrong and he didn't care—but not in a bad way. All he cared about was me.

'I will not let you do this, Alice.' He pulled back the duvet and hauled me out of bed; he did a lot of flapping with his hands and told me I smelt and I didn't even care.

All I knew was that my body ached like it did when I had the flu. I knew that I could not walk down the massive hall—even though our flat is tiny—I could not turn on a tap, let alone stand and have needles of water on my skin.

The thought was exhausting.

'You're having a shower,' Dan said as I shuffled down the hall. He turned on the taps and I stood there. 'Don't make me have to undress and wash you. Have you any idea the damage it would do to me?'

The muscle in the bottom of my lip stretched—I couldn't call it a smile. My lips, I'm sure, barely moved, but I felt a tiny spasm of a muscle and, no, I didn't want him washing me.

Every button took for ever and I could hardly lift my feet out of my pyjamas.

I stood naked for ages before I summoned the strength to step into the water.

I stepped under the shower but I wanted a bath; I wanted to lie and soak and remember feeling her, but we didn't have a bath, so I stood.

'Wash your hair.'

He was guarding the door.

I understand depression; I understand now complete fucked-in-the-headness, 'cos I stared at the bottle of shampoo and it seemed too heavy to open.

I thought my arms would fracture.

I could not do this.

I could not get through this.

I couldn't even wash my hair.

I stood as the water pelted me.

And then Dan shouted through the door, 'Wash it, Alice, or I'll come in.' And though I wanted to sink I think it was then that I realised I wouldn't, then that I started a painful ascent to the surface. I did wash my hair, but it exhausted me.

Wrapping a towel around myself exhausted me.

But I did it.

Energy depleted, I sat on the bed as Dan handed me clothes, or rather, some awful maroon leggings (I have no idea to this day where he got them from), and then he tucked me into a bed where the sheets had been changed and I braced for him to leave.

He put on pyjamas.

The sexiest gay man in the southern hemisphere had come armed with designer pyjamas and brought his own toothbrush along just for me.

'I'd never wear these for a man,' Dan said, and he climbed in beside me.

'Matthew...' I sounded drunk but I wasn't. It was my first word in hours.

'He knows where I am,' Dan said. 'He's worried for you too.'

I stared at the Russian dolls Hugh had given me. I had them all lined up on my bedside table.

Maybe I should put them all together, tuck them all inside.

It was too much effort.

Dan didn't ask what had happened.

He didn't go to sleep either.

He turned off the light and he guarded me.

I don't know, and I still don't, how to define Dan.

There is not another man, or woman, on earth I would have allowed to see me like this.

No way did I want Nicole or Roz climbing into bed and holding me, and I didn't want Hugh either. So why was it okay with Dan?

'Remember the night I told Dad?' Dan pulled me in.

'I couldn't tell him at home 'cos he'd beat the crap out of me. Remember how scared I was of my brothers?'

In fog, I remembered.

Standing at a bar.

Hovering as he had the dreaded conversation.

Feeding him gin.

Then a strange fight broke out—a mass of brothers and trucks and testosterone. His dad was crying and I took Dan home.

Brought him here.

To this bed. And he was disgusted with himself but I was so proud of him and I knew there was nothing I couldn't tell him.

'I had a baby when I was seventeen,' I said, and he didn't answer. 'Lydia.' Still he said nothing. 'She died and no one knew.'

'Poor baby,' Dan said.

Yes, she was.

'You,' Dan said, and kissed my head. 'You poor baby.'

For the first time as I lay there with Dan I remembered the bit I had never remembered before.

Not once.

I hadn't been fighting it, like I had the memory of her birth; I had never, since that day, thought about it.

Fifty-Four

Bonny and Lex rang us from their twenty-four-hour stopover in Singapore, which they loved, apparently.

And then on their Monday night, which was our Monday morning, they rang to say they were in Melbourne.

Bonny hadn't seen anything because it was dark, but his family seemed as nice as they had at the wedding.

No, there were no kangaroos or koalas, no beach she had glimpsed—in fact, it was the middle of winter in Melbourne, which meant it was freezing.

It was hot here.

And I had my final exam.

My music practical, which had once been my centre.

The most important hour of my life.

But I was so zonked out that I almost missed my bus stop.

My breasts didn't hurt and I didn't need a pad any more.

There was nothing at all to show for her existence, which was what I had wanted, I reminded myself.

The music A-level is a complicated exam—it stretches for ever—and today was the final part.

To this day I can hardly remember the theory or the aural exams, or my English Lit that had come in the weeks before, but for ever I will remember sitting there at the practical.

You see—I had given her up for this.

For this vital day, for my vital future, I had denied her existence.

So, it made sense, surely, that I should summon the magic now, should play from my heart, should play for her, should make the loss somehow worth it.

I played.

But I just played.

Technically, I think it was okay, but all it was was fingers that made a noise that sounded like a tune that somebody brilliant had once written.

I *just* played.

And then, when it was finished, I collected my music and closed the piano lid and swore I would never play that piece again.

That part of my life was over.

Fifty-Five

How come I don't get to have a nervous breakdown?

I got two days in bed and then I was hauled to the sofa.

And Big Tits was wrong, I had no self-control, because when Dan made me soup and toast, one bite of that lovely buttery bread and I wanted more, more, more.

I want to say that the days passed and I got thinner and paler and more interesting, but I got bigger and ruddier from crying, and probably I was really rather boring.

Lex came over and I couldn't look at him.

Bonny was beside herself—apparently she'd come to the door and had glimpsed me in my catatonic state.

'You need to tell her,' Lex said as Dan held my hand.

'I know,' I said. 'I'll leave you out of it.'

'No.' He shook his head. 'Alice, I can't live with it any more…it nearly killed our marriage once.'

My eyes jerked to his.

'That fight when we first got married.' His face was grey with the memory. 'When I got arrested.'

'Gus?'

He nodded.

'I beat the crap out of him. I think I would have killed him if someone hadn't pulled me off. She was my niece!'

No wonder Gus had looked so petrified when he saw me.

'It's been eating me up,' Lex said. 'I even went to see my GP.'

Christ, so Dr Kelsey had known too.

'Can I be the one to tell Bonny?' Lex asked.

I nodded.

Can you guess what happened next?

Bear in mind I'm trying to have a nervous breakdown, I am probably clinically depressed and that she's seen me catatonic on the bed.

So she came over and burst into tears, cuddled me, loved me and held me, right?

Er, no—this is Bonny we're talking about.

She burst into the flat about two hours later, pushed past Roz and stood there, all big and jiggly and white with fury, and scarily angry.

Dan was holding my hand, but I was holding his too.

She really was scary.

'You selfish bitch!'

She called me a few other names, and Lex told her to calm down, but she wouldn't listen.

'Have you any idea the damage you caused? No, because you're so fucking selfish. Don't ever ask my husband to keep a secret from me again.'

'I'm sorry.' I glanced over at Lex, who gave a grim smile, and I knew there had been a row about something that had happened ten years ago.

'She was seventeen and scared and didn't know what

to do. I've got four younger sisters,' Lex said, and Bonny closed her eyes and breathed out.

'We don't have secrets. We don't have any secrets—that was the deal,' she insisted. Her eyes opened and flicked to mine and she closed them quickly, because maybe she was realising that they did have secrets.

Maybe I was realising it too.

And then, when she'd calmed down, she burst out crying and she loved me again.

Lex went home and so did Roz. Nurse Dan got a night off and Bonny stayed.

I didn't know what bits to tell her—or what bits to leave out. I told her about Gus and I told her about the pregnancy and when she was born—and how I'd begged Lex not to tell (I exaggerated that part a bit).

And Bonny hates silence; Bonny always fills in the gaps or pushes me to get to the point. But she didn't this time.

I couldn't look at her. I just looked at my hand, which she was holding. I saw tears that came from us both.

'You could have come to me...'

'I didn't want Mum to know.' It wasn't quite true. 'I didn't want to stop you going to Australia.'

And then we cried, because at the centre of it all was a girl, just a girl, who hadn't known who she could turn to.

I really don't think I'm physically wired to be able to have a nervous breakdown.

And even if I was, no one would bloody let me.

Because they had problems of their own. It was, *Sorry, Alice, I know you've got some stuff on your plate, but I kind of need you too,* and when I'd stopped telling my story, Bonny suddenly needed to tell me hers.

'Nothing happened!'

I frowned over at her. I was so deep in *me*, I had no idea what she was talking about, no idea that there was something other than me at the forefront of her mind. 'That night. With that pilot…' Her lips were white and I realised she was sweating. I could see the fear that I had felt so many times mirrored in her eyes as she spoke on. 'He tried it on and I said no. I told him I was happily married.' She started to cry and I put my arms around her. 'Which I am—well, sort of… It's just sometimes… sometimes…'

'Sometimes what?'

'Nothing.' She righted herself. 'It's nothing. I'm fine.' Bonny sniffed. 'I just had too much to drink that night, and Lex would freak if he knew that we had guys chatting us up.'

'Bonny?'

'Leave it,' she begged.

And, for now, I was relieved to.

Fifty-Six

'I took your advice.'

Roz was opening my bills and going through them.

'What advice?'

'That night, when you said I should just let her say it…let her talk to me.'

I had no idea what she was talking about.

'That the worst thing that can happen is if your kids can't tell you how they feel.'

Oh, God, I sort of could remember—now she said it…

'Er, Roz, I was roaring drunk and probably mentally ill…'

'Well, Lizzie certainly told me!'

I winced for her.

'She hates me; she's ashamed of me; she thinks everyone will think she's gay too. And I smell, apparently.'

'Oh, Roz!' God, I wished I'd been the one to tell her. I'd have done it so much better.

'I stink, in fact, and my clothes are disgusting.'

I waited for tears and I blinked when they didn't come; instead, she turned her attention back to my mail.

'It's a mess.' She had been collecting my closely guarded post for days now and was starting to see the true picture.

Not once did she admonish me.

Okay, once.

'Botox!' She stared at the statements littered round the table. 'You bought home-brand everything and then you went and spent a grand on your face!'

And then she laughed.

I was a shell on the sofa and she wheezed and laughed.

You either understand or you don't, but my fear of envelopes was real.

You get it or you don't.

And even if she didn't, Roz did her best.

'I'm sorry for what Lizzie said...'

'No,' Roz said, 'you were right. She cried and ranted and raved but do you know what? She was there. She keeps getting on that train to see me, to row with me, to try and tell me how she feels, and now she finally has.'

I didn't understand.

'I told her some stuff too,' Roz said. 'I'm not dressing like a dyke.' There was a flash of tears in her eyes then. 'I just didn't care, but I do now.' I watched a big fat tear spill on her cheek and I wanted to wipe it away, but instead I sat there. 'I want to look nice for Karan; I want to look nice for me—I told Lizzie that I don't know where to start.'

I still sat there.

'I told her I was sorry.'

'You shouldn't have to say you're sorry for being who you are.' (Gawd! The thing was, I actually meant that.)

Roz disagreed.

'I am sorry. Sorry for what I did to Andrew, what I did to Lizzie, what I did to me...' She gave a wobbly smile. 'I think I need to go and see Big Tits.'

'Maybe you should,' I said.

There was no skirting issues with Roz: she looked me straight in the eye. '*You* should,' she said, and she didn't add maybe.

Yes, I supposed I should.

My hand was shaking so much I had to dial twice, but I needn't have worried, I wasn't going to get to see her. Big Tits was on four weeks' annual leave.

And, because it was all I seemed to be doing these days, I burst out crying.

'We can put you in to see someone else.'

I didn't want someone else; I didn't want to have to go through everything again, and I said the strangest thing.

'Lisa's the only one who will understand.'

Fifty-Seven

It was my first trip out of the flat.

My hair was in chaos; I was wearing those awful leggings and a big jumper, and shoes that should not be worn with leggings. It seemed a long way from the flat to the car, but I got there and Roz drove. As we pulled up, so too did Big Tits.

I could not believe she would break her holiday for me.

After the way I had spoken to her, the way I had been, I could not believe that the receptionist would call her and that ten minutes later she would call me. (I didn't go to the phone, as I was—as you can probably guess—on the sofa, crying.) Instead she spoke to Roz and Roz spoke to her and then apparently she said that she would meet me.

So Roz brought me.

And because she was so nice to break her holiday like that, I won't call her Big Tits any more.

Well, not so often.

I wasn't angry with her any more either; rather, I was relieved to see her.

Roz sat on the sofa and I saw the receptionist's curious look as I stood by Lisa while she took a message. Then she got her keys out of her bag, opened up her office and spent a few moments arranging furniture, opening a window and pouring me some water.

'Roz seems nice,' Lisa said. 'She seems like a very good friend.'

'She is.'

And I told her.

I told her and I watched for her reaction but she just sat there.

So I told her some more.

And then I told her some more.

I told her everything I have told you and do you know what she said?

'Thank you for sharing that part of your life with me.'

It sounds so wanky and false, but it was said very kindly. Reading that back, it makes me gag, but it was actually, to hear, rather nice.

And then I told her some stuff that I haven't told you.

You see, I had read all those self-help books and, as I have said, I'm not stupid. I get the bit about low self-esteem and self-loathing and why I did some not very sensible things and didn't do things that, in hindsight, I wish now that I had.

I waited for her to nod, but she didn't.

I understood, I said, that even though I had refused to analyse it for a long time, well, now I had and because of what happened with Lydia, I didn't feel that I deserved a nice life.

And she just sat there and I rambled a bit more.

She had to get up at one point and turn on the light because it was getting dark outside.

She didn't once look at the clock.

I told her I felt things would be better now.

Still she didn't nod.

Now that I had told her, now that Bonny knew, now that I was dealing with it—well, now finally I understood why I was like I was.

Please nod.

We sat in silence.

Please say that I'm almost sorted.

'I think, or rather, I'm sure,' Lisa said, 'that you're grieving. You know there are stages to grief?' I felt my lips tighten, a smart response on my tongue, but I swallowed it. I wanted her to skip the long-winded explanations, to get to the bloody point.

Which, I might add, I already had.

I'd done her work for her, in fact.

'Denial, bargaining, anger, depression and acceptance—they don't happen neatly, they often overlap, but I would say that you are coming close to acceptance.'

Phew.

'And to go through all that you did, practically alone, must have been an awful experience.'

It was, it was, can we be done now?

'The thing is…'

Are we nearly there yet?

She glanced at the clock.

We were almost over.

Oh, I knew I'd have to see her again, probably quite

a few times, but the hardest part was over. Any minute now, she'd wrap it up.

'While I agree with you, that you have low self-esteem and that's, in part, why you do the things you do…or don't do the things you should.' She gave me a pussycat smile, to tell me she had made a little joke there. 'It's not about your pregnancy or grieving…'

I blinked.

I mean, I had told her the deepest, darkest part of me, and she still wasn't satisfied. There still had to be more.

'Why did you let Gus sleep with you?'

Oh, God!

'Hormones?' I suggested. I mean I had been a teen-ager then.

'Alice, the self-loathing started long, long before Gus came along. And though, absolutely, we need to work through your pregnancy, there are other things that need to be sorted out.'

Big Tits!

I shot her a look that said it.

'My guess is you were a highly anxious, eager-to-please child—a sensitive child with superstitious thinking.'

Please, please don't say it.

'I think we have to get to know Little Alice.'

'You mean I have to learn to love my inner child?' My words dripped sarcasm.

'Absolutely.' Big Tits smiled. 'Perhaps you could bring a photo.'

'I don't have one.'

'You don't have any photos of you as a child?'

'Because I emigrated.' I whistled through my teeth. She read something into bloody everything.

'Speak to your mum?' Lisa said. 'I'll see you at my home on Thursday.' She stood up and wrote down the address, and I paid her (with the money Roz had lent me) and she wrote a receipt and thanked me again for my openness today. Then she led me outside to Roz, who was asleep on the sofa.

'How was it?' Roz was all anxious as we got to the car. 'Do you feel any better?'

'I don't know,' I admitted, and then thought about it. 'I really don't know. I just need a few weeks to get myself sorted.' I could feel the bubble of panic building—I hadn't been to work all week, my sick leave was up, the bills were still pouring in, but, worse, I didn't know that I could face going in to work. A trip in the car with Roz driving was making me anxious enough.

'You will get it sorted,' Roz said, and glanced over. 'But you do feel better?'

It was easier to just say yes.

Fifty-Eight

'I went to the gym...' Roz was sitting, *still* going through my paperwork, when Bonny rang that evening. Dan was over for a quick check on his patient. Actually, Dan and Roz were friendly now—he had known about Roz, of course, but given what he'd been through, he wouldn't be the one to out her. 'And I'm back on Weight Watchers,' Bonny chatted on. 'You're sorting yourself out and I've decided that so am I.'

'That's great,' I said, but maybe I'd had too much contact with Lisa, because a little voice in my head told me that it wasn't just a diet or gym that Bonny needed.

Still, it was a start.

'So what did you do today?' she asked.

'I went to see Lisa.'

'Lisa?'

'My psychologist.'

There was a silence as she struggled to make the right response.

'Oh.'

Bonny's very English.

There was another silence before she spoke again.

'So what did you talk about?'

'This and that,' I said blithely.

'Nothing about me, I hope,' she said with a friendly laugh, but it was just a touch shrill.

'Just me,' I said, and then, because it was Bonny, I got off my high horse and had a bit of a giggle. 'I have to learn to love my inner child.'

'You're not serious!' Bonny snorted. 'That's so old.'

'Lisa *is* old,' I said. 'She wants me to ask Mum for a photo of me—no way.'

So we chatted on as she clattered about, talked about the gym and about her weight and how Lex was going away on another business trip soon. She sounded happier than she had in a long time and I was relieved that she knew now. I felt closer to her, I guess. And also relieved that it wasn't all that we spoke about.

'Done,' Bonny said.

'What?'

'Go and check your email.'

I hadn't turned the computer on in days and we chatted as I waited for my emails to download. There were loads to go through but I deliberately started at the end and there was one through from Bonny with an attachment.

'Open it,' she said. So I did and felt my stomach go tight; I felt my lips clench and the sting in my nose as Little Alice stared back at me.

Flaming hair, flaming cheeks and I was red, red, red—even my eyes were red from crying because I hated having my photo taken. I couldn't stand it. I mean, how the hell was I supposed to love that?

'God.' Bonny's voice seemed to be coming from a long way off. 'You've got your work cut out.' She laughed. 'Pre-product Alice—I'd forgotten what an ugly little thing you were.' Then she must have remembered that I wasn't in the best place right now and quickly she added, 'You know I'm joking.'

The thing was, I didn't find it funny.

'What are these?' When I came off the phone, Roz held out two forms from envelopes I hadn't even bothered to open. 'From universities?'

'Shred them,' I said, but Dan took them and had a look and I cursed the night that I'd sent them off—too many lime margaritas and, fired up from Dan, I'd started to think it might be possible.

'Close of applications next week.'

I let out a breath of relief. 'So throw them.'

'You can still do a late entry.' He made light work of the forms. 'That would give you more than three months before you sat the entrance—'

'Dan,' I interrupted. 'Three months is nothing—it would take a year at least.'

'But you already know those pieces.' Bloody Roz interrupted me. 'I've heard you.'

'I'm nowhere near exam standard. Nowhere near. I'd have to practise every hour of every day.' I wasn't making excuses; it really was impossible. 'Shred them,' I said, and when Dan still held onto them I did it for him and fed them into the shredder.

'Next year,' I said.

I think I meant it.

Next year, when everything was sorted; next year,

when I was out of the mess I'd got myself into, I'd think about it.

'I'll do it next year.'

Fifty-Nine

From: Nicole Hunter
To: alicelydiajameson@hotmail.com
Subject: News
Hi Alice
I have tried to ring a few times. Hope this means you are busy and having fun. It is great to be home and I am busy catching up with everyone.

Alice, I don't know if this will come as a surprise or a shock—I hope it will be a nice surprise!

Paul asked me to marry him. I was hoping it would happen—in fact, I was on high alert the week before as he took me to this really romantic place (a castle). Anyway, it didn't happen then. It was when he was opening up the shop—I was yawning and he turned around and just said it. It was actually very romantic.

As you know Rita is here, and I have been offered a permanent position at the London branch, which is very exciting. We have decided to get married on New Year's Eve—I remember you saying that your sister did—well, it makes sense—that means you guys can come out! You said you were hoping to get back and see your mum, and Roz is always saying she wants to bring Lizzie to the UK for a holiday.

The thing is, what with the wedding so soon, I can't afford to come back. I know I have to sort out the flat and rent, etc., and I will do that properly with you, but for now I am still on a buzz and wanted to share it with you.

I know you will be happy for me.

Nicole

She was telling me what to do—the appropriate response.

How come everyone seemed to move on with their lives, and I just stayed the same?

I hit 'Reply'.

From: Alice (alicelydiajameson@hotmail.com)
To: nicsalawyer@hotmail.com
Subject: Re: News!
What a surprise—I knew this was coming.
Well, good luck.
Are you sure you will be happy?
He's a barista for fuck's sake.
You don't even like sex.
Why is it everyone who leaves me ends up happy?
Alice

I didn't hit 'Send'. I'm not that unlucky. I hit 'Cancel'.

Are you sure you want to move away from this page?
OK

I hit 'Reply' again.

From: Alice (alicelydiajameson@hotmail.com)
To: nicsalawyer@hotmail.com
Subject: Re: News!
Ohmygod
Fantastic!
I knew, I knew, I knew. I know you two are going to be so happy.
New Year! How romantic!!!!!!!!!!!!!!!!! Will do my very best to be there, but am a bit broke. This has to be quick as I am on my way out.
Will email properly soon.
A xxxxxxx
PS Have you heard from Hugh? I think he is back in UK.

Okay, so now I didn't have a flatmate.

I knew Nicole would do the right thing and chuck in a month or so's rent but I felt the bubble of panic rising. I went to the bathroom and I looked through the cupboards—right at the back where I'd kept a few— but Hugh had been thorough in his locate and dispose mission.

I wanted a drink. I knew Roz would be here soon, but if I dashed out I could make it back. I had my jacket on, I was checking for cash in my bag, and then Roz came to the door.

I almost didn't answer.

I just wanted her to fuck off and leave me alone.

I was sick, so sick of her asking if I was okay. Or was I feeling better yet? Fed up with her telling me it would be okay, when I still felt like *this*.

'Where are you going?'

'Just...' I couldn't think of anything to say. 'For chocolate.'

'I'm on a diet, remember.' Roz rolled her eyes. 'Lizzie's orders. Come on,' she said, 'we need to talk.'

The books were wrong—the universe was not kind, it didn't reward hard work.

I had hauled myself out of bed.

I was getting dressed by now, going into poxy work each day. I was seeing Lisa; I was staring at that shagging photo and trying to like her—did I get a reward?

Did the universe treat me gently as I struggled to recover?

No, I lost my flatmate and when I sat down with Roz I found out I had to lose my car too.

'I need a car!' I had nothing—nothing to show for the spending except a car that I had, despite everything, kept up the payments with. There was just a year left on the lease and then I could pay the balloon and I'd own it.

'There's no hope of you paying off the balloon,' Roz said, as I sat firm.

'How am I supposed to get to work?'

'Public transport.'

'What about when I go away?'

'You can't afford to go away.'

Roz, I realised, would make a very good tax inspector, because lovely, lovely Roz, when it came to work, when it came to figures, was just—immutable.

'You need to ring all the credit-card companies and sort out a plan.'

'I can't.'

'You can.'

God, but I needed a drink, except I didn't have one. I did everything she said and I'm not going to say it was nice, it was awful, but I was still trying.

I really was trying.

And did I get a reward? Did anything get easier?

No, it got harder.

Every day it just got harder.

From: Nicole Hunter (nicsalawyer@hotmail.com)
To: alicelydiajameson@hotmail.com
Subject: Re re: News!
Alice

You *have* to be there.

I know you can't afford it, but since when did that stop you? Please, please don't think of not being there.

Paul's brother has backed out of the coffee shop. The day before signatures, can you believe? Paul's upset, of course, but he's being amazing—he's not going to give up. I'm sure it will still happen.

Nic x

PS Yes—so sweet—Hugh couldn't stay away from Gemma. Aunty Cheryl is planning the wedding! He said you were great—so thanks for being so nice.

I felt like a plank with bits of nails being hammered in.

At some level I had known and accepted it was temporary. Even as we'd made love, even with everything he'd said, in my heart of hearts I had known that Hugh and I weren't *real*. That I would lose him, just as I was losing Nicole.

It hurt far more than it possibly should, though.

And just when it couldn't get much worse, I lost my job as well.

I gathered up all my self-help books and all my New Age stuff and put everything in the recycle bin, except for Yasmin's book which went in the shredder.

The universe sucked.

Sixty

It wasn't *that* dramatic.

I wasn't asked to clear out my locker and escorted out of the building.

But the meeting I had been dreading for close to two years now was called. I could feel the sweat beading on my forehead as they spoke about voluntary redundancies and packages and though they said voluntary, really, there was no guarantee, they said, that this type of package would be offered again.

I could feel Roz's eyes on me when I came out of my one-on-one meeting. Roz's job was okay, because she was a casual (yep, thanks a lot, universe).

'This is good,' she said, dragging me over to a coffee bar and going through the details of the package. 'You can get another job.'

'Doing what?' Okay, I hated my job but I'd been there years, it was my place, it was what I did, where I went. I couldn't stand the thought of applications and interviews and meeting new people.

'You can pay off some of your cards.' She squeezed my arm. 'Alice, you can pay off most of your debts.'

'And keep my car?'

Roz closed her eyes and for a horrible second I thought she was going to get cross, but she didn't. 'Maybe. But...' She didn't finish. I took a sip of coffee and lost the roof of my mouth it was so hot. 'This is the best thing that could happen,' she said firmly. 'You'll get another job— you can start over again.'

Bonny agreed.

Lex was away and I ended up there for dinner. She drank wine, and I did too, I mean I *had* lost my job.

And I wasn't an alcoholic. I hadn't had a drink for ages and Lisa said it wasn't for her to say that—only I could decide. Though she was happy to add that I had an unhealthy relationship with alcohol.

So would she tonight.

I had just lost my bloody job—I was surely entitled.

Well, Bonny got the kids to bed and we sat on the sofa and it was so nice to relax.

'Lex will put in a word for you,' Bonny said, because he was high up now at the pharmaceutical company. 'I know there aren't loads of jobs, but they are hiring.'

'I don't know anything about drugs,' I said, and then we both started laughing.

'You won't be doing anything like that,' Bonny consoled. 'He'll find you something in Reception or something easy.'

'I'm not thick.' I bristled.

'No,' Bonny said, 'but you need to be concentrating on you now. The last thing you need is some high-stress job.'

Which made sense.

'Things are looking up, Alice.' She was being so nice, except I didn't feel much better.

'Dan said I should think about going back to study music.' Bonny looked at me for a long time before responding.

'Would you get in?'

'Probably not,' I admitted.

'Why would you set yourself up for a fall, Alice?' I could see the concern in her eyes, her struggle to say the right thing. 'Alice, you can't support yourself *with* a job—how on earth would you manage as a student? How long's the course?'

'Three years.'

We chatted some more, and the more we chatted the more I realised the impossibility of it. It was a relief when she changed the subject. 'You said Roz was thinking of moving in?' Bonny said. 'But I thought she was serious with Karan.'

'She is. They just…' I didn't want to tell Bonny everything. 'They're just not ready to live together yet.'

Okay, I won't tell Bonny, but I'll tell you.

It's fascinating, actually.

They have all sorts of problems that we don't have to think about.

Gays, I mean.

Roz is fresh out of the nest, according to Karan.

And Karan is her first love.

Well, it's complicated, because though Roz is sure that Karan is 'the one', and Karan is sure that Roz is 'the one' too, Karan has been burnt by someone just fresh out of the closet once before and she isn't ready to take the risk yet. So while Karan waits for Roz to suddenly realise there are thousands of women to choose from, and while Roz tries to convince her that she won't, the answer is simple.

Roz would move in with me.

'This is the best thing that could have happened,' Bonny said firmly. 'Roz is great, she's just what you need right now, and I know it must feel awful to lose your job, but think positively: you'll have your car; you can pay off some of your debts.'

I slept on the sofa—there's no spare room at Bonny's thanks to her amazing ability to reproduce—and even though it was my first drink in ages I couldn't sleep. I lay there for ever, telling myself it would all be okay, that Lex would find some work for me, that my money would get sorted, that I got to keep my car.

I felt shocking in the morning.

I felt like I used to feel *every* morning. Bonny wasn't looking too hot either. Somehow she got two kids off to kinder and the babies were in their pen in the corner like little monkeys at the zoo.

'Stay a bit longer,' Bonny said.

'I can't. I've got an appointment.'

'With your counsellor?' (She didn't like the word 'psychologist'.) When I nodded she gave me a worried little smile. 'Surely you can reschedule it? Come to the gym with me.' Her face lit up. 'You should join!' she said. 'Exercise is supposed to be good for depression!'

'I'm broke,' I reminded her.

'You can pay as you go.'

'I can't afford to.' Except she wouldn't hear otherwise. She would pay for me, buy me some gym gear. We were the same shoe size. On and on she went, but I hate the

gym, even the thought of the gym makes me feel ill.
Even with my obsession with staying slim I couldn't
bring myself to go there. Oh, I know she meant well, I
am sure that for most people it is great for depression
and that exercise is good and all that—it's just not for
me.

'I don't want to go to the gym, Bonny. I want to go
and see Lisa. It helps.'

'Alice.' Bonny took my hands, 'Don't you think…?
Well, aren't you seeing a bit much of her? I mean, I'm
glad you can talk to her and everything, but…'

'She helps.'

'There's nothing wrong with you,' Bonny said. 'You
had a shit experience ten years ago. And, yes, Mum and
Dad got divorced. All this self-analysis, I think it gives
you problems that aren't even there.'

I didn't go to the gym. I was very good and went to
see Lisa, but privately I was starting to think that Bonny
was right.

Nothing had gone well since I'd started seeing Lisa.
If anything, my life was just a whole lot worse.

Sixty-One

'Are you sure that's a good idea?'

I hadn't come to see Lisa to talk about Roz moving in—I was there today to talk about Hugh, but the second I mentioned it in passing, she jumped in, uninvited.

'Roz is moving in?' She sat there peering at me for a long time and then asking if I had thought this through.

I had. It was a brilliant idea, on so many levels.

Roz was a friend, one who supported me. It showed how much I'd come on—I couldn't care less that she was gay (well, occasionally, I did, when we were out and I just knew people were assuming we were partners). She gave me unconditional love and I was grateful for it and, apart from that, I needed a flatmate!

And I told Lisa the same.

'Another injured bird,' Lisa said. 'You've amassed quite a collection. And what do you mean by "unconditional?"' Still Lisa peered. 'What exactly do you mean by that, Alice?'

'What I said.' I was flustered. 'And I give the same back.'

'Till they leave you.'

Bonny was right—Lisa saw problems when there were none.

'You love people with problems, don't you, Alice? And the juicier the better, because it makes you feel better about your own. You pour all your energy into helping them, but the funny thing is, when they start to get better, you resent them.'

'I don't.'

'Roz is finding her feet. She has to come to terms with being a gay woman, a mother. She is dealing with her family's rejection of her. She's in a relationship, and soon she won't need you as much, Alice, and you will resent her.'

She was wrong—there was nothing I wanted more than to see Roz happy.

'After all you did for her,' Lisa said, and for a second I thought she was impersonating me. 'After all the times you were there for her.'

Er, actually she was impersonating me!

'All the support you gave her—'

'I'm not like that now,' I interrupted.

'Roz will leave, Alice,' Lisa said. 'Just as Nicole did, just as Dan came out of the closet and moved on. Now, you can be stuck in that flat resenting her, or you can be so busy with your own wonderful life that you're able to be genuinely happy for her.'

I didn't respond, but bloody Lisa did.

'If not, I guess there'll always be another little bird to take in, another little broken thing to fix,' Lisa said, and she looked at me. I think she was waiting for me to say something or ask a question, to ask who, but I just sat there.

Didn't want to go there.

'If Roz moves in, there have to be conditions.'

'Conditions?'

'That you allow the other to grow and that, at any time, you are both free to leave.'

And then she went round and round the houses, spoke about sodding boundaries. Nicole was building them now, apparently, Lisa said, and Dan was just starting to.

'And Roz?'

'Roz,' Lisa said, 'arguably has a greater self-loathing than you—which is why you can so easily manipulate her.'

'Oh, so I'm manipulative now?'

'I find you extremely manipulative, Alice.'

What?

'When?'

'Consistently. You try to control the universe with your wishes and your cosmic orders, and when that doesn't work you turn your attention to the human race.'

What the hell was she talking about?

'You try to manipulate everyone.' She stared at her pad as my cheeks burnt. 'Well, almost everyone.'

I didn't ask who she was referring to.

The strange thing with Lisa is she doesn't really give out answers. Oh, she's extremely delighted to voice her opinion when asked, but generally she questions things, questions me, which in turn makes me question myself.

She sort of leads me, not to conclusions, but to a place where I can see.

And often I don't want to.

'As you grow,' Lisa said, 'as you change, there are people who aren't going to like it. People you think will automatically support you are actually going to do everything in their power to hold you back. They like having you around, Alice. They like watching the train wreck of your life, because they get to feel better about themselves.'

Sixty-Two

'Hey.' Roz was lounging on my sofa (she'd practically moved in anyway), looking as fed up as I did. Karan wrapped Lizzie's hair in foil. 'How was it?'

'Enlightening.' I rolled my eyes and Lizzie giggled.

'You've got roots,' Karan warned, as if I didn't know.

Two inches of ginger roots, and my straggly, half-straightened hair was tied back in a ponytail and I was also, as Roz kept telling me, completely broke.

I was (and this shows how far I had come) thinking of buying a mid-brown hair dye from the supermarket. Blonde was bloody hard work, and anyway all the celebs went brown when they got serious.

'Dan dropped round,' Roz said, 'and left something for you.' She gestured to the table. 'And can you talk some sense into my daughter? I'm offering her three weeks in the UK and she's refusing.'

'I can't,' Lizzie said. 'I promised I'd spend New Year with Vince.'

'Then fly out after...' Roz said, then shrugged, but I

could tell she was hurting. 'You're too embarrassed to be seen with me?'

'It's not that.' Lizzie squirmed.

They had come on a long way.

They still fought a lot, but Roz was right: Lizzie kept turning up and clearly wanted a mother. She was just struggling a bit with the new one she'd suddenly got. The thing was, Karan made things easier. It wasn't just that she shamelessly bribed Lizzie with free foils, it was more she was so assured and girly and ahead of the game with it all that she put everyone at ease with the gay thing.

And I think I helped too.

Lizzie seemed a bit fascinated with me really, but, as Lisa had said, watching someone else's train wreck of a life can be quite a relief at times. But Roz had told me that Lizzie thought I was a bit glamorous.

Me.

Anyway, glamorous or not, I'd been seventeen for a very long time—about ten years, in fact—so I knew that scary place well.

'I was the same when I found out about your mum,' I said, and Lizzie looked over. I sort of knew when I caught the plea in Karan's eye that I had to get this right. 'I was so embarrassed; I thought everyone would think that I was as well.'

'I did,' Lizzie said. 'I thought you were her girlfriend.'

And my throat was so tight I didn't even try to swallow, because that had been what I had dreaded except it didn't seem so important now. Maybe I was growing up, but she was still seventeen.

'Really?' Karan pitched in, perhaps seeing I was struggling. 'It never entered my head that Alice was.'

Only she wasn't saying it to appease me, she was giving me the words to give to Lizzie.

We all want to fit in. Even when we rebel we want the rebels to like us.

And if Lizzie was, or one day found out she was, gay, then she'd got the best mum to help her deal with it. But my guess was that she was as straight as an arrow and petrified of what her friends thought. I tried to help her with that.

'I'm the same with Lizzie.' I shrugged and spoke to Karan. 'She's so *not* gay.' Out of the corner of my eyes I watched Lizzie's cheeks pink, and it wasn't a blush, it was relief. I thought about saying more, I thought about elaborating, but it was safer to just leave it there—leave the conversation right out in the open—the best place for it.

They were waffling on, but I wasn't really listening. There were the forms I had shredded. Well, not *the* forms. Dan hadn't rescued them from the shredder and spent the last few weeks piecing them together—no, he'd got some fresh ones, *several sets* of spare ones, and what was more he'd filled one in as best he could.

For personal reasons I emigrated to Australia. For those same reasons, despite passing, I did not achieve the results I had hoped for in my A-Levels.

I have missed music; I have missed exploring my talent and I feel ready to embrace it again.

Dan had stuck a Post-it note on them.
Do it, Alice. x
I looked over to Roz, who was watching me.

'I can't.'

'You can,' Roz said. 'Just.'

'Just?'

'If you sell the car, spend time practising, getting ready for the entrance exam, you can survive for three months.'

'On what?'

'On nothing.' Roz winced. 'You might need to do a couple of casual shifts at the paper.'

'And then what?'

'You get a job for a few months and save up for being a poor student.'

'Do you want some foils?' Karan had finished wrapping up Lizzie's hair.

'I can't afford them,' I said in a martyred voice. 'Actually…' I had a wonderful plan coming together. 'If I get the Brazilian keratin treatment…' Roz was frowning, but I rapidly thought this through. 'If Karan can do that for me, I can manage my own hair. I'll save a fortune on blow jobs.' (That's what we call them.)

'Foils or nothing.' Karan smiled. 'For free.' And I guess she was thanking me for my words to Lizzie. 'Seeing as you're going to be a poor student.'

Ooh, I liked being poor.

Free foils. I bounced over like an eager puppy. All was okay—my friends would look after me!

'If we put in a few at the part line…' Karan was examining my hair '…just to take the edge off the roots.' She was going through my hair like a mother monkey, like she was searching for nits. 'And some around your hairline…'

'Fine.'

It was free; she could do what she liked.

'It will take a few weeks,' Karan said, 'and I'll add more when I can. I'll try and save a bit of product as I go—it's going to take a while.'

And then I watched her squirt orange into a bowl and then she measured out two inches of a colour I don't like that was called red—and where was the lovely pale blue peroxide? Why was she slicing great long strips of silver off when she was only supposed to be doing my roots?

'You can't afford to be blonde any more,' Karan said.

I felt my stomach tighten. 'Then I'll be a brunette.'

'Fine.' Karan shrugged. 'But I'm not doing it.'

'I'll do it myself.'

'This,' Karan said, 'is a one-time offer. I'll take you back to your roots.' She smiled. 'For free.'

'Slowly?'

Karan nodded and I watched as she picked up a length of strawberry-blonde. I watched as the comb weaved through the sandy shade and picked up a few strands and laid them in foil and I felt sick—I swear, I felt sick as I watched her plaster it in red.

Lizzie didn't even dash off when her free foils were done. I could see Roz shining with delight when her moody bitch of a daughter flopped on the sofa and asked for a drink.

Just a normal family, really (these days).

'I thought you were doing this slowly,' I said when Karan's little tub ran out and she mixed up some more.

'There are shades of red—lots and lots of shades of red,' Karan explained impatiently. 'I'm the colour technician!' So she squirted out a nice safe caramel-looking colour and then I felt my throat dry as she added what was surely three inches of red while Roz sliced off more foil strips.

We sat for what seemed like ages. Roz and Lizzie were talking; Karan was painting her toenails. And while in the scheme of things I was just getting my hair done, for me this was huge. Karan refused to let me wash it off in the shower. Instead she did it over the kitchen sink and then she dried it off with a diffuser.

My knee was starting to bob up and down—I just wanted to see.

They were all cooing and nodding and murmuring about a great colour match, as Karan smeared dollops of product through my curls and finally I was allowed to look in the mirror.

I walked into the bathroom and turned on the light (it was dark by now), and I stared at my new reflection.

Think Ronald McDonald meets Shirley Temple.

The funny thing was this time around I kind of liked it.

Sixty-Three

From: Nicole Hunter (nicsalawyer@hotmail.com)
To: alicelydiajameson@hotmail.com
Subject: DELETE THE SECOND YOU READ THIS
             AND CAREFUL HOW YOU REPLY

Hi Alice,

Please don't reply to this. Paul doesn't check my emails or anything, but you know how paranoid I can be.

I haven't been hearing from you much at all lately and I miss you a lot and can't stand the thought of you not coming to my wedding.

I know we weren't getting on so well before I left, and I'm sorry if I was moody—I know I was a pain but I had a lot of trouble at work and I can't tell you how relieved I am to have left the Australia office.

I know you won't believe this, I KNOW how old and sleazy he is, but a few months back, when I was in a bad place—well, I won't go into detail, but Ice Pick Man and I…

I wasn't with Paul then. In fact, we met just after

that. It's just been hell, fronting up to work each day since then. He's never made mention of it, I just couldn't stand working there and seeing him every day knowing what I let him do to me.

I wish I'd spoken to you about it at the time. I was so ashamed, though, I didn't know how.

Please email me or, better, pick up the bloody phone when I ring.

I miss you.

Nicole

I wish she had been able to speak to me.

Or that I'd been able to speak to her.

There's so much I want to say.

Do these men just know when we're feeling like crap? Do we have some invisible sign that only bastards can see?

I could see now how she ran straight into a relationship with Paul. I don't know that Paul's a bastard, but I know Nic deserves better than him, and I am honestly not talking about money.

You went straight into a relationship with Hugh. I can almost hear Big Tits' response if I talk to her about this, except I *know* Hugh's not a bastard. For him, I kept up my façade too well—maybe his guard was down?

Maybe he was so confused about Gemma that he didn't see the nice guys' invisible sign that should have warned him this woman was trouble.

From: Alice
To: nicsalawyer@hotmail.com

I'm sorry I've been quiet. I'm honestly not sulking.
I've had some stuff...

Then I stop writing and I hit 'Delete'.

I don't know what to say. It's not something I can put
in an email and not something I can say on the phone. I
don't know, even if she was here, that I could tell her.

That I even want her to know.

She's one of my best friends, yet I don't want to tell
her, so I fire back an email, taking care not to hit 'Reply'
and making no mention of Ice Pick Man, just in case
Wanker Paul checks it (I'm quite sure he does). I just say
that I'm sorry for being a moody bitch too, and always
glad to hear from her.

I don't want to tell her.

'You don't have to tell anyone anything you don't want
to. Apart from me.' Lisa gives her pussycat smile that
means she's just made a joke and I find myself smiling
back, but she clarifies, because there are so many things
I clearly don't get. 'You don't have to tell me anything
you don't want to.'

Instead of dwelling on Nicole, though, I talk about
my decision to cram for my music entrance exam and
my hope of studying further.

It was going to be, I told Lisa, the hardest three
months of my life.

But since when did she agree with me?

'I think you've already done the hardest bit, Alice.' She
gave me a brief upturn of her lips. 'And you survived it.'

And she wasn't talking about Dad or Hugh, or my
sort of breakdown, or the bank or the job loss or...

She was talking about Lydia.

Okay, that should sustain me, I decided as I paid the annoying, perpetually bubbly receptionist.

I would do this for Lydia; I would practise and practise and practise some more—and it did sustain me, for a few days.

Then dark clouds gathered and I took fifty minutes off to prepare two-minute noodles and pore through endless emails about Nicole's shagging wedding. I was an expert in procrastination and the wedding proved an excellent distraction from advancing my future. She had a coffee theme. I thought at first she was joking. I truly did.

I fired back witty one-liners, or words like latte, cappuccino or frappucino.

And, bloody hell, suddenly the bridesmaids were to be dressed on that theme.

Yes, I knew I should practise more.

I had D-Day coming up soon after all.

Do it for Lydia!

This was my chance, my one chance I had fought so hard for, and I should practise.

And I often did.

Hour upon hour I *did* practise. Just not enough.

I saw some improvement, but I was a 'mature student' (bloody cheek), and I would be getting in on my ability rather than my results—I had to offer more than a technically correct piece.

There was one piece in my head, one piece that maybe I could play well enough. It was the piece I would rather curl under the duvet and hide than attempt again.

I hid under the covers for way too many hours.

Roz would come home from work—and she loved me and she wanted me to do well—but she was scared for me too.

She had the pep talk written for when I failed.

And my hair went redder, thanks to Karan, but Lisa never commented. She didn't comment either when, red in the face, I handed over a copy of the picture of Little Alice. She just clipped it into my (rather thick) file and started talking about my father.

And nothing got any better.

Six weeks into my three-month retreat I knew that I'd left it too late.

'January' from Tchaikovsky's *The Seasons* was the only thing that could possibly save me and I still hadn't looked at the sheet music.

'I can't do it, Bonny.' I sat on her sofa and she offered me wine and I said yes. 'There's no way I can play it. I haven't practised it—I haven't looked at it for ten years. I should be working. I should just give up now and get a job.'

'Alice.' She held my hand and as always she supported me. 'Do you want me to speak to Lex?'

I shook my head; I had let so many people down I couldn't stand to let him down too.

'I put in an application at the supermarket,' I said. 'Look, it won't be for ever...'

'Just till you get your confidence back,' Bonny said. 'Alice, you've tried. I am so proud of you for trying, you've given it your best. You know I'm always here.'

I hadn't given it my best, though. 'Maybe I should give it one last shot?' I swung back to hope. For a second I danced in my head, for a tiny minute I glanced at those examiners hearing my piece, hearing my soul, and then I turned to Bonny. 'If I give it everything, I've got nothing to lose...'

'Whatever you decide,' she said. 'Just don't build up your hopes.'

I slept on her sofa and I felt like shit the next morning.

I always felt like shit after a night with Bonny.

As Dan had felt like shit after a night with me.

I called Dan and he came over, bearing double-shot coffee. He sat with me as, shaking, I told him how little I had actually practised. How the only piece that could really sway things was 'January'—that, in the past, I had worked on it so hard that maybe, just maybe...

'Play it,' Dan said, 'and let's hear what we're dealing with.'

I was shocking.

No kidding—it's a lovely piece but there are some challenging bits (remember the hand crossovers?), and I stuffed it all. It isn't even that hard, but it was one piece that I had excelled at and now I clearly didn't.

'I can't.' I shook my head at the hopelessness of it all.

'Play something else,' Dan said. (That was how bad it was.)

'I don't know anything else well enough.' I screwed up my forehead (easily now my Botox had long since worn off). 'Not at that standard.'

'But you play other pieces so well.'

He didn't understand but he tried.

I sell on emotion—that is what I do best—and, quite simply, I could no longer convey it. Even if I did, I was so far behind technically...

'How often did you used to practise?' Dan's voice broke into my despair.

'Every night.' It was useless; it was hopeless; I wasn't really listening to Dan. I knew I'd left it too late.

'That piece?' Dan pushed. 'How long at night did you practise it for?'

'An hour.' There had been other pieces I had had to work on, but 'January' had always got an hour. 'At least—maybe even two.'

'Let's call it an hour,' Dan said, 'because you *have* played it to standard.'

'Not in a decade.'

'Seven hours a week,' Dan said and he still didn't get it.

'Sometimes I just played it for me.'

'Okay…' He took a breath. 'Let's say ten hours on that piece a week.'

'Five hundred and twenty hours.'

He stared at my bleached skin. 'But you already know it, so say four hundred.'

I had no idea what he was talking about.

'If you work for ten hours a day and take one day off a week, then in six weeks you'll be at three hundred and sixty…'

'You can't play for ten hours a day.' He did not have a fucking clue.

'Says who?'

Said everyone.

Roz had been reading a book on psychology and was worried I was tipping into mania (I had a peek at that chapter and rather hoped that I was—at least I'd get a lot done). Bonny—well, Bonny said that she was seriously worried now, that I should just let it go. And do you know who else didn't think it was such a good idea?

Go on; guess who else wasn't too keen on me giving it my absolute best?

From: Nicole Hunter (nicsalawyer@hotmail.com)
To: alicelydiajameson@hotmail.com
Subject: Worried
Alice
I don't like the sound of this. I've really given it some thought. If you do get in, you've got three maybe four years of study and then what? You'll be over thirty and just starting out. Maybe you should think about getting that job—how nice it will be to get on top of your finances—I know I'd love to have no debts. It's scary the loan Paul's taking on for the coffee shop—I am thinking of cutting down my hours to part-time to help out—early days yet. Anyway, enough of my stuff, this is about you. You have the chance for a clean slate—please think carefully.

I know you are probably thinking this is because I want you to come to my wedding—and, yes, of course I do, but it is not about that, Alice. This is about you.
Nic xxxxxxxx

From: Alice (alicelydiajameson@hotmail.com)
To: nicsalawyer@hotmail.com
Subject: Re: Worried
Hi Nic
Actually your email has nothing to do with me, and neither does it have anything to do with me

coming to your wedding. In fact, I'd go as far to say that it is all about you.

Do you remember when you accused me of being jealous? You were right. I was.

Well, I'm not jealous now.

Can I suggest that you are?

That you are really struggling with the realisation that you are thinking of giving up a fabulous career to work in a fucking coffee shop that, yes, you will own, but why can't he just hire someone?

Yes, I know he needs cheap (slave) labour for a year or so, till the business is running, and that you are hoping you can resume your career, but there might be a baby too by then, or your job will have gone. You'll be barefoot and pregnant in the sodding kitchen, Nic, and you know it.

Alice

Do you want to save the changes to this message?
No.

From: Alice (alicelydiajameson@hotmail.com)
To: nicsalawyer@hotmail.com
Subject: Re: Worried
Hi Nic

I know you are worried about me, and I do appreciate it, but I have given this a lot of thought. I have one last chance to pursue my dream—yep—it might not work, but I'm going to give it my best.

I know how hard you worked for your wonderful

career and the hours after hours you had to put in to get to where you are. I'm just doing the same, Nic, albeit a condensed version. Don't ask me to give it up.

Alice xxxxxxxxxxxxx

PS—how's the dress coming along?

And I hit 'Send' and hoped she read it carefully, because just as her email hadn't been about me, that email was actually all about her.

I had six weeks left.

For six weeks I had to let them all take care of themselves.

No booze, no gossip, no drama.

For six weeks I had to play.

I had a kitchen full of baked beans and two-minute noodles, but do you think they'd let me get on with it?

'You're doing too much.' Bonny was worried. She came over and saw my ravaged face and unwashed body. I was six kilos heavier, thanks to all the carbs, and all I could talk about was 'January'. I don't blame her for being concerned—I mean, I was coming out of a mini-breakdown and had locked myself away with a piano.

She had every right to be worried.

I just didn't need her to be.

I wanted her support and instead I ended up reassuring her. Always her visits drained me.

Roz was twitching about it too, though I don't think it had anything to do with holding me back. It was more that she had moved in and had to listen to it over and over and over and over.

I avoided Lisa as well.

I didn't have time to focus on anything. I was in the zone and I played it, slept it, hummed it.

Dan insisted on one night off a week.

Karan added more foils to my hair on those nights; we ate pizza and we drank wine. But when Dan scuttled back to Matthew at eleven and Roz went off to bed with Karan (Ew! I was still a bit uneasy with that), instead of roaming the flat for more booze and distraction, I went back to my piano.

It was all I thought about.

The neighbours complained.

They banged on the walls; they came to the door. I had a man from the council come and finally, two weeks before my recital, the neighbours cracked and...

They called the police!

I stood in my dressing gown and I laughed when I opened the door.

I stood there and laughed as a policewoman gave me a warning and then the sexy copper beside her grinned too.

All the debauchery that had gone on at the flat and the police had been called when I was finally being good.

So good I didn't slip him my phone number.

(I was, I admit, tempted.)

Sixty-Four

I was at the Conservatory. Roz and Dan were there too, hanging around in the gardens as I did my aural and theory and then it was time for my recital.

As I set up my music I had a sudden panic—with good reason.

'January' is about winter and January is in summer in Australia.

Gawd! Why the hell didn't I think of that?

Then I blew out a breath and realised it was too late to do a thing about it.

My moment was here.

I got through it. Most of it, I think, rather well, at least technically; and then it came to 'January', my last piece. If I wanted to nail it, I had hopefully left the best till last, because even if the other pieces were more complicated, this was the one where I shone.

Or rather, I had shone.

Did I play it for Hugh or for Lydia?

No.

Because no matter how much I loved them, it didn't count if I didn't first love me.

So I played it for myself.

I wasn't that eager little girl begging for them to please just choose me.

I could hear the music I was making and it was the very best I could do—it was the very best of me. If it wasn't good enough for them, then that was okay; my best was the best I could do. My fingers stretched and they slid and I was back in January, when she had been made. I was there with the cold and the lows and the still that is winter, the light and the dark and never-ending grey. It was like a transfusion, that is what music played from the soul is like, like my bone marrow was being infused. I was the best I could ever be, I was in the zone, I was over the rainbow. I wasn't Alice Lydia Jameson— for a moment there, I got to be Dorothy.

I knew I had stepped into my future; I could see it in their faces and I knew it had moved them, because no matter how many times you hear a piece, when it comes from the soul and it vibrates up to heaven, it is more than music, it is like oxygen.

Roz burst into tears when we stepped outside and even Dan's eyes were glassy. They had heard me and knew I had held the room and I knew something else too…

My life was starting again.

Sixty-Five

Here's a shocking fact for you.

You know those stools the checkout chick sits on when you pay for your groceries?

Well, in Australia she stands!

Can you believe it?

I couldn't.

I had lived there for ten years and never noticed.

On my first day at the supermarket I asked for my stool and the fifteen-year-old who was training me up just laughed.

It was fun, though, in a back-breaking, ankle-swelling way.

Beep, beep, beep.

And after two days there I had worked out that I wasn't the first, neither would I ever be the last, who had their credit card declined.

I wore my red blouse and my name tag with something very close to pride, even though it clashed horribly with my hair, which was tied back all the time but still managed to work its way out to form an orange halo by the end of my shift.

I was an official redhead again.

I had the type of hair that caused little old ladies to look up from their shopping and tell me how wonderful it was, though of course, they beamed, I probably hated it.

Some days I did and some days I didn't, it all just depended.

Lisa had never mentioned my changing hair colour or my curls and neither had she mentioned the photo of me as a child, until a few weeks after my recital. I had a five p.m. appointment after a very long shift (standing). I was quite relaxed about going. In fact, I had bought a large latte and smiled and stood when she came out and called my name.

I followed her into the little room, sat in my middle seat, didn't take a sweet because I was *really* putting weight on. It wasn't just about vanity. I couldn't afford a new wardrobe.

We chatted and had an update. I had seen her only once since my crazy six weeks; I had told her about the recital and said that I was still waiting to hear. I also told her about my job. I had made a couple of friends, or rather friendly acquaintances. They were older than me and had children and really we did not have much in common, but we went and had coffee together in our twenty-minute mandatory break.

I don't know why she chose that day. It was late, I was tired, but instead of banging on about my dad or the divorce or her latest favourite—*boundaries*—we spoke about me.

Or rather Little Me.

She handed me the photo of myself and asked me what I thought of her. I filled up with tears because I wanted to say that I loved her, that, hey, actually, I had been quite cute. But all I could see was a pinched face and scruffy hair and eyes that were angry.

'I don't know.'

I could feel her thinking. I could feel her tentative silence, feel her weighing things up, deciding perhaps whether to leave it for now, and I fervently hoped that she would.

'I've had to bite my tongue these past few weeks...' I stared at the photo as Lisa spoke. 'I didn't know you had curly hair till Roz brought you in that day—I was aware you always made an effort with your appearance, but I hadn't quite grasped to what extent. Every time I have seen you since then, my first instinct is to comment on your hair.' I sat there and stared at the photo. 'I think it is gorgeous, by the way, but I am telling you this because I have given it some thought. Always, I want to comment on your hair. I expect you get that a lot.' I gave a shrug. 'It's striking, Alice—you have red hair and wild curls and it is, however you feel about it, the first thing people notice. People comment, strangers discuss it in front of you—I am quite sure of that because, when I spoke to Roz and she told me you were in a bad way, when you stepped out of the car and walked into the office, despite all that was going on, I noticed your hair. Despite your obvious devastation, still I felt inclined to comment, and I'm very glad now that I didn't.

'Sometimes I am sure you didn't need the attention, especially growing up. You stand out. No matter what sort of day you are having, no matter what is going on in your life, your hair is the first thing people notice.'

It was true.

It was true.

'I hated my hair.' I stared at the photo and all I could see was why.

'Alice, you seem to think your first sexual experience was when your hair was straight and you were sleek and groomed.'

'It was.'

'No.' Lisa's voice was firm. 'Gus was grooming you already. You could have looked like Worzel Gummidge that day and the outcome would have been the same. He had already been completely inappropriate.'

I stared at the photo but I still loathed that little girl.

'I don't see an angry little girl when I look at that picture. I see a very worried little girl.'

I shook my head, because I hadn't been worried—at least I don't think so—I just hated having my picture taken.

'She knew a secret,' Lisa said, and my heart stilled. 'A secret that would completely destroy her family.' I felt my intestines turn to liquid. 'And she knew that for a fact, because it had happened once before. If she told anyone what she had seen that day at the pub, if her mum found out her father was doing those things, then her family would surely break up again, her mother would be devastated...' I could hear someone crying and I realised it was me. 'What a terrible burden for that little girl.'

'Mum would have fallen apart.'

She ignored what I said.

'What a terrible burden for a little superstitious child

who catastrophises everything to think she held her family's destiny in her hands.'

'But I did.'

'Alice.' For the first time ever I heard sympathy in her voice. 'I'm quite sure that your mum knew your father was cheating again.'

'No.'

'Yes.'

'No.'

'Your mum had long since realised that nothing, *nothing* she could do would change him.'

'It would have broken them up.'

'Maybe,' Lisa said, 'though I doubt it—I'm sure your dad had a good few years in him still, of making sure your mother felt like shit.'

I know I swear like a sailor, but Lisa never does and my eyes jerked up.

'Even if it had ended the marriage, that wasn't your problem. You should have been allowed to be busy getting on with your childhood. They were grown-ups, it was their marriage to either make or break.'

And I stared at the photo and remembered, because if I got to be Dorothy, then they'd both go out together. They'd both come and see me, and I'd dazzle and be wonderful and it would all be okay.

'Then a few years later you had your own secret. A secret that would ruin your life, end your promising career, devastate your mum, break up your sister's marriage, your father would track down Gus and kill him...' I was crying but it was just a choking sound. 'Another catastrophe.'

'Because it would have been.'

'Why?'

'I'd have ended up a single mum in a crap flat, with a crap job.'

'Says who?'

And I was really crying then, because I'd fulfilled the prophecy, just minus Lydia.

'Alice, your mother's a nurse; she sometimes worked on Maternity. She should surely have been able to cope with a teenage pregnancy.'

'She wouldn't have.'

'Then that's her problem,' Lisa said. 'The same way if your pregnancy stopped your sister from moving to Australia, threatened her marriage, it would not have been your problem either. And if your father had managed to put in an appearance, he wouldn't have killed Gus. Oh, he'd have made a few noises to petrify you...' She shook her head. 'Alice, with the right support you might have been just fine. You might have chosen an abortion, or you might have decided to keep the pregnancy; you could have looked at adoption, or you might have considered deferring your studies.'

'It was more complicated than that.'

'Of course it was,' Lisa said. 'Because you make it so, because that is the way you are wired and no one ever took that into consideration when they were dealing with you.'

And then she did something she had never done before, even when I told her about Lydia, or since, when I've had other stuff come out. She came and sat next to me and gave me a cuddle and I wept into that sixty-year-old crepe chest and *how* grateful I was for her understanding.

Sixty-Six

I was weary from revelation; it was twenty-five past six when I got home.

I would have killed for a drink, and I think I did deserve one, but for the shagging greater good and all that I chose to check my email.

From: Nicole Hunter (nicsalawyer@hotmail.com)
To: alicelydiajameson@hotmail.com
Subject: Re: Update
Hi Alice
Loads to tell you!
Not sure where to start.
I know I said that my job's been great, and I guess it was. The thing is, the hours are ridiculous.
Part-time there would be like a full-time job anywhere else! As Paul pointed out, with the coffee shop opening in two weeks and the hours he'll have to put in we would hardly see each other.
We want kids ASAP—and there is no way I can work and be the mum I want to be, so I have decided to

go in with Paul—just for the first couple of years. That way if we do have children I can bring them into the café and work as well. Then, once the café is more established, I can go back to law.

I've given this loads of thought and to tell the truth, now my decision is made, it's actually a relief. Work has been so stressful. It's going to be bliss having time with Paul and at least I'll be able to concentrate on my wedding now.

I have enclosed the hotel prices where the reception is being held and a list of a few local pubs that are a bit cheaper. If you stay at the hotel you will need to book soon.

Love and hugs

Nicole

PS—give me some gossip about you. You've gone terribly quiet again. How is work at the shop?

Nicole's love life was like a really bad soap opera. Every week night at six-thirty she flew through the flat door with the latest instalment and, even though you knew how it was going to end, knew it was heading for disaster, still you found yourself watching from behind your fingers, scarcely able to believe someone could really be so stupid where men are concerned.

And she was *surely* heading for disaster.

Big time.

Which meant, yet again, yours truly would be left to pick up the pieces.

I'm sure you've noticed I'm repeating myself lately.

I understand now that that's what people do.

We make the same mistakes over and over.

We repeat and repeat and we fuck up and we mess up in the same old ways…

The universe *is* kind, though—it gives us chance after chance to grow, to put right, but it's up to us to take those chances.

Well, I'm sure I've read it somewhere, and I tell Roz that when she comes in and swears and bitches as she reads the email from Nicole, and Dan does the same. 'This has nothing to do with the universe and second chances,' Dan says. 'I told you—Paul's just a wanker.'

'So what should I do?' I asked. 'What should I say to Nicole?'

And it was then I realised the answer—precisely nothing.

Oh, I could point out that surely her full-time wage would be a good thing to fall back on, or that her fantastic new husband could surely afford an au pair if ever she did have kids, and, hell, it would have two sets of grandparents nearby, but I knew Nicole knew all that already.

The truth—if it came from me—would cost our friendship, because Nicole, quite simply, didn't want to hear it.

This lesson wasn't mine. It was Nicole's.

Sixty-Seven

It didn't come when I was least expecting it.

Because I never *stopped* thinking about it.

I was hanging out for the post if I was home, racing back to the mailbox if I wasn't.

I'd always avoided envelopes but I was *desperate* for this one—and then here it was, the big white envelope with my official confirmation. It was the first envelope Roz had let me open in months, and I stared at the offer and I was so proud and humbled and scared and I didn't know what to do.

'Let's tell Bonny!' Roz said.

'I'll ring her.'

'No. Let's go over tonight—ring her and tell her that we'll pop over.'

I didn't think too much about it, Roz and Bonny had become sort of friends and Lizzie sometimes babysat the kids. It wasn't till I walked in and saw the cake and balloons and my nephews dancing around in little hats all excited that I realised this was a party.

For me.

Bonny gave me a hug but then she was busy dealing with the monkeys. Lex said he was very proud too—and then we rang Mum, who cried, and Eleanor, who was out, and life couldn't get any nicer. It got more complicated instead.

Lex called Bonny down and she was so pale and almost shaky that for a moment I thought they were going to say they were breaking up.

'We've got something for you,' Bonny started, but then her voice was wobbly and she turned to Lex. 'You tell her.'

'We're proud of you, Alice,' Lex said. 'It almost killed us not to help you out, but you had to do it yourself.'

'You've helped me out enough.'

'But you did it.' Lex smiled. 'You've dug yourself out of that hole, and you deserve a bit of a break.' He handed me an envelope and I opened it and there was a plane ticket. Ten days in London and I was flying out with Roz.

'I've booked the pub over the road for the wedding,' Roz said. 'You can share my room, so long as you don't mind...'

'You can see Mum and Eleanor and the kids.' Bonny smiled, but her eyes were glassy, and I was quite sure she and Lex had had a row about this, and I got it then. I fully got what Lisa had been trying to tell me that day.

Because I repeated her words to myself, not quite verbatim but enough that I finally understood.

Stuck in that house, worrying about you, doing everything she can to help you, doing everything she can to keep you from leaving.

'You just make sure you come back,' Bonny said when

it was time for us to leave. She hugged me tightly, told me she was proud of me, but I could feel her shoulders shaking and I wanted to fix her, I wanted to comfort her, I wanted to tell her I would stay the same and never ever change—but that had come close to killing me.

I beamed at Roz when we were home.

I did a little dance with my ticket in hand and told her I was delighted.

Had a little tinkle on the piano and sang 'Maybe It's Because I'm a Londoner...'

And then I crawled into bed and I curled up into a ball. For the first time in weeks I wanted a Kalma.

But I didn't have one.

And I didn't have a drink either.

I curled up in bed and told myself what Lisa said to say when I got scared.

That this too will pass.

And it would. In a few short weeks I'd see Hugh again, and then I'd be back to restart my life.

I'd dealt with it all—the banks and the taxman, my hair, work, the mental stuff. I'd mapped out a future...a real future...but the hardest part was going to be facing Hugh.

Seeing again what I'd lost.

This too will pass.

Except I didn't want it to.

I didn't want closure because then it would really be over.

Sixty-Eight

'What's an MR?'

Roz, who was cleaning up before we headed off, and who had read every bill, every demand, every receipt had, while cleaning, found my pyramid and order to the universe.

Did she fold it up and put it back under its little pyramid? Did she do the polite thing and pretend not to notice?

No, she stood and read and tried to decipher for a while, and then she had the nerve to ask me how to break my secret code.

'It doesn't matter.'

'"Sexy. Rich. Professional. Doctor. Lawyer. Good looking. Fantastic dress sense. MR. Brunette, raven or blond…"' She started to laugh. 'What is it? A shopping list?'

'Leave it, Roz.'

She started really laughing. Then she saw my face and tried not to, and when I walked off she followed me into my bedroom. I sat on the sofa with my head in my hands. She didn't have to try not to laugh, she was serious now. She sat down beside me and I took the list and stared at it.

'He was *it*.'

'There'll be others.'

'I don't want others.' Or maybe I did. 'You know…' I wasn't crying, just shaky, and there was a flare of anger too. 'He went—he knew the state I was in and he just…' I balled the list in my fist and then I flicked those tiny Russian dolls off my bedside table as easily as he had discarded me. 'Not a phone call, nothing; he didn't care how he'd left me.'

And I felt Roz still.

I felt the silence and looked over at her, at lovely Roz, who stopped lying the day she came out; I looked at her little pink face and the worry in her eyes and I realised I was missing something.

'He emailed me.'

'When?'

She couldn't look at me, so she covered her face with her hands and pressed her fingers into her eyes. 'A few times,' she said. 'Quite a few times.'

'Saying what?' I begged. 'Fucking show me!' I demanded.

She was all sort of nervous and shaky as she logged in.

I was beside myself, desperate, demented; I was peering through a foggy window and finally there would be answers—finally I would be able to see.

But there was nothing.

Or a little, and it revealed nothing.

You may not know this sender. Mark as safe | Mark as junk

From: Hugh Watson (hughdrwho@hotmail.com)
To: andersonrosalind@hotmail.com
Subject: Re: personal
Hi Roz

I hope you don't mind me emailing you, especially as I am asking you not to tell Alice that I have.

I was wondering if you could let me know how she is. I was concerned...

I won't go on, but that was pretty much it, and Roz hadn't replied at first, but then he sent another one, saying he was *very* concerned this time.

From: Roz Anderson (andersonrosalind@hotmail.com)
To: hughdrwho@hotmail.com
Subject: Re: personal
Hi Hugh,

I'm going to be honest: I'd prefer that you didn't email. It puts me in an awkward...

There were lots of them and I'll spare you all the details and let you race through them as I did. I just read them like the Bionic Woman (my mum had every episode on video and when we were little she watched them over and over), trying to get to what I did not know.

He was very concerned, he said again.

He'd been concerned for a while before the row.

I was no longer his concern, Roz had replied to him. He had made that perfectly clear.

Go, Roz!

Should he email Alice to ask, perhaps? Hugh had suggested.

It was then that Roz had told him that I was doing okay and perhaps it would be better not to contact me.

He appreciated her response and he told her some more.

He'd been increasingly concerned (okay, we get the picture).

He had tried to ignore, on many occasions, and to give me the benefit of the doubt. When I'd wanted to go back to the hotel that day his phone had broken it had hit him—I was like the patients on the ward waiting for drug time. He had seen my agitation and he had tried to ignore it, to justify it.

But he couldn't apparently.

He was aware he had overstepped the mark in his assassination of me (okay, he didn't use *that* word, but I think that was what he meant) and he would appreciate knowing how I was doing.

I was getting there, Roz had told him—it was stressing her, and she felt very conflicted, and, really, she would rather not give updates. Alice was doing fine. He could stop worrying now.

And he had.

There was no more correspondence.

Sixty-Nine

I can never decide how I should display them.

All apart.

All together.

I scrabbled on the floor and found them, worried I'd lost the teeny-tiny one, but I found her in the join between the carpet and the wall.

I put them all back on my bedside table but I was worried about losing the little one again, so I slotted them inside each other. They were safer together while I was away.

They belonged together.

Nesting inside each other.

And then I went for my appointment with Lisa.

I hadn't even realised I was lost when I had met her and, when I had realised I had wandered around in circles for what felt like for ever. But with a lot of guidance, an eventual humongous effort from me and loads of help from my friends, suddenly things were becoming clearer.

Suddenly I was on the edge, looking in at the centre, and I was able to see what my father's leaving had done.

I could see how his treatment of women had affected not just his wife but his children.

All of it I could see.

That when my hair was straight and I was thin I felt sleek and groomed and in control.

I could see the personality I had been born with and how it struggled with a sometimes cruel world.

All of it I could see now, but Lisa and I differed on one vital point—well, it was vital for me.

I obsessed about men—any male attention and I glowed. With Gus, with my dad when he had taken us out, with the best man at Bonny's wedding and the many, many that had followed on from there. Hugh had been the last, Lisa pointed out, so I was still stuck: I still hadn't learnt how to move on.

She read all the emails I had printed out.

I had pored over them and she read them in a minute at best, then folded them up and handed the little package that contained my heart back to me.

'You went out for a few weeks—Hugh admitted from the start that he wasn't sure if it was over with Gemma.'

'He ended it with her before he slept with me.'

'Even if that's true,' she said carefully, 'clearly he didn't end it well enough because Gemma got on a plane.'

'She was upset,' I argued. 'If I'd passed on the message—'

'Alice,' she interrupted, 'this isn't about a message being passed on. This is about how you were falling apart. Hugh couldn't have made it clearer when he left that it wasn't anything to do with Gemma flying over. He was building up to leaving anyway.'

I hated that the most.

'And you've heard from Nicole that he's back with Gemma? That they're planning a wedding?'

Correction—I hated that bit the most.

'I know it's over...' I hadn't cried over Hugh and still I didn't, still I couldn't. There was a piece of me that couldn't even let myself mourn him, because it was such a black place; I didn't think I could go there yet and carry on. But I stood on the edge of that circle and stared at it for a moment, stared at me and Hugh and what for a little while we had been—the glimpse of what a relationship could be—and I didn't think I could ever get there again.

'You will,' Lisa said. 'When you're ready.'

'But not with Hugh?'

'What do you want me to say here, Alice?'

Not the truth, my eyes pleaded, so I bargained instead. 'Do you believe in love? I mean, love can be real, even if it only lasts a few weeks...'

'Alice.' She stepped in then. My hour was nearly up and she wasn't going into the red for Hugh. 'Real love doesn't end after a few weeks.'

The snake-shaped sweet I was holding in my hands and playing with snapped then. It just snapped and so too did the last bit of hope I had for Hugh and me.

'Your future is waiting for you.' I gritted my teeth. She was daytime TV and a trip round the garden centre looking at the water features all in one.

A book of clichés but with very big tits.

She was also right.

She wished me well for my trip away, booked me in

an appointment for the day after I got back (after ten days with my family I would no doubt need it), and she even gave me a copy of the Serenity Prayer, to read, she said, when things got a bit too much.

I just prayed I didn't have an accident on the way home from my appointment and some well-meaning paramedics found it in my purse and assumed I had *issues.*

Which I did, of course.

It just wasn't all that I was.

So Hugh and I were over and it was right and healthy, and of course I had to move on, but not even the sweet snake in my mouth as I paid my bill and then walked to the tram could take away that last taste of bitterness.

It tasted bitter because I was bitter, bitter and angry with myself, because I had lost him. Sort of Bonny's Lex and the straight version of Dan all rolled into the perfect guy for me.

He had been that good.

Seventy

We were an odd little crowd at the airport.

Bonny said she had a migraine, but I knew the dark glasses were there so I didn't see that she was crying, yet the tears kept trickling out.

'You go and have a ball,' Lex said, and hugged me goodbye.

'I'll get there one day! Give Nicole my love.' Dan grinned and he cuddled me. I was against his chest and I could hear the thud, thud of his heart, and I loved him— just not in that way. I gave Matthew a hug too.

I kind of liked him now.

Maybe.

Okay, yes. I liked him. (BTW, you'd certainly have no trouble spotting it with him. He's too ordered, like Nicole actually, but I now realised Dan needed a bit of sensible order because, for a while there, he walked on the wild side too.)

'Come back.' I closed my eyes as Bonny held me tighter.

'Of course I'll be back. It's just ten days, Bonny.'

And then it was my turn to walk through the doors and I knew how my sister was feeling as she watched me leave.

You have my absolute permission to shoot me if I ever describe myself as jaunty, but I was shiny and *ready*, as my time came to go through the doors.

I can't even remember what music the customs officers were playing. You'd have to ask Bonny.

I was going back.

I was moving forward, by going back.

I was ready.

Seventy-One

My paranoia as to people thinking I'm gay when out with Roz has been slightly merited.

I mean, had I been trying to pull on this trip home, it would have proven difficult.

Roz was finding her own style now—lots of linen trousers and blouses and flat shoes.

She smelt great. She even wore make-up, but it was still—well, kind of obvious.

I accepted the quizzical frowns when she cuddled me because I started bawling at Singapore Airport because Hugh had once said he liked it, and when I had a little panic on the descent to Heathrow and she held my hand, I didn't care that two horrible teenagers nudged each other and giggled.

I guess they thought I was the girly one.

Mum had known I was bringing a friend and the second she opened the door I could tell she was petrified of Roz, but Roz was so used to that, that she soon put Mum at ease. I left Roz chatting away with her in the kitchen as I roamed about the house, checking out the changes.

It was the day before Christmas Eve and we were too excited to sleep so we took the tube to Oxford Street. Even Mum came along, and Roz took a hundred photos and we bought last-minute presents and enjoyed the mayhem, and then it was back home and Mum refused Roz's offer to help with dinner, but gave me a wide-eyed look and nodded her head towards the kitchen.

I had been summoned.

I was in my old room, she explained. Roz was in Bonny's till Christmas night, when she'd have to have the sofa because Eleanor, Noel and the kids would be staying. Mum would sleep on a camp bed in the back room, so Eleanor and Noel would have hers and the kids would be in Bonny's, which had once been Bonny's and mine. Eleanor always had her own room—it's really too confusing to explain.

'That's fine,' I said patiently, because Mum always gets in a lather about room arrangements.

'Why don't I put the camp bed in your room tonight?' Mum said. 'I could set it up now.'

'Why?'

'Well, it would save us all moving our things around. You and Roz can share. I can set up Bonny's old room for the kids.' (I will spare you all the logistics of the conversation—I'm sure you've had one similar.)

'Just leave it as it is,' I said, turning to go.

'It would make things easier,' Mum said.

I don't know why, but though I'd matured a great deal over the past months, a few hours back home and I was seventeen again.

'I don't want to share!' I whined. I didn't. No matter how much I hated having the flat to myself, I loved having my own room—and it was the same here. Roz chats till she's unconscious and then she snores and then she gets up at some ungodly hour like seven. I'd put up with it for the wedding 'cos I couldn't afford otherwise, but I didn't want to share my bedroom.

I almost stamped my foot.

It was like being in a time warp, really.

'I'm trying to make this easy on all of us,' Mum said.

'Why can't you just leave it as it is—?'

'Alice!' she interrupted. 'It might take a bit of getting used to, but Roz seems lovely. You're the happiest I've seen you in a long time.' *She doesn't...?* a little voice said. *She doesn't actually think...?* 'Now, I'll put the camp bed in your room. I'm not going to come in and say goodnight, so what your arrangements are behind closed doors...' *Yes, she bloody well does!*

'Mum,' I said, 'Roz and I—well, we're not...'

'Alice, I'm not blind,' Mum said.

'Roz is,' I said, 'but I'm not.'

'I'm not going to get upset.' Mum was very patient. She was putting on a very reasonable voice. 'You don't have to pretend to me.'

And I stood there in the kitchen and realised how far we'd come.

I wasn't hysterical that she had dared to think...

Mum wasn't having kittens that maybe I was...

I started to laugh.

'Mum...' I was laughing so much I was crying and in the end Mum was laughing too. 'I'm not a lesbian!'

We were a bit hysterical really.

'Oh.' She looked a bit disappointed once she had calmed down. 'But if you were,' she checked, 'I mean if you had been, did I handle it well?'

We had the best evening.

Mum and Roz just hit it off. So much so I went and had a bath.

I could hear Roz and Mum laughing and chatting and it was nice to be able to relax, to know they were getting on. I came downstairs and they didn't stop their conversation.

'I've had three,' Mum said. 'I know exactly what it's like.'

'Yeah, but Lizzie had to put up with a lot,' Roz said. 'So did mine.'

I was combing my hair and pretending to watch the TV but just listening.

'You weren't gay!' Roz pointed out.

'No, but I had loads going on when they were teenagers—all the way through, really. To tell you the truth, Roz, I was in a right mess, trying to keep tabs on him all the time, and then he went off with some lovely young thing. He was always stalling with money. I know I wasn't great with the girls, but I was trying to keep things going...' Mum said.

And they chatted on, about how hard it was dealing with your kids' issues when you had issues of your own, and I felt not jealous, not excluded, but an outsider. I heard a different side to my mum and a different side to Roz too.

'You need to get out there,' Roz said later, and Mum just harrumphed.

'I wouldn't know where to start.'

'I didn't either. Get your hair done,' Roz said, 'join a social club.' Mum just shrugged. 'You should do something just for you.'

'I keep meaning to ask Noel to do my teeth,' Mum admitted. 'That's Eleanor's husband—he's a cosmetic dentist.'

'You should, Gloria.' Roz nodded furiously.

Yep, Mum does have a name, and I listened as Roz used it.

I have a pretty spectacular friend.

I could never have had the night I had with Mum without Roz there. Could never have learnt so much about Gloria.

We showed Mum YouTube and she was delighted. She kept asking if it was legal as she typed in her searches, pushing the enter button as if she expected the police to jump out of the screen and arrest her, but she soon got over it.

There was even the *Bionic Woman* there.

I lay in my bed that night. I could hear Roz snoring across the hall, Mum was back on YouTube. 'I Wanna Go Back' wafted up the stairs, and then it stopped and I could hear Mum flicking the lights off.

It felt good to be home.

Seventy-Two

Christmas Eve, was...well, Christmas Eve.

Hand up turkey's bum, dashing to corner shop for Sellotape, and then at two p.m. Roz asked what I had got Mum for Christmas. I showed her the perfume I had bought at the airport and the next three hours were spent with the last of the last shoppers, choosing a necklace and nice jumper for her.

And Christmas Day was Christmas Day at the Jamesons'.

I will spare you the details except to say it was nice and, like any family at Christmas, it had its share of drama.

I worried that Roz would get bored. I mean, it was her first time in London, but she was so genuinely happy to be around us mad lot that I realised how much she must miss her own family.

Eleanor was a misery—excused herself three times during Christmas dinner.

I could see Mum's lips disappearing; saw my niece and nephew getting awkward when she had been gone one puke too long, and went upstairs to check on her.

'Everything okay?' I asked as she came out of the loo.

'Fine.' She brushed past me and I had that terrible repeat feeling again. I saw Eleanor rinsing her mouth in the sink and then she went to go downstairs, and just as Lex had to me, at this very spot, I called her back.

'You *can* talk to me.'

I never really expected her to.

Eleanor is an enigma, this distant older figure who happens to be my sister.

I never expected her to start crying.

'I'm pregnant.'

This time last year I'd have congratulated her. This year I stood there.

'I can't tell Noel.'

We sat in her old room, filled with her kids' presents. The kids are twelve and thirteen. Maybe she and Noel didn't want to start over again.

'Doesn't he want any more?'

'He'd be delighted.' She was crying in earnest now. 'It might not be his.'

Is it just mine, or are all families like this?

I stood there as she crumpled and asked myself that question. I got a very rapid answer.

Yes.

Yes.

Bloody hell, *yes*!

If you look, if you take your blinkers off, if you dare to be honest, if you dare to ask and stop for long enough to hear.

Well, I stand corrected.

My family isn't dysfunctional—it's crazy, yes, but completely normal.

'I can't have an abortion…'

'Okay.' I sat with my arm (awkwardly) around her. (I've never cuddled Eleanor before.)

'I don't want to break up the marriage,' she sobbed, 'but if he finds out…'

'Do you have to tell him?' I was all for honesty (well, not really, but I was trying now), but if it had been but a moment's madness… I guess I was offering options— but you may have realised by now that when my family fucks up they do it in style.

She stood up, went into her bag, pulled out her purse and her shaky, skinny fingers dug inside and she took out a picture.

She wanted to be caught, I realised.

I mean, you don't carry a picture of your lover in your purse if you don't want to be found out.

'What if the kids went in your bag? Or Noel?' I said as she handed me the photo.

I looked and looked and I looked again.

There was going to be no mistaking who the father was when this baby arrived!

'He's my personal trainer,' Eleanor said and I started to sweat because was I supposed to not comment that he was black?

I honestly didn't know what to do. I should have just stayed quiet, I suppose, like Lisa does, but I stared at the photo and then I looked at Eleanor.

'Whatever happens…' I watched her flinch as she braced herself for an incoming platitude '…your baby is going to have beautiful teeth!'

We laughed.

On her worst day, with more to follow, we sat on

the bed and laughed, a sort of hysterical laugh, because sometimes that's all you can do.

I told her to tell Mum.

She said Mum wouldn't understand.

I said try her—Mum's a lot stronger than she seems. And if she doesn't understand when you tell her, find someone to help who does understand, and that included me.

And by the time we were down the stairs and back in the dining room I realised I had another sister.

It was Christmas and it was fab and then it was the lull that preceded New Year. There was some place I needed to be and I did not want Mum to come with us.

I made some vague excuse, and I could tell she felt left out as she waved us off, but there was no question of bringing her.

It was a fifteen-minute walk to the hospital. Roz had rung from Australia and there was a package for me to collect.

The medical records department was suitably dreary. The miserable clerk said that it was only skeleton staff on over the Christmas break and that I'd have to come back in a couple of weeks. I nearly turned to go, but Roz was insistent. She had it already arranged, she said. Could she check again if there was a package for me?

I stood there sweating, sure I would hear that due to an administration error those little pieces of paper that had meant so little at the time but seemed vital today were lost.

And I promised I wouldn't make a scene.

I didn't exactly have the right to, ten years on.

Whatever happened, I had promised I would just accept it.

But I got a large envelope that I wasn't ready to open, so we walked to the cemetery.

I had no idea where to go, but Lex had given Roz instructions and off we headed—to stare at some signature in a book of remembrance, probably.

I was determined not to fall apart—not just for me. I wouldn't do it to Roz.

The grass was icy and it crunched under our feet. We sat on a bench and I opened the envelope.

There was a little armband, 'Baby Jameson', and it had the date.

There were photos too—I looked so young and scared and she looked so tiny and perfect.

There were footprints and handprints and I traced the outline of her toes just as I had that day, and suddenly I wanted to hold her.

There was the little yellow blanket too, a sort of nappy square in faded lemon, and I buried my face in it and inhaled. There was no scent of her, but there was the feel of her, and I held it on my face for a while and I wanted to hold her so badly, how much I cannot adequately describe.

Roz sat in silence till I was ready and then we headed over to a little wall.

And there it was.

There, amongst so many plaques, we found it easily.

> *Lydia Jameson*
> *You are loved*

Not *were*.

I was so grateful that Lex hadn't written *were*, because

till now, by me, she hadn't properly been. I didn't want love to be past tense, some proxy love I would later read about and agree with—I'm glad for the time Lex gave me with that single word to catch up.

To grow up.

Lydia Jameson, you *are* loved.

Seventy-Three

I don't think I could have done this trip without Roz.

Actually, I know I couldn't.

Dad, Lucy and Charlotte had been away over Christmas and were heading off skiing for New Year and could cram me in for a couple of hours on our way to the wedding.

After the wedding I was heading back to Mum's for a couple of days and Roz would be picking up Lizzie and doing the touristy stuff.

'Stay for another week?' Mum asked, and I really wanted to. I wanted more time with her, but I had shifts lined up at the supermarket and I knew that I couldn't.

'You should think about coming out soon for a holiday,' Roz said for the umpteenth time, only this time I realised that Mum was actually considering it.

'Where are you and Lizzie staying?' Mum asked.

'Bed and breakfasts and a couple of pubs,' Roz said, and her face was going pink with pleasure and pride as her new friend Gloria continued.

'Why don't you both stay here?'

* * *

Dad wasn't home.

Nope, he was freezing on the golf course, but Lucy assured me he would be there soon.

She made us coffee, and she'd bought nice cakes from Marks and Spencer and made a little selection plate for us.

And then she offered us some wine.

'No, thanks,' I said.

'Sure?' she checked, sloshing some into her glass.

'Not for me,' Roz said.

And it had nothing, *nothing* to do with being strong. I just knew that if I scraped even the top off my inhibitions I would rip in two.

Charlie came home.

She has a pony, you see, so couldn't be there to greet us.

All long-limbed and buck-toothed (not the pony, Charlotte, but the teeth were about to be corrected by Noel, Lucy hurriedly pointed out), she opened the present I had bought as an afterthought at the airport, then dashed off. She had Lucy's tiny frame and Dad's air of confidence and she was quite a stunning mix.

It was pretty tense, like sitting in the dentist's waiting room, so I excused myself and headed to the loo, then came back down the stairs and Lucy was waiting.

'He just rang.' She gave a too-bright smile. 'He's on his way; he'll only be five minutes.'

'No problem.'

'Alice…' I so did not need this, I so wanted to keep walking, but she didn't read the signs and kept talking. 'I'm sorry this is awkward.'

'It's not,' I assured her. 'Dad will be here soon.'

'Yes,' she insisted, 'it is awkward.'

'It's really not,' I said.

'I know you hate me...' And thank God I hadn't had a drink or I'd have punched her lights out. 'For taking him from your mother.'

I didn't say the first thing that came into my head. There was a pause, because that's what I do now—I employ the pause where I think, where I stop, where I step back before I speak.

You took him from me, you stupid bitch.

You justify it because my mother was too fat, too lazy, too slow. You don't blame him for not wanting her, but what man doesn't want his kids?

Did you think about that?

When he should have been a father, when he should have been dealing with teenagers and angst and doing what a father bloody well should, you took him from that. You took him away and you stopped him from being the father he should have been.

You had your baby while his grandchild died.

Thank God I hadn't had even a thimble of wine. Instead of punching her lights out, instead of saying all that, I just looked at her. And Lisa had taught me well—too well, perhaps—because in that slice of time I knew it wasn't really about her. It wasn't, in fact, her fault. He was probably treating her just as poorly as he had my mum—the blame lay with my dad.

I understood all that, and I might have learnt a lot of lessons, but it doesn't make me Mother Teresa—I can still be an utter bitch.

'You didn't take him.' I frowned, and then there was a strange, almost sympathetic laughter in my voice, as if to say, *You poor deluded fool, is that what you've thought all these years?* 'You don't *take* people.' I watched her blink. 'Clearly my dad wanted something else—all through the marriage he wanted something else and he regularly got it. You didn't take him, Lucy, he just walked away—from his wife, from his children, from his responsibilities—to someone younger, sexier and prettier. *You* were just the one who happened to be there. It wasn't even about you, Lucy, so why would I hate you?'

I might as well have slapped her, because I knew the words had hit, but then the door opened and there he was.

'Hi, Alice.' He didn't say *Hi, baby girl*, because I wasn't his baby any more. He had Charlie.

We chatted—a bit but not much.

About how well his work was going, though regrettably it took him away a lot—lots of weekends away, which he hated, of course—I glanced over at Lucy, who sat there rigid.

We couldn't talk much because his phone kept bleeping.

A few texts that he had to answer, and one call that he had to go out into the garden to take.

People do change, of course.

Just not my dad.

'It's been great…' He ruffled Charlie's hair instead of mine. 'Maybe we'll try and make it over there.'

I doubted it.

'You enjoy the rest of your holiday,' Dad said.

I hugged him goodbye and gave a small smile for Lucy; I felt a bit sorry for her. I didn't resent Charlie now: she wasn't the baby I could have had, but the step-sister I'd ignored. And Christ knows what she was dealing with, with that pair as parents—and doing it without siblings too.

Eleanor and Bonny are right royal pains, but I wouldn't want to do this life without them.

'Here.' I wrote down my email address and gave it to her. 'I'm good at email.'

And then we were out through the door and it was a relief.

A relief to walk to our little hire car and head for the motorway.

'Nearly there,' Roz said a couple of hours later.

Yeah, just the wedding to get through.

And then the best bit. I had to face Hugh.

Some bloody holiday.

Seventy-Four

The hotel where all the wedding party were staying was something like three hundred pounds a night if you added early check-in and late check-out. Two nights in the pub over the road only cost about half of that.

And it was a lovely old-fashioned place that smelt like a pub, and I remembered when I was little and Dad would take us to a pub for lunch and I'd have steak and kidney pudding or ice cream while he chatted up the landlady. And it had been a nice memory, but it wasn't at all nice now—he should have brought Mum.

Or at the very least left his kids at home.

We knelt up on our single beds and watched the wedding party arriving.

Nicole directing them with military precision.

Roz noted her hips and her boobs and so too did I.

There were bags, dresses, flowers and relatives, and though I watched in glee and chatted with Roz, all the time I looked for Hugh—but I never saw him.

'We should ring Nicole,' I said about nine p.m., when I was desperate to know for sure whether or not he was coming. 'Let her know where we are and maybe catch up for a drink.'

'She'll be busy tonight with her family,' Roz said.

So I read one of Roz's self-help books and learnt precisely nothing.

I was bored with self-help—I didn't need help any more; I just needed it to be the day after tomorrow.

I am rather ashamed to admit that I slept marvellously. In fact, I was out like a light by ten—no fitful stirring, no waking up and thinking that soon I would see him.

According to Roz I snored my head off, and was woken at seven a.m. by the tiny kettle and Roz swearing like a sailor as she tried to divide three sachets of powdered coffee into two mugs.

Sorry—it really was as boring as that.

Seventy-Five

Roz had bought American Tan stockings.

I found them on the morning of the wedding laid out on the bed as she had her shower and I confronted her when she came out.

'You'll have to go to the shop,' I said. 'You need nude.'

'I haven't got time.'

She was dripping wet and my hair was done (well, almost), and my make-up was on, so I hauled on some jeans and a T-shirt and coat and raced to a shop that I thought we might have passed.

I was hyper-vigilant, just in case Hugh had run out of whatever it is that guys run out of a couple of hours before a wedding—nothing—so really I knew he wasn't in there. I bought Roz some nude stockings and stood in the queue as the slowest cashier in the history of slow cashiers (I'm much faster, and I can smile while I do it too, and she had a bloody seat: I didn't see what her problem was) took her time to scan some frazzled woman's shopping. She had a baby strapped in the trolley who was wrapped up so tight that his arms stuck out in front of him, and he had one of those caps on which covered the ears. I just sort of glanced over him and then I saw *her.*

She was about four, maybe five, and had the same affliction as me.

Worse, even.

She had a wild mop of ginger curls, all frizzy and knotty, and the poor thing looked as if she had the slap-cheek virus her face was so red. She had too the runny nose that often seems to come in red-headed children, and she must have been on her way to her ballet lesson because her coat was open and her little fat legs were in pink tights and she had a pink leotard on, which clashed badly with her hair.

And I can promise you she hated the lessons and didn't want to go, because beside the skinny, neat perfects she would stand out.

She was lost in her own little world for now, as her mum packed up the groceries, hop-hop-hopping on one leg, and I knew what she was doing before I checked.

Hop-hop-hopping on the floor tiles and trying to avoid the cracks.

Bear in mind I had wedding hair (loads and loads of product and a hot wand through some of the curls) and a good layer of foundation to spare my blushes from Hugh, and I was, apart from the clothes, dressed for a wedding. But we afflicted kind of stand out, because when she looked up I saw her do a double-take. And then I felt her staring at me as I paid for Roz's stockings. I glanced over and her little pale blue eyes were staring at my hair and my face.

Normally I hate kids who stare; normally I'd have

poked my tongue out at her while her mum wasn't looking. But I did the strangest thing. I smiled.

Not an embarrassed half-smile, but a proper smile.

She looked at me closer, a smile on her (ugly) little face, and I could almost hear her mind whirring.

She thought I was beautiful.

She was looking at me and thinking, hoping, praying that one day she might look as lovely as me.

I felt as if that pinched, embarrassed, cringing face that looked out of my photo was staring back at me too, that they were both pleading that one day it would all be okay.

So I gave a little nod.

That told her I understood.

That told her she would be okay.

Then I watched her mum yank her arm and drag her away and she kept turning around, staring and smiling, forgetting to avoid the cracks, and do you know what...?

She wasn't ugly. She was, I suppose, kind of cute, striking, curious and funny.

Do you know something else?

I felt a bit lovely and beautiful too—a little like Cameron Diaz .

I felt as if I'd made it.

Almost.

Seventy-Six

I did Roz's hair. Karan had taught me a thing or three, and I did an excellent job, if I do say so myself. Roz ditched the linen pants and put on the nude stockings I had bought and the palest grey dress and make-up. With a little flowery feather thing in her hair that was grey, black and white, and a splash of pink lipstick she looked like a different person.

I almost fancied her—well, not really, but she roared with laughter when I told her.

So we took a picture and texted it to Karan and then she put on a dressing gown because she's always spilling things.

And it was my turn to get ready.

I didn't have much left to do with my hair; I'd washed it last night and put in loads of stuff and now I just ran my fingers through it and added a bit more serum. I did use a curling wand and took a few strays and added several heavy ringlets. And my make-up was done, so I slipped on my dress and I would have killed for a Kalma, but I'd have to settle for a pep talk from Roz instead.

'You look great.' Roz gave me such a proud smile as I came out of the bathroom she could have been the mother of the bride.

'Thanks to eBay!'

I was wearing an Emilia Hill fake—but a very good fake—willow-green, it clung in all the right places and had a sort of Spanish ruffle at the bottom, which matched the rather red ruffle of curls at the top. I'd put on weight and was feeling a bit of an Amazon, really, and was minus my usual spray tan—if Hugh actually recognised me he'd be prescribing iron tablets.

My stomach was in knots, but it was only eleven a.m. and good girls don't drink at that time.

'Here!' Roz pulled out a bottle of champagne and expertly opened it. The bubbles fizzed over my hand because it was shaking so much that she struggled to line up the neck of the bottle with my glass.

'You said I couldn't have a drink before—'

'That was before I had to face Andrew.' We sat on the bed, in our dingy little pub room, drank champagne before eleven a.m., and never had we been more clean or more honest.

'I rang Lizzie while you were out and she told me that Trudy's pregnant.' Roz took a big swig of her drink. 'Which is what I wanted to happen—I mean, I want him to be happy, I just never expected it to hurt. I don't fancy him, our whole marriage was a sham, but...' She screwed up her face and for the first time I saw that, despite a serious lack of effort on Roz's part, despite the fact she was a Botox virgin, there was hardly a wrinkle. Roz, now she was actually taking care of herself, was a very beautiful woman. 'I couldn't figure out why it would hurt—then I realised that...' She couldn't finish, so I did it for her.

'You love him?' And I waited for her to laugh, because once again I'd said the wrong thing, only it wasn't funny.

Roz nodded.

'Have you ever told him?'

'Yes,' she gasped, as if the word was choking her—the admission killing her. 'We went out for a drink before I came away.'

'And what did he say?'

'That he loved me too.'

I'd seen Roz cry—it was a regular occurrence—but she really cried now, huddled in her little white hotel dressing gown, with her party clothes underneath. She was all bunched up and she cried like the plug was being pulled, sucked in air and dragged it down the gurgler, then it came back out in a shrill wail. Like a Jamaican woman keening, she wailed a lament.

'I don't want to go back—not that he'd ever take me back—but I do love him, and knowing that he did love me...that it wasn't all bad...' She crumpled. 'The good bits were good—like when Lizzie was born, like when he used to bring me home noodles when I couldn't manage dinner, like when we laughed and we bitched...' I was holding her shoulders as she ranted and raved. 'When she was a princess in the nativity play. When we got so drunk we had sex on the beach...when my mum got ill and he cuddled me...' Roz sniffed and dribbled on my beautiful Emilia Hill fake. 'He cuddled me every night for a week when I was sobbing, even when I woke him... He loved me. Ninety per cent of me he knew, and he loved me—he just didn't know the sordid, messed-up bit.'

And I wasn't a psychologist's bootlace, but in that second I understood.

He *had* loved me.

In that moment, in *our* moments, even if he hadn't truly known me, still he *had* loved me.

'It wasn't all a sham,' Roz implored, but she was preaching to the newly converted.

Whatever Lisa thought, I knew I had tasted—albeit briefly—real love.

And I'd lost it too.

And now it was time to face him.

Seventy-Seven

I hate weddings.

More than that, I particularly hate good weddings—watching the happy couple and knowing it isn't me. Knowing that someone has that other half—for now at least—someone to lean on, someone there. And I've never had that, or I did once, but Lisa said it didn't count, that a few weeks was too short to call it a relationship.

I beg to differ.

My eyes scanned the pews for him, as if I was turning and looking to see if Nicole had arrived, but really I was looking for him—and he wasn't here. Maybe he wasn't coming...

Maybe he knew I was coming and has feigned other plans.

I have never stood at a wedding happy.

I loathe being a bridesmaid—Eleanor's wedding I don't really remember, but Bonny's was hell and so too was Nicole's.

Only it wasn't hate and jealousy that filled me

today—I was sad, a deep sadness as the organ played the background noise and the church hummed with chatter and colour and hats.

'I hate weddings.' Roz rolled her eyes and made me smile, made me feel less alone. 'They always remind me of mine.'

'They always remind me of mine too,' I said, and, because it's Roz, I didn't have to elaborate. She picked up the service card.

'Coffee-coloured,' Roz said, and we smiled, and then, even before I glanced up, even before I heard or saw anything, I knew he was there. I knew that when I looked up I would see him. I was staring at the words of a hymn, my face was on fire and I knew that the next thing my eyes would see would be him. And I wasn't ready—I would never, ever be ready to face him, to see him and to not have him.

> *The King of love my shepherd is,*
> *Whose goodness faileth never*
> *I nothing lack if I am his*
> *And he is mine for ever.*

I just kept reading this verse over and over.

'Guess who...?' Roz started, but I shook my head. She didn't have to tell me, I already knew. I could hear his lovely voice saying *Excuse me*; I could smell him. Despite all the cologne, the perfume sprayed on people today, I could smell the man who'd just walked past. Only it wasn't a smell, it's him, the carbon dioxide he breathed out that I breathed in. And finally I stopped staring down at the hymn and looked up. He was moving into the pew two rows ahead of us, dressed in a morning suit and looking stunning. Gemma was beside him, pale and dainty, and it killed that it wasn't me.

He knew everyone, of course. He was in the pew, shaking a couple of hands, and then a man tapped him and Hugh turned around and shook the man's hand, leant over and kissed the cheek of a woman, and then his eyes met mine. Just for a fraction, as he pulled his head back he gave me, I don't know what to call it, a short grim smile is the best I can come up with. It was a brief, polite acknowledgment, and I gave a very brief one back and then he turned his back to me.

He went to sit but the bridal march had started so he stayed standing in a room that rose and Gemma rose to stand with him. We all turned around to watch Nic enter, but I didn't turn quickly enough. I watched him lower his head as he said something to Gemma, I watched her hand slip into his, and I watched him hold it tightly, and my heart was shredded, but still beating.

And I would get through this.

This too will pass.

Hugh sings loudly.

Funny, the things you learn. Two pews in front of me and I could hear his voice, and even Roz nudged me and we shared a grin, 'cos he really does sing loudly.

It came to the verse I love, and I love music, singing, and if I closed my eyes I could hear only Hugh—a gorgeous deep baritone voice that I hadn't known existed.

> *'Perverse and foolish oft I strayed*
> *But yet in love he sought me*

> *And on his shoulder gently laid*
> *And home rejoicing brought me.'*

And I heard his voice waver for a second and I wondered if he was thinking about me, because when I had strayed (oft) Hugh hadn't sought me; he had left me to it.

Which was right and everything.

I just wanted his shoulder now.

But it wasn't mine—so I let him go.

I did what Yasmin said I should do ages ago, I stood there and cut the strings and sent him off with a smile—and I made a wish too.

A sensible wish rather than an order.

That when I was ready, when the universe thought I was ready, it would send me another perfect guy.

The universe's choice this time—I gave it full leeway—yes, even a redhead.

And then it got to the *'In Death's dark veil'* bit...

The bit I was dreading. And something happened—something I wasn't expecting—and, given my history, you may put this down to a slightly manic moment, a teeny psychosis, even, but it wasn't.

I was past all that.

I know there is a heaven, or a place like that, and that I will get to hold her again.

I found out at Nicole's wedding.

I stood, sharing a hymnbook with Roz and hearing Hugh's voice, and doing my absolute best to hold it together. I looked up to blow out a breath—that sort when you're trying not to cry—and I heard the organ and the words, saw the sun on the stained-glass windows and felt the music vibrate and rise to the heavens, and heaven sent something back to me.

And I know I will get to hold her again, because for a second, as that line was sung, I was holding Lydia.

Sounds mad, I know, but it is my second clean-and-perfect memory and, even though I love the one with Hugh, if I only get one memory to take to the nursing home with me, I want it to be that one.

When I got to hold her again.

Fuck, I hate weddings, especially good ones, with bells and the organ and Nicole. And, yes, maybe Roz was right, because Nicole *did* have a rather large bouquet covering her, er, suddenly ample figure—and I especially hate that bit when you sort of got stuck in the crowd spilling out, and I ended up, for this clashing second, walking down the aisle next to my ex, or whatever I was supposed to define him as.

And I loathe photos, especially watching Hugh, throwing his head back and laughing over something Gemma said. And it was freezing. Lovely and frosty and romantic—but freezing.

Now just the night to get through—oh, and the speeches and dinner.

Thankfully we weren't at the same table. He was up with his mother, Aunty Cheryl and all the Watson clan, and Roz and I were stuck with friends of Paul's who would make your eyes cross, they were so boring.

We had bonbons.

A little glass cup and saucer filled with not sugar-coated almonds but sugar-coated coffee beans.

'Alice.' Nicole fell on my neck later in the night and held me. 'I love the hair.'

'I love the cleavage.' Nicole blushed and her mouth opened to tell me, to share, but she blew out a breath, and I know they'd probably decided not to reveal till after the wedding, but this was me.

I didn't want it in an email.

I was happy for her, and I was sad too.

I wasn't jealous about her baby.

I can say that is the absolute truth.

I was sad for her for different reasons, but I hoped it was wasted—that she really was as ecstatic as she said she was.

We chatted for a moment and all she gave me were details, details, details.

About how they'd wanted the Billy Joel version but it had been Barry White who had sung 'Just the Way You Are'.

Why didn't she listen?

Not to me, or to Billy or Barry, but to the words of the song she had chosen.

And then she got called away.

'You'd think he'd discovered the shagging coffee bean!' I was savage as Roz and I stepped into the cool night air. And the universe was supposed to be kind, but sometimes I wonder. I mean, I am so much nicer now, so much less bitchy and judgmental, but the one time I allow myself a brief respite, the one time I let myself shine in a rather non-glorious fashion, Roz went red in the face and I was caught in mid-bitch with the man who thought I was the world's biggest...

'How are you doing?'

'Great.' I smile, cringing, cringing inside. 'It's a lovely wedding.'

'Really?' Hugh gave me a strange look. 'It's fucking awful—the cake is coffee-flavoured—she's a lawyer and they've themed the wedding on coffee.'

Thank you, universe!

'I'll go inside.' Roz smiles, a few idle minutes of chatter later. 'You stay and have another cigarette.'

And I was alone with him.

'It's good to see you,' I said, because it was good— and bad and horrible—but mostly bloody good.

'It's hell seeing you.' He stared right at me and I could see his anger and it was merited.

'I'm sorry.' More sorry than he could ever know, in fact. 'I really am sorry for what I put you through, Hugh.' There—I'd said it. 'I'm going inside.'

'I thought you were having another cigarette.'

'I don't smoke any more.'

'But Roz said…'

'We still nip outside.' I gave a thin smile. 'When it gets too much it's a good excuse to get away…'

'You've really given it up?'

'Yep.' I just wanted away from him, couldn't stand to be so close and not touch him.

'Is it too much tonight?' Hugh asked. 'Did you need an excuse to get out of there?'

'Yes.'

'Because of me?'

'Because of me,' I said, and I'd promised I wouldn't cry in front of him, I'd promised I wouldn't make a fool of myself, but I'd also promised to be honest. I could feel my nose burning, feel my throat tighten as I nodded, and I didn't boo-hoo, but a couple of tears shot out as I answered him. 'It's hell to see you too.'

'I'm sorry too. I just…' He scrunched his eyes closed. 'I was crazy about you, Alice, but it was too hard. I shouldn't have said all that I said. I wanted to help you, but…'

'You get enough at work…'

'No.' He shook his head. 'Maybe I just couldn't stand watching you self-destruct. I should have…'

'You couldn't help me, Hugh. I had to do that bit myself…'

I had.

How many psychologists does it take to change a light bulb?

One.

But it has to want to change.

It is a stupid joke—and I hate jokes—I never get them, but this is one of the few that I understand.

It isn't actually a joke—at least, I no longer find it that funny.

It's true.

For a while I had wanted to lie with Dan for ever, but he had made me get up.

For ages it was better that Roz answered the phone.

Roz had let me shelter in victim mode.

Roz would have loved me if I'd stayed there for ever.

Truth be told, Roz didn't like her baby growing up.

But she worked on herself too.

And there was Bonny and Nicole and Hugh and all things complicated, but the only person who could do the big bit was me.

The only person who could change me was me.

We walked twice around the lake, our breath white in the cold winter air, and then we sat down and I told him—all of it. I told him about Gus and what had happened, and I spoke too about Roz, about the choices that she'd made and about her daughter and Andrew and I sort of jumbled it all out. And given his job, he was a good listener. Well, he had to be because I couldn't stop. I told him—about my music and my hair and the money and the chaos, how Roz had helped me and how I had helped myself.

How the worst thing that could happen was that you couldn't talk to your parents—and that Roz and Lizzie were getting there now. And that Lizzie was seventeen too and we could just hope to God that by talking, by being honest, by being able to come to Roz, she wouldn't make the same mistakes we had.

Earlier in this conversation I had told him about Lydia, but when we stopped at a bench I told him properly.

Not all.

It wasn't about him.

There are bits of me so private, and I don't have to reveal all to anyone.

I told him what I chose to.

'I miss her.'

I felt his hand on my shoulder.

'All she could have been...'

Then Hugh said something. 'All that she was.'

He sounded like a sympathy card and my throat tightened around some caustic retort, but I accepted his words.

She was.

She is.

She will always be my baby.

He was ridiculously proud that I had been accepted

to study for my bachelor of music, so proud and encouraging, and there was almost a wistful note in his voice when he asked me what I want to be.

And I told him something I haven't told you yet.

I no longer want to teach.

Remember that night playing Mika?

Remember how Roz laughed, how we were suddenly free?

I had thought about all that music gave me, how it took me to places I could never usually go, and I wanted to give it to someone else.

I wanted to climb into some poor bastard's locked brain and give them the key.

'Musical therapist...' I gave a tiny shrug. 'I think.' And I saw the flare of interest in his eyes. There was a conversation, many conversations we could have had, but now we wouldn't.

I shifted the conversation.

I had boundaries now, you see.

My future wasn't his place.

And he told me about him. He told me that he hadn't fled back to the UK because of me—the woman on maternity leave had lost her babe and had wanted to come back. He told me that this week he had, in fact, been offered a job in Melbourne, that it was breaking him up to turn it down, that sometimes he wondered if things could be different—but he'd been so worried, broken so many of his own rules by staying with me, by trying to ignore what was under his nose.

He was worried that he might enable me.

And I understood.

It hurt a lot, but I understood.

And if that was hard and brave, as we came back to Reception, as we headed inside, I said the hardest bravest thing of all.

'I'm happy for you and Gemma. I want you to be happy, so I really am—happy for you.'

And a kiss goodbye would be too dangerous and too sad and I really wasn't going to cry, so I smiled instead before I turned to go.

'We broke up.'

I looked back at him, saw him rake his hand through his hair, and could see he was torn as to what and how much he should say to me, lest I burn his bunnies on a boiler.

'We lasted a couple of weeks. But, well…' He gave a thin smile. 'We're friends, just really good friends with a whole lot of history—hey, she was seventeen too.'

'Lucky Gemma,' I said, because to lose your virginity to a guy like Hugh made you a very lucky girl indeed.

'So what's she doing here?'

'She's supposed to be protecting me from you, except she's making eyes at the best man.'

I had done that once too.

I just hoped Gemma was a little more sensible than I had been.

'You don't need protection from me,' I said. 'I know that it's over and I understand why.' And I smiled. But I did start crying, a little bit, because it was true you had to be careful what you wished for. I had demanded from the universe the perfect guy and the universe had delivered—I should have read the small print. It wasn't anyone's fault except my own that I'd been sent the perfect guy, as requested, and I hadn't been ready.

'I wish I'd met you later,' I said, 'when I was all sorted and...'

'But you didn't.'

He pulled me into his arms and didn't kiss me, thank God, because my nose was running; he just hugged me and held me and then, because he had to, he let me go.

'Hey.' Roz was in the loos waiting, worried and kind and armed with make-up and tissues—not to mop my tears but to help me be brave. 'Blow your nose and let's get back out there. You can tell me about it after.'

I didn't want it to be after but I accepted that it had to be.

So I blew my nose and painted my face and walked back out there with my head held high. Roz headed for the bar to buy me a bloody grapefruit juice this time— only of course Karan rang, and Roz dashed out.

And I sat alone in the darkness, watching all the couples dancing.

But I didn't feel like a wallflower on New Year's Eve.

I was just a woman sitting, pausing, watching others dance, some alone, some in couples, some in groups. I knew that one day, when I was ready, I might join in.

And then I saw him watching me, saw him look away and then look back. I smiled, to let him know that I was okay, that he really didn't have to worry about me, that he could let me go.

Only he didn't let me go.

He put down his orange juice and walked in a completely straight line towards me.

He walked right up to me and, just as Yasmin had said the right man would always come back, just as Big Tits had said a man should, Hugh walked up to me and asked if he could have the pleasure of this dance.

* * * * *

Acknowledgements

Mostly I have loved writing this story, but there are times I have just wanted to walk away—actually, a few times I did walk away, so there are loads of people to thank for helping me to keep going till I felt Alice's story had been told.

First of all I want to thank my children (not that I **ever** want them to read my work)—I have to confess that it worries me a little that they think it's perfectly normal to have a mum crying and laughing at the computer keyboard and that they have all, over the years, individually asked how Alice is doing!!

I have a brilliant friend, Helen Browne. There is no way I would have finished without her—not only does she help with the ups and downs and logistics of my life, but she also has an amazing ability to keep her eyes from glazing over as I bombard her with my plot and to nod in all the right places —better still, she tells me the bits that she doesn't like (brave woman indeed)!

I want to thank the wonderful team at MIRA for taking Alice's story on, especially Kimberley Young and Jenny Hutton, who have pushed me to make it the best that it can be and who have been so patient.

Thanks, too, to my mum and my sisters Anne and Helen, who put up with my long phone calls. I have the best mum and despite the distance we are so close and she comes over and is a huge support. A special thanks to Anne and my gorgeous niece Hannah, who came all the way over to Australia from the UK when I needed it the most.

I have a wonderful group of friends, they go by the name Maytoners—we push each other and support each other, well, they do me and I hope I give the same back—they all know who they are, but I cannot not mention Anne Gracie, who read a shaky draft of this book at a time when she really had every reason not to and then took the time to contact me and give me words of encouragement—it meant an awful lot. Nor can I leave out Marion Lennox, who lent me a very patient ear as I worked out where Alice's pregnancy was going.

I would like to thank Stuart MacDonald for his enthusiasm —he is a wonderful friend and an endless source of wisdom. Thanks, too, to Shane Burns, a gifted musician and all around nice guy and also thank you to Annemarie and John for breakfasts, lunches and love and also to Raelene and Leanne too.

Yasmin Boland has been wonderful—not only letting Alice read from her fantastic book *Cosmic Love*, but also providing me with insightful, wonderful horoscopes every day at www.moonology.com

Then there's Sarah Morgan, a brilliant writer and an amazing friend. If there is one advantage to living on the other side of the world, then it has to be the time difference with e-mail. I can pour out my worries at night—when the book has stalled, when things catch up, when life feels hard—and then wake up the next day and it is as if the fairies have been and I have a reply filled with love and support and an awful lot of laughs.

Anyway, these are my thank yous—they really are heartfelt, but first, last and always my love and thanks goes to my children.

putting

Alice

back
together

MORE ABOUT THIS BOOK

MORE ABOUT THE AUTHOR

Read all about it...

QUESTIONS FOR YOUR READING GROUP

1. Alice is a normal woman who is on the edge, pressures of work, love and everyday life pile on to the secrets buried in her past. Are there aspects in Alice that you can relate to? How many of us, do you think, are hiding our biggest fears?

2. Alice is almost fanatical about her hair. How significant do you think this is to the storyline and her turbulent emotions?

3. Music is extremely important to Alice; what role do you feel music plays in the narrative?

4. Lisa plays a key part in Alice's journey of self-discovery, as do the self-help books and the universe! Did *Putting Alice Back Together* change your opinions about asking for help? Could Alice put herself back together on her own?

5. Hugh stays with Alice for a long time before he confronts her about her addiction. Why do you think he doesn't see the warning signs earlier?

6. Alice is battling addiction, her relationship with her family and, most importantly, her relationship with herself. How do you think the book deals with these three elements?

7. If Alice could write a letter to her mother now, what do you think she would write?

8. There are so many poignant moments in the story and also laugh-out-loud scenes; which passages stood out for you?

9. Do you think that Alice and Hugh should have their happy-ever-after?

Read all about it...

Read all about it...

READ ON TO FIND OUT MORE ABOUT CAROL MARINELLI...

What inspired you to create the story and character of Alice?

Alice ☺

She just kept knocking on my head and on a Thursday night I would write a little. At first just a page or two, or sometimes I would read her back, but more and more I started looking forward to Thursday nights and getting to know her.

Did you have Alice's character mapped out before you started? What surprised you most about her along the way?

I didn't have her character mapped out at all. She surprised me at every turn. When I first started writing it, the book was a lot lighter—in fact it was very much more about hair! The more that all faded, the more Alice started to show herself.

Were you ever worried about creating a heroine who was quite flawed, and being able to keep her sympathetic?

Absolutely.

I struggled for a long time—a very long time, until I took that shackle off. I really liked Alice, even if she drove me insane at times. Once I got past attempting to give her flaws that might be more acceptable, or trying to please, and I just let her be herself, I found a far more interesting person. I think the same is true in life.

How important do you think the notion of family is to Alice?

Family was vital to Alice and still is. I do

think that she needed their approval too much though—so much so that she felt she had to protect them from her real self, which, as it turned out, was really rather nice.

Apart from Alice, who was your favourite and also who annoyed you the most?

I love Roz—funnily I didn't when I started writing the book, but, finding out a bit more about her journey as I went along, she just changed before my eyes and became so much more a part of the story. She made me laugh so many times—and had me tearing up too.

Nicole, on the other hand, was *always* annoying—when the book was more about hair she was around a little bit more and really got on my nerves! It was quite pleasurable deleting her at times.

If Alice could go back now do you think she would tell her mother the truth?

I'm sure she would—with the benefit of hindsight and a whole lot of growing up and psychology—but she can't go back and somehow, I hope, she is now accepting of that.

Do you think Alice gets her happy-ever-after?

I hope for a few glimpses of Alice in future books—I love her too much not to find out for myself. I do think that she got her happy-ever-after at the supermarket and then later at the Church. That said, after writing the end, a part of me really, and I mean REALLY, wanted her to go back to the pub with him and kick Roz out so that I could write a whole chapter on that last night, but I also felt it was right to leave it there—that no matter how badly I wanted to sew it up, in the end their future was up to Hugh and Alice.

Read all about it...

Can you describe your writing process? Do you start with the characters? The plot? Do you write the last chapter first?

Do you really want to know my writing process??!

I eat cornflakes.
I see something.
I start.
I get all excited and am convinced it will be done in a few short weeks.
Nothing happens for variable periods.
I finally see the end (I can only write when I know the ending—even just a little peek at it).
I write the end.
I read the end and hopefully get goosebumps.

Then I go back and have to write the rest, trying to work out how on earth they got there.

Can you tell us a little about your next book?

I was so in love with Alice that I was concerned I could never fall so heavily again—I'm happy to say that I have. I'm staying quiet, except to say—I don't think that it's the story you're expecting. ☺
I have the start.
I like her so much that I've stopped worrying if she's likeable. I'm past the variable and have written the end and am now working out how on earth they got there! I am also very glad to report that I got goosebumps.